SHARED BLOOD
Book 1: Discovery

by David Erasmus McDonald

PART ONE - The Big Drink and Beyond

***

CHAPTER 1

Gedrec Kirkland was invited to the Captain's table on the *Ship Elise* out of Bremen the night before they docked in Baltimore. The other guest was Jacob Mueller, a middle-aged, affable Boston merchant of timepieces. The food was solid Bavarian fare, the conversation a little stilted—both Captain Ahlhorn and Mr. Mueller were native Prussians and spoke in their dialect from time to time—but Gedrec was fluent enough in high German and held forth admirably, recounting his experience on the HMS Beagle some years before.

"Your Mr. Darwin sounds like a peculiar fellow," Ahlhorn said after a few moments of astonished silence.

"*Ja,*" Mueller agreed, adding dubiously, "Descended from *apes*? Man has no divine spark?"

Gedrec was used to this reaction and patiently explained the proposition that all primates had ancestors in common, not just a single hereditary line.

"Millions of years back?" the Captain asked with an arched, bushy eyebrow.

"That is the argument," Gedrec responded.

"*Argument* is the correct word, my friend," Mueller chuckled, and shot a knowing look to the Captain. "And you may expect quite a vocal one in return from the clergy!"

The Captain then remarked that the manifest showed Gedrec's last place of residence as Dusseldorf—what was his business there?

"Excavating in the Neander Valley looking for ancient relics," Gedrec said.

"What did you discover?" Ahlhorn asked. Mueller was all ears.

Gedrec admitted that there was nothing conclusive yet, deciding not to mention evidence of an older culture—much older—than previously thought. Instead he said it was the future that concerned him now—that, and his teaching post at the newly opened Naval Academy in Annapolis.

"A professorship!" Mueller exclaimed.

Gedrec nodded, remarking that he had received his doctorate from Cambridge five years before.

"Not in religion, I'm thinking," the Captain commented with a laugh.

"Not quite," answered Gedrec with a smile. "Chemistry and natural philosophy."

"Such weighty topics, for one so young!" Mueller commented through a mouthful. Despite his world travel, Gedrec did in fact look younger than his twenty-seven years, as if the sea itself were his fountain of youth.

Captain Ahlhorn mentioned he'd heard that a coach service to Annapolis from Baltimore was now available, and he would be more than happy to find out the particulars.

Gedrec thanked him.

Then the conversation turned to landfall the next day, the good weather, the hospitality of Baltimore, and Mueller's plans to expand his dry goods business in the Northeast. After port and cigars, Gedrec bid his companions good night.

In his cabin he found Klaus, the ship's cabin boy, lying on the bunk, bare-chested, a sheet covering him from the waist down. Gedrec had learned it was not out of modesty, but to titillate, a strategy that worked admirably. Klaus' wide, boyish smile was as provocative as his lean body and cock swelling under the sheet.

Klaus also acted as steward for the *Elise*, and when Gedrec walked up the plank they had exchanged knowing eye-signals as Klaus had hefted Gedrec's trunk onto his shoulder. Gedrec had been captivated by Klaus' fresh, Teutonic beauty, and struck up a casual conversation— mentioning that he had been a cabin boy himself—hoping to end the necessary sexual hiatus imposed by his work. Excavating was a lonely business. Fortunately, Gedrec's German was much better than Klaus' English, but only a few words were necessary, wrapped in euphemism, leaving no doubt about their mutual attraction and Klaus' availability most evenings.

Klaus flung off the sheet, propped himself on one elbow and extended a well-muscled arm. *"Komm her,"* he whispered in gruff, thick Bavarian. But Gedrec didn't need to be encouraged. Moving toward the bed, he ripped off his collar and fumbled with his silk tie. Klaus went right for the trousers. With calm, deliberate movements he undid them and yanked them down, fondling Gedrec's erect cock and nipping it with gentle bites through Gedrec's underpants. *"Sehr gut,"* he murmured as Gedrec let out a long, low moan, that deepened to a growl. Gedrec lay down beside Klaus and reciprocated, hoping that the waves surging against the bow drowned their cries of lust.

Gedrec kept a written account of all his conquests, so as Klaus snored softly, Gedrec penned an entry in his journal by the soft light of the lantern: *19 September 1845. Met the young steward aboard. Very eager to please, and his expertise matches his enthusiasm. What a peezle! And he was such butter to my bread . . .*

As scholarly as Gedrec's lectures were in the classroom, he was just as crude when describing his trysts.

Afterward Gedrec crept in beside Klaus and slept soundly, as he always did on sea voyages, if not for very long that night. As usual, Klaus had been enthusiastically obliging, incredibly limber, sensual, and in no hurry to finish.

Gedrec had been awakened especially early by the echoes of Mueller singing Beethoven's *Ode to Joy* down the passageway—in surprisingly good voice. He looked up at Klaus' strapping form wriggling into tight trousers, buttoning them with quick precision. He gave Gedrec a quick, wide grin as he pulled the jumper over his head and chest. The grin was still there when his head popped out. Klaus seemed to be doing better than Gedrec on three hours' rest.

Klaus pointed upward toward the deck. "Time for muster." He gave Gedrec a playful smack on the face, tweaked his nipple and slipped out into the passageway. There was no goodbye. Just then it had occurred to Gedrec that they hadn't kissed once.

Gedrec shaved and dressed quickly, then closed the single trunk that contained his attire, personal hygiene items, and the several folios containing notes and drawings documenting his five-year exploits in digs around the world. He went to the galley, where a silent, smiling cook served him an ample breakfast of salt pork, cheese, hard tack, and half an orange followed by a cup of wonderfully strong coffee. He ate alone in short order and then went up on deck for a breath of fresh air and to survey the Baltimore skyline as the ship prepared to dock.

Long journey, thought Gedrec as he stood on deck, watching the bustle around the docks of Baltimore's Inner Harbor. It was a perfect early September morning, clear and breezy. Gedrec closed his eyes and took a deep draught of the salt air.

"Herr Kirkland!" Mueller's hearty voice called out behind him. "Excuse me," he corrected. "Herr *Doctor* Kirkland." He smiled broadly "Quite a night!" he said in German. "Did you sleep well?"

"Not long, but well," he answered truthfully, recalling the events of the previous night.

"I hope I did not awaken you too early with my singing," Mueller said.

"Not at all, I awoke in good time. And to good music, well sung."

Mueller beamed a smile. "As a youth, I aspired to the concert stage, but one must earn a reliable living." He paused, pulling a cloth-wrapped packet from his coat and holding it out. "If you please, allow me the honor of presenting you a memento of our journey and stimulating conversation."

Gedrec took the packet with obvious delight, offering a slight bow. "So generous. Thank you, Herr Mueller." He undid the loose wrap, revealing a small, round object, about the size of a silver dollar—indeed it seemed made of silver, with detailed engraving on its surface. A delicate chain was fixed to the stem.

"Press that latch." Mueller suggested, pointing to a small projection. Gedrec did so, and the cover flipped open. Inside was a small clock, its moving hand ticking away the seconds.

"As you know, I make and sell timepieces. This is called a pocket watch."

"Pocket watch," echoed Gedrec with a hint of awe.

"Yes," replied Mueller, as he demonstrated how the watch was to be tucked away in a vest pocket and anchored through the fabric with its substantial metal fob. "The inside of the cover may be engraved, or hold a picture, if you so desire."

At that moment Klaus strode over and saluted Gedrec. *"Guten morgen,* Herr Doctor," he said. Not a glimmer of recognition. His face was impassive. "The Captain wishes to see you at your convenience to discuss the arrangements for your coach to Annapolis."

"Of course," answered Gedrec. He turned to Mueller. "Thank you so much again, Herr Mueller. May the rest of your journey be without incident."

Mueller regarded him with a speculative gaze. "You are an interesting young man, and I believe your journey will be filled with adventure. Farewell, and may God go with you." He gave Gedrec a hearty handshake, and Gedrec never saw him again.

Gedrec followed Klaus, who was was stoic and proper—polite, in a curt way—to the Captain's quarters. He looked busy, but broke into a smile. "Good news! There is a daily coach to Annapolis that leaves at ten o'clock each morning. But I'm afraid we will not dock in time for today," he added with some regret.

No matter, thought Gedrec. He had several days before he had to report, so he decided to stay in Baltimore and "see the sights" until then.

He found lodgings at a small hotel on the Inner Harbor, close to a pub that seemed both popular—especially among the sailors, Gedrec was pleased to see—and very welcoming to handsome travelers like himself, in pursuit of distraction in leisure moments.

CHAPTER 2

Cezar Balanescu didn't discover the name of his cellmate right away, since he shared the Istanbul dungeon cell with him for only a single night. He was astonished at the man's casual, almost humorous demeanor, considering that they both faced the firing squad the next morning. Cezar didn't know the nature of his cellmate's crime and didn't much care—he had plenty on his mind already. He sat in silence, considering the past events that led him down such a grisly path. While he couldn't be as cavalier as his cellmate, he still had no regrets. He loathed the Ottoman Empire and joined the Russian forces in the Crimean War as an officer.

With Russia's defeat, he now faced a traitor's death, which only justified his passion for liberation from the Ottoman yoke—the same passion which he now felt all the more in the face of his liberation from the earth.

In truth Cezar had already been something of a rebel even before the war, slipping hints at insurrection into his lectures at Istanbul University, using double-talk wrapped in flattery and cloaked in duplicity to mask his insults against the Empire.

His cellmate sprawled comfortably on his bunk, poking with a spoon at the lump of petrified porridge left over from that morning. Cezar had wolfed down his own in seconds. The cellmate hadn't taken a bite—merely examined the bland, pasty mess. But he seemed far from starving—in fact, he grew even more robust in the dank cell as the daylight faded through the tiny barred window. "Deep in thought?" he asked in Russian.

Cezar shrugged.

The cellmate was already there when Cezar had been brought in that morning, and even though he had felt the man's keen eyes watching him. They hadn't exchanged a word thus far. Still watching Cezar, the cellmate stretched his arms and back. Cezar watched him from the corner of his eye and noticed for the first time his lean, powerful form, hoping his glance wouldn't be noticed. The cellmate offered Cezar a knowing grin and pulled up his sleeve, flexing an impressive bicep.

Cezar stared straight ahead. To hide his growing erection, he brought his legs against his chest—no easy task, since his legs were both long and strong, with a muscular torso to match. His skin was supple and smooth.

"You *are* a shy one," the cellmate remarked. He arose from the bunk—oddly, as if he were levitating—and strolled across the cell and leaned over Cezar, arching his body, one knee on the bunk. He held out his hand. "Ivor Sokolov."

Ivor's crotch, sporting an impressive bulge, was inches from Cezar's face. Cezar turned his head.

"No need to look away. I believe we understand each other."

Cezar remained silent.

"You don't understand Russian?"

"Yes, I understand you. I just don't know what you mean," Cezar said defensively.

The cellmate laughed—a hearty laugh, so out of place in such dismal quarters. The guard ambled over, peeked in, then shuffled away again. Ivor's face went blank. In a serious tone he said, "Yes, my friend, you do. You understand very well." He lowered himself onto the bunk. Cezar scooted away with a few quick, furtive, fearful looks. The cellmate leaned over, but Cezar halted him, hand against Ivor's chest.

"It is true enough, what you say," Cezar began. He paused, then said, "But . . . but we're barely acquainted."

"Quite right," replied the cellmate. "But I told you my name. If you believe in formalities, isn't it proper to return the courtesy?"

After a moment, Cezar looked into Ivor's face, which was pale and framed by sheaves of light brown hair. He held out his hand and said, "Cezar Balanescu."

"Pleased to make your acquaintance, Cezar." He took Cezar's hand and pulled him closer, and leaned over to kiss him. Ivor was only mildly surprised when Cezar backed against the wall and brought knees against his chest.

"I've never…" Cezar began, but Ivor understood.

Ivor was fascinated. "Never?" He gave Cezar a speculative look. "How old are you?"

"Thirty-nine." For some reason, Cezar felt ashamed, adding, "Bachelor schoolmaster."

Ivor felt more curious than lusty. "What did you teach?"

"Mechanical engineering. Slavic languages."

"Where?"

"Istanbul University."

Ivor was startled. "For that, you receive death?"

"No. For defying Ottoman rule. I fought for the Russians."

There was so a long silence that Cezar believed treason had precluded friendship, until Ivor spoke. "And you 'never'?"

"Never with someone else."

Ivor went wide-eyed with surprise. "Saving yourself?" The corner of Ivor's mouth curled up, amused but not unkind. "For the right moment, perhaps? The right person?"

Cezar lifted his head in defiance. For the right moment *and* the right person. His ideals in politics *did* extend to his private life—or would, once he had one. There was no point, he decided, in bedding anyone who didn't feel as he did, passionate about both life and love, dedicated and unifying. He would have it no other way. He had felt a mixture of pity and disgust as he watched his fellow soldiers go with anyone remotely suitable who happened to cross their paths, all with false promises of everlasting devotion. *Intimacy is a sacred bond*, Cezar thought with contempt. *Can't they understand that?*

"Of course, I understand," Ivor whispered in his ear. "And perhaps we met on death's doorstep just in time—that I may be the one you have waited for. Have you considered that?"

Cezar hadn't, not until that moment. He thought he would recognize his partner at once. Somehow, he had always known he was destined for something more sublime. And isn't that what he felt now, with Ivor so close? He was beginning to think so, and he was more certain as he met the cellmate's penetrating eyes. They seemed to reach into his soul.

Ivor put his arm around Cezar's shoulder and pulled him close. Cezar's cock stiffened under Ivor's gentle hand. His head lolled to one side as Ivor nibbled on Cezar's ear, slid his tongue down his neck, then a delicious, piercing sting at his throat, lingering there, softly milking the spot that soon drove Cezar to an edge of excitement that he never dreamed possible. Then Ivor pulled away and gazed down at his friend. Cezar was startled to see the red smear on Ivor's mouth, and then the ruby-colored rivulets on his own shoulder. But Ivor dismissed it casually, licking it up with a small, quick smile. Cezar paid little mind, mesmerized by the grip of passion as Ivor sucked on one nipple, then the other, then tweaking them between his fingers as he traced a trail with his tongue down toward Cezar's loins, gently biting the strong thighs, nuzzling the dark thicket of hair around his cock.

Meanwhile Cezar had not been idle. No lack of experience stood in his way as he tended to Ivor's body, stroking lightly at first, as though he might crack the smooth, white flesh, then carried along on the wave of his mounting passion—Ivor was sucking him off—and Cezar found himself reciprocating with furious abandon, exploring Ivor's swollen cock—*how rock hard it is, like velvet on hot steel*, Cezar thought— and wondering if it would choke him. But he didn't wonder long. Whether transported by desire or realizing a hidden talent, Cezar took Ivor's full hardness with no trouble. It seemed only a minute had passed when he heard Ivor's deep groan of satisfaction and to his surprise, felt a burst of warmth at the back of his throat, and the rich, sweet-salty taste right afterward. Then he released Ivor's still-hard cock and shouted out as he reached his own climax, Ivor sucking it down.

The guard either didn't hear or didn't care.

They lay in silence for a few minutes afterward. Cezar felt gratified and confused, wondering what, if anything, he should say, when Ivor leaned over and kissed him, nibbling his ear—his teeth were so *sharp*— and whispered, "That was lovely."

"What was lovely?" Cezar asked, then said, "Oh, yes. Yes, it was."

Ivor chuckled. "Not the sex, although that was lovely, too." Ivor paused for a moment, looking deep into Cezar's eyes. "You shouted my name."

Cezar didn't remember that, but since Ivor was saying, "Cezar…Cezar," and stroking Cezar's hardening cock, it didn't matter. Neither of them were in any hurry for the lovemaking to end. To Cezar, it seemed that the fateful sunrise would never come.

Ivor had in fact planned to leave right at dusk, but he was determined to stay and find out more about the intriguing, dark, brooding man who had been condemned to death for treason. He couldn't take his eyes off the newcomer, studying the aquiline nose, square jut of jaw, full lips slightly parted, and the deep-set eyes with their pensive expression—not to mention his strapping physique. Ivor had brought many to his bed, and some into eternal life. But this man's passion brought him to a peak of excitement he had never felt before. He first toyed with him, but felt guilty at once. And when they finally fucked, Ivor almost felt young again.

They slept in each other's arms until early morning. Hours until dawn, Ivor started to slip out of their embrace and caught sight of Cezar's face, bathed in moonlight. After a moment's hesitation, as if trying to remember how, he leaned down and kissed him on the cheek. Indeed, it had been many years since Ivor's kiss had been anything but deadly.

Cezar awoke, his eyes bright, inquiring.

"Time to go," Ivor whispered.

Puzzled, Cezar opened his mouth to speak, but Ivor silenced him with a gesture. Quietly they got to their feet and dressed quickly. Ivor grasped the ring handle on the door. A *snap*—and the door swung open with a soft creak. *The guard must have left it unlocked*, thought Cezar.

As astonished as he was, Cezar didn't utter a sound as Ivor disabled three guards in a matter of seconds. The first two were taken by surprise, snapping the neck of the first as he napped, and strangling the second. The last one was alert, but his truncheon didn't leave his sash—Ivor leaped forward in a blur, or so it seemed to Cezar, and ripped out the guard's throat.

Cezar stood frozen with shock. Ivor nudged him, but getting no response, grabbed his arm and pulled him along. Cezar couldn't help but look back at the guard, a red lake pooling underneath where he had fallen.

Fortunately, the compound was small, and the door from the courtyard to the street opened readily with Ivor's quick, strong tug. They slipped out into the street and vanished among the shadows.

CHAPTER 3

Though he was no stranger to battle and fearless in his own right, Cezar was still amazed at the calm he felt as they crossed the Bosporus into Europe, then maneuvered through the streets, city after city, avoiding police, sentries, soldiers, and sundry. "We move by night, sleep by day," Ivor instructed, which made perfect sense to Cezar, who was himself a good tactician, but what their destination was he had no idea—and decided he didn't care. He knew now that Ivor was his lifemate. And where he went, Cezar would follow.

Cezar felt little hunger or thirst. At one point Ivor darted out of sight and returned in seconds, handing him a slab of raw meat, still warm, which Cezar promptly ate with appetite.

Two nights later they slipped aboard the hold of a sizable merchant ship docked nearby and had no problem hiding among the cargo. They remained below for the entire trip, slept in the day, made love at night, and Cezar partook of the meat scraps that Ivor had provided, still warm from the kill. Ivor didn't say where the meat had come from, and Cezar didn't ask. It was satisfying, and that was more than enough; he'd never felt more fit. Otherwise Ivor's devotion was all the sustenance he needed.

They docked in Piraeus, penniless and without prospects, to find Greece in the midst of religious turmoil under Catholic King Otto and his Lutheran Queen Amalia. On the outskirts of the city Ivor and Cezar found an abandoned building in the middle of a field. It was in dreadful disrepair, missing one wall and part of another, no glass in the windows that remained, which were unshuttered against the elements. A portion of the roof had caved in as well, but the remainder provided ample shade and protection from the sun and rain. The rooftop of a large building could be seen behind a line of trees, not far away, but distant enough that they felt fairly confident holing up for a short time without being discovered, "So long as we lay low," Ivor cautioned.

It was their second night there when Ivor returned with Cezar's meager repast—along with an announcement. Cezar swallowed the meat after a few fast chews. Cezar found it curious that Ivor never ate with him, but for some reason could never remember to ask, and once again it slipped his mind.

"Excellent news. We have a solution to our money problem."

"What solution?" Cezar asked.

"Let's fuck first."

"We don't *fuck*." Cezar said the last word as if he'd bitten into a bitter almond. "We make love," he insisted.

"Of course we do," replied Ivor, with a touch of amusement. "And now it is time we make love in a special way. To celebrate." Ivor leaned toward him with a peculiar lust in his eyes. His head dived down as he stroked Cezar's cock, then pushed it aside. "It's better than fucking." Cezar opened his mouth to protest, but was silenced by the sweet pain in his loins. After a moment Ivor lifted his head, his mouth was red, his expression blank. "Third time lucky," Ivor whispered, cradling Cezar's chin with his hand.

"Lucky?" Cezar's heard his voice, but it seemed to come from a distance.

Ivor's reply was barely the echo of a whisper. "Yes, lucky for us. We'll have eternity."

"I don't understand."

"Three times I have fed on you. No longer must you take scraps from this hand." He reached out to Cezar and took his arm. "Hereafter, we will feed as equals."

At that moment Cezar's vision cleared. He felt himself lift off the ground, his back stiff and straight, hovering as Ivor looked on, his face still blank. Cezar's arms hung limp at his side, his hands slack and hovering inches from the ground. Cezar saw nothing but black for a moment, but soon saw a blazing violet sun, pinpoint at the center of the void. It reached toward him until he was enveloped in a purple mist, which wafted away, like tatters of a lifting fog. It was a moonless night, but Cezar had never seen the world with a vision more clearly or bright as he did now. Ivor held his hand and pulled him to standing—but to Cezar's surprise, he saw his own feet hovering in mid-air.

The next thing Cezar realized was the maddening emptiness in his middle. He had never felt so ravenous. He knew that scraps of meat would no longer suffice. But what would?

"Come along," Ivor said, his hand still in Cezar's. As Ivor tugged gently, Cezar realized they were both indeed floating above the ground outside the ruined building. Ivor beckoned Cezar to take his other hand, his legs gliding in circles through the air, weightless. The feeling was so delightful that Cezar forgot his gnawing hunger for a while. They held hands and hovered above the ground, spinning around with mutual joy.

CHAPTER 4

Kurvat had sucked the blood from seven rats before he remembered the specific edict of Hemera, his benefactor and Lady of the Manor, to fill a larder with partridges before sunrise, and now that was four hours away. On this occasion the request was special. Hemera was with child.

There were plenty of partridges on the game lands abutting the Manor, so tonight's task should have been a simple one, but for the fact that he had misplaced his quiver (he, like his littermates, was forbidden to use fang or claw) and couldn't find it anywhere. It was no use asking to borrow from the other residents of the Manor; they treated their own weapons like their own kin and never gave them up. He began to panic as he loped through the Great Hall with the perpetual fire in its huge open hearth, past the Sanctum, a small anteroom where the residents held special gatherings, always behind closed doors, and which were always locked when not in use. But now the door was ajar.

Kurvat crept over, poked in his head, and spied an ornate quiver, silver filigree on shiny dark leather, lying on a marble pedestal, packed with arrows whose black tips sparkled violet in the half-light from the Great Hall.

Emboldened, he loped over, slung the quiver over his shoulder and trotted out of the room, as quietly as the rats had done before he snared them for his supper.

CHAPTER 5

Ivor and Cezar were still engaged in their whirling reverie when they heard the sound of a trotting horse down the lane. They set down on the ground, and Ivor looked in the direction of the sound. "That must be she," he whispered.

"Who?"

Ivor motioned him to keep quiet, then said in a low voice, "Stay here." He strode to the front of the building, where the clopping hooves stopped, punctuated by a horse's nicker. Cezar crept against the wall, making sure to stay out of sight. Then he heard the sound of a woman's voice, deep-throated, cultured—and unmistakably British. "Here you are. It's good to see you again."

"Lady Ellenborough."

Cezar was surprised at the tone in Ivor's voice, a drawing room formality he'd never heard before.

"Please," answered the Lady, "in such surroundings, it would not be improper to call me Jane, especially since we're keeping to first names only, Master Ivor."

Cezar couldn't resist his curiosity; he peeked around the partition. He saw the tall young woman who stood before Ivor, wrapped in a dark cloak. Even in the gloom she appeared uncommonly pretty and, it seemed to Cezar, twice as shrewd. She spied him and said, "You didn't tell me you were bringing a friend. Show yourself, sir."

Ivor beckoned to him with a look of forgiving irritation. "Jane, this is Cezar. My . . . companion."

Cezar emerged, joined Ivor at his side, and bowed. "My Lady," he said.

She accepted his courtesy with a graceful nod. "Fine manners. Are you of gentle blood?"

"He is," Ivor said, "but now we are both strangers here, destitute and skulking like rogues, and very much in need of coin, as you know."

"That will be remedied forthwith. As soon as the General arrives," she replied.

A tall, swarthy, mustachioed man strode around the corner of the the building.

"And so he has," said Lady Jane.

Cezar thought he certainly had the bearing of a General. He addressed Jane as he indicated Ivor. "Is this the man?"

She nodded. He turned to Ivor. "Major General Kristopolos. Greek Independent Forces," he said, and then relaxed somewhat. "Jane tells me you fought against the Ottomans in Crimea. Tell me of that." In the space of a minute Ivor described the battles he fought and the field promotions he'd received. Cezar was as impressed as the General seemed to be. Jane looked on with a knowing smile.

"Well, young man," said the General, "your skills are of certain value to us. But I gather these skills are not just for asking. Name your price, and then…" The General spread his arms wide. "Let us haggle."

But before Ivor could reply Cezar pulled him aside and hissed at him. "Using purse-strings to strangle the future of an oppressed people! How can you?"

Ivor was only momentarily surprised to hear the indignation in Cezar's voice, the glint of challenge in his eye. They had discussed the religious and political unrest ravaging their host country, but in abstractions, teacher to soldier. But Ivor had also come to recognize the foolish, albeit, charming romanticism that seemed bred in Cezar's bones. He was gentle as he replied, while the General chafed nearby.

"Consider our state of affairs. I too feel for the noble citizens of this ancient land. But we are strangers here, with no resources or comfort. Besides," he whispered into Cezar's ear, "these are persons of means and influence. If we refuse, no doubt they will find someone with greater greed than need. Are we not more deserving than they?"

Cezar could find no answer to his argument, so in the end, haggle they did, and in the end agreed on a fair price—which equaled two full years of Cezar's salary as an instructor. The General took out a leather coin purse and opened it, digging inside.

Suddenly, Ivor drew in a strangled breath and cried out in pain. He looked down and saw the arrow that had pierced his thigh clear through, its black tip dripping blood. With one hand he grasped the shaft of the arrow, then reached out to Cezar, as if begging to be pulled out of a chasm. Cezar started toward him, but in a matter of seconds Ivor's body vaporized in a burgundy mist which hung momentarily in the air, then suddenly wafted away.

Frozen where he stood and open-mouthed with astonishment, Cezar couldn't take his eyes off the ash left behind, or the arrow that had taken his lover's life lying in the midst of it—until the General retrieved it, rolling the shaft in his fingers. "You!" he called out, "Over there in the thicket! Come over here!"

Cezar looked up. The General's face was stern as he watched a creature, as much bear as man, approach with extreme deference, almost cowering.

"Kurvat," said the General.

Kurvat nodded, averting his eyes. The General held up the arrow with one hand and stretched out his other. Kurvat handed over the quiver.

"Go back and wait."

At the General's command Kurvat loped off in the direction of the manor. The General trudged over to Cezar, whose disbelief was written all over his face. The General put his hand on Cezar's shoulder and gave it a gentle squeeze. "Most unfortunate." His voice was soft and solicitous. "The wages of war often go beyond money. Still, unless you wish to make good your friend's promise . . ." The General's voice trailed off to silence.

Cezar stood mute from shock, his eyes still fixed on the ashes.

"I see." The General put away the purse. "Very well then. Good luck to you." He leaned toward Jane and whispered into her ear, "I must attend to Kurvat." To his surprise, Cezar could hear the General's words as if he had shouted them. "Later, then," he added, "at the usual place." With a quick nod at Cezar, the General made off after Kurvat.

Jane went to Cezar, who stood frozen with grief. She looked deep into his eyes with sympathy. "I know too well what it is to love and lose by the thread of fate." She reached in her cloak and took out a purse and held it out to him. "Take this," she said. "It is no longer safe for you here. You must leave Greece at once. Take this road west and embark at Patras." She gave him the names of a ship and its Captain. "Show him the purse, and he will know you as my trusted friend. The ship sails in three days." He floundered for proper words to express his gratitude. Evidently none were needed; she kissed him on the cheek instead. He escorted her to the pony cart, intending to help her up—when suddenly the pony, neighed, bucked and backed away, trap and all, as Cezar approached.

"No matter," Jane said, "I can manage," as she hoisted herself into the trap with little effort. She took the reins and said, "Good fortune go with you, sir." With that she reined the pony toward the road. The pony's brisk trot seemed to say how very glad he was to part company with Cezar.

CHAPTER 6

The General stood before Hemera. She was stately and commanding despite her garment of simple weave, and since she was lean and well-formed, it was hard to guess her age. She sat in the wooden cross-framed chair, the only furniture in a small anteroom off the Great Hall of the Manor. Sunlight streamed in through a window of leaded glass, glinting off the arrow that lay in Hemera's lap. The same arrow the General had retrieved from Ivor's death site. Even though Kurvat was clearly Ivor's murderer, he had been questioned briefly and then dismissed.

"There can be no doubt, Hemera," the General said emphatically, "the one called Ivor must have been of a higher order. As was his companion. Without doubt."

Kurvat had speared Ivor on instinct, that much was clear; as a lower-order vampire, he wasn't capable of much more, yet he had touched the point of the arrow and had been unaffected—a fact that greatly interested the woman.

"And I do not doubt *you*, Christos," Hemera replied. "Whether by fate or chance, it seems our ancient duty has been thrust upon us once again." She fell silent in contemplation. "Where did the Lady Ellenborough send this companion?"

"To the port at Patras. He will board ship there for America."

Hemera fell silent again. "Then we shall follow him." Hemera patted her belly. "Our child will usher in a corps of the Vanator on new soil, and take my place as Burgess." She held out her hand, and the General gently pulled Hemera to her feet. "I must make haste."

"*You* must make haste?" asked the General. "Am I not to accompany you?"

She shook her head. "Greece needs you here." She squeezed the General's arm. "You have given us Vanator a great gift, a new beginning, a child of the New World to continue our vigil of the vampire nation, which clearly seeks to spread."

This made sense to the General. As King Otto's military leader, he was too embroiled in the battles of his beloved homeland, at odds with itself over religion, while foreign powers squabbled as they chipped away the Greek political landscape. He knew his duties. As a son of Greece he must protect his native land. As a progenitor of those who kept the peace between the warring vampire factions—the Primes and the Sympaths—he must father the next Burgess of the Vanator in the New World and spread his tribe's seed to foreign soil.

CHAPTER 7

Though Gedrec had had some reservations about fitting into the regimented structure of the Naval Academy, he had found the faculty to be welcoming, and the administration to be more open-minded than he anticipated. He even had some hand in designing the curriculum, despite the fact that he had no battle experience, apart from fending off pirates on the HMS Beagle and the ordinary rigors of life as a sailor. He was a popular instructor, despite his youth—or perhaps because of it. He was an exacting taskmaster, but far from a rigid one. He had a good sense of humor, but still demanded diligence, good form, and sound judgment from his students. Thus far, after eleven graduating classes, he hadn't been disappointed. *Or disappointing.*

In the beginning the staff would inquire occasionally if he was courting, but he always insisted his work came first, and would attend to that when opportunity allowed. Eventually they stopped asking, and began to notice his regular excursions to Baltimore, jibing him, calling him a rake, and perhaps, which several gentlemen said with a leer, a little too handy with certain "exotic" women. *Half right*, he thought, with an inscrutable smile of his own that his colleagues took, wrongly, as agreement.

In the late spring of 1856, however, Gedrec had even greater—and quite understandable—reason to smile: he was given a year's sabbatical to continue his research, partially subsidized by the Academy and supplemented with his savings. In one week's time he would board ship and return to the digs in Neander Valley. But until then he would keep company with some sturdy sailor, who was able and willing to share all the diversions the busy port had to offer—including his own special attentions to the lucky lad he would happen upon.

His private rooms were comfortable and spacious at a quiet hotel whose keeper was as discreet as he was pragmatic: "Your business is your own, sir," he assured Gedrec, taking the full week's payment with a smile. "So long as you don't go makin' clamor and bustin' up the place." The hotel was tucked away on Liberty Street, just outside the Inner Harbor and well within walking distance of the pubs there. It was late afternoon when he arrived. He took a light meal and then rested in anticipation of a raucous night.

But he was wrong.

His favorite pub—usually loud and lusty with sailors and sundry in various states of intoxication—was relatively quiet. He counted two dozen or so people, and the conversations were hushed. The atmosphere was gloomy, and no one was more somber than the barkeep himself, Clyde, whom Gedrec considered a friend. Clyde brightened considerably when he saw Gedrec, who strolled over and asked, "What happened? Where is everyone?"

"It's been nigh on two weeks when business started falling off," the barkeep replied mournfully.

According to Clyde, evidently a sort of wasting sickness seeped throughout the harbor, one that affected the strength, complexion, and—oddly—memory; victims couldn't recall entire days, even though the fever was light. It eventually spread to enough people that the officials had gotten worried, as much about revenue as public health. They had even considered a quarantine. Fortunately, the effect seemed to have leveled off, and those stricken seemed to be recovering. But there were a few deaths—among whom was Clyde's wife, Maisie. The news greatly saddened Gedrec, because he genuinely liked the tough-minded, plain-spoken Celtic woman, and said so to Clyde, adding his condolences.

"Aye, much obliged," Clyde said, his eyes filling with tears. "Always believed naught but a hurricane would put down me Maisie." He forced a bright smile and handed Gedrec a whiskey. "Here you go. Your usual."

Gedrec, crestfallen, had reconciled to spending the night alone when he spotted a brooding dark man sitting alone in a dark corner. The man seemed to be about his own age. Gedrec took note of the broad shoulders and lean torso, the long and muscular arms, with hands which were large and shapely, yet graceful as he poked his glass back and forth. Suddenly the man looked up and leveled his gaze at Gedrec without pause—or surprise. Gedrec saw the glint in the man's deep-set eyes. A beard several days old accented his square jaw and framed his thin but firm lips. After a moment, the man offered Gedrec a broad smile—but a rather sad one, Gedrec though—his teeth even and white, glistening in the dim light of the tavern. Gedrec strolled over, as much mesmerized as encouraged.

The man leaned back in his chair and appraised his guest.

Gedrec got right to the point. "How do you do, sir." Gedrec bowed slightly and tipped his hat but did not offer his hand. He was, after all, a son of Victorian gentry and bred to its etiquette, and this was no rough-hewn sailor.

"Gedrec Kirkland at your service."

"Cezar Balanescu," the man replied, abrupt but friendly.

"May I assume you are on your own?"

"You may," Cezar answered in stilted English, "and you would be correct." Underneath the table he pushed the chair opposite, sliding it out, evidently inviting Gedrec to sit.

Which he did. Cezar related the unexpected loss of his devoted friend in Europe and his subsequent flight to America. Gedrec apologized and rose from his seat, assuming that Cezar's obvious grief precluded companionship.

With a sudden reach across the table that astonished Gedrec, Cezar grasped Gedrec's wrist. "No, please, good sir," he pleaded. "Forgive my bad manners. Your company is most welcome."

Gedrec sank back into his chair. He put his hand on top of Cezar's, who still held tight to his wrist and didn't let go for a full minute—which for Gedrec was full of promise. They shared their stories with easy confidence. An hour sped by, then two.

In the meantime, more patrons strolled in, one or two at a time, among them a pair of women, looking pale and doing their best to appear frisky. The tone of the conversations became lighter. One seaman even serenaded, "My Love Is Like A Red, Red Rose." Soon the plaintive sound of a fiddle joined in, and the pair listened with the rest, and the mood had changed from solemn to nostalgic. At that point the two men exchanged a meaningful glance. Without a word, they rose and slipped out of the tavern together.

They walked side-by-side, close enough to rub shoulders as they walked through the streets, glancing at each other now and again. They said nothing as they entered the inn and made their way to Gedrec's rooms. They spoke with their eyes as they undressed each other, purposeful and deliberate, then with their bodies bare chested, grinding their cocks together.

Gedrec would find that, in Cezar, he met his match and more—endowed with energy, endurance, and daring. They pulled off their drawers as they grappled, unable to restrain themselves, spilling their seed on each other's flesh in minutes, ending the tryst with a deep kiss, which only brought their cocks once again to full mast. Gedrec lay back as Cezar snuggled against him, stroking the shaft of Gedrec's now fully erect penis and gently jerking his own.

"This won't end here, will it?" asked Cezar.

Gedrec stroked his hair. "Of course not," he replied, then smile. "I'm not through with you yet, sir." And with that remark he leaned over and gently grasped Cezar's cock, now hard as his own. They screwed hard until shortly before dawn, when Cezar announced he must leave. Gedrec made him promise to return. "This evening, seven o'clock, right here," Cezar agreed.

After a nap, Gedrec breakfasted in his room, then went to purchase a bottle of wine. He turned a corner and literally bumped into a rather short and bear-like young man leaning against the wall. His attire was peculiar—more like a hunter than a sailor or merchant.

"I beg your pardon," Gedrec said, tipping his hat.

"Quite all right, sir," said the man, watching Gedrec until he disappeared.

Then the man made off in the opposite direction, down one street and up another. He went through an alley into a small courtyard, where a stately woman, obviously with child, sat on a wrought-iron bench, reading a book. She looked up, closed the book and waited.

"He is here, Burgess," the man said. "Went with a gentleman who has rooms on Liberty Street last night."

The Burgess Hemera was silent for a few minutes, considering. "Very good. Continue the watch."

"The rooms are well out of the way, ma'am. If we dispatch the gents in the room—"

"No!" Hemera's tone was sharp, and her eyes flashed. "Remember, that is *not* our role!" At once her expression softened. She continued in a calm voice. "Understand this, Kurvat. This is a fragile time. You are not to harm Cezar or his companion, either by intent or mischance." She rose and towered over him. He bowed his head. "You are a faithful servant to the Vanator, Kurvat, and a valuable one besides. Without you, Ivor and Cezar almost certainly would have slipped by unnoticed. There is much work ahead. I should hate to lose you. Do you understand?"

"Yes, Burgess," he answered, contrite. "No harm to Cezar. Just watch and report."

She nodded. "All hangs in the balance," she said, as if to herself. "If there is one like Cezar, there must be more. But how many? And where?" She looked Kurvat in the eye. "Go now and feed," she told him, "then rest. Return to your post after sunset."

Kurvat bowed and snuck away.

She sighed and eased herself down on the bench and sat in silence, contemplating.

CHAPTER 8

Seven o'clock couldn't come soon enough for Gedrec, yet he dreaded it, as he had all week, and Cezar picked up on that mood when he arrived—late, which was unusual.

"I am behind my time, I know it," Cezar said, nuzzling Gedrec's neck. "Forgive me?"

Gedrec slipped from his embrace and avoided Cezar's eyes. "It's not that. Something I must tell you."

Cezar held onto Gedrec's hands and regarded him closely. "Yes?"

Gedrec took a deep breath. "It's to be our final night together." They had never discussed the future, too absorbed in the passions of the present.

Cezar struggled to hide his surprise and dismay. In a quiet, reasonable tone, he asked, "Have I displeased you?"

"No! Not at all," Gedrec reassured him. "I thought we had assumed we would go our separate ways…" His voice trailed off. "When the time came."

"Why must that time ever come?" His words were measured, his tone flat and steady, full of warning, it seemed to Gedrec, and it unnerved him.

"Because it must," stuttered Gedrec. "As we must return to our daily lives." Only then did Gedrec realize the depth of his own heartbreak and knew that Cezar felt the same. "What else could we do?"

It seemed Cezar had an answer. "We could have a life together."

After a pause to absorb his surprise, Gedrec said, "Not possible."

"Why not?"

"Tomorrow I leave for Germany. It's all arranged."

Cezar glared at him for a few leaden seconds. "Tomorrow?" *Like an accusation,* thought Gedrec with sudden sadness; he couldn't find his voice, so he nodded.

Cezar began to pace, stealing quick glances at Gedrec from shining eyes. Gedrec decided to give him some privacy and moved toward the door. In a blurry motion that Gedrec had seen several times before—and dismissed as a trick of light—Cezar seemed to vanish and then reappear, blocking the door, barring his exit. He regarded Gedrec with a peculiar combination of grief, hunger, lust—and love, then pounced toward him and wrapped Gedrec in his arms.

* * *

Gedrec was slow to awaken. The dusky light hurt his eyes. He gathered all his strength and tried to sit up, when he found himself nude—and restrained. Through his blurred vision he looked side-to-side and saw that his wrists and ankles were tied to the bedposts with his own stockings. He tried to shake the bleariness from his mind, but it stuck there like damp salt. He felt feverish. Had he been ill? Had Cezar been a concoction of his mind?

He heard the sound of stirring underneath, and the mattress bumped. A hand groped over the edge of the bed, followed by Cezar's bearded face. He got to his feet and stood tall, his erection tenting his nightshirt between his muscular legs. Cezar's brow creased with concern and contrition, his eyes sad and pleading. Despite his fright and confusion, Gedrec felt his own cock harden. With his erection came an overwhelming desire to hear Cezar's voice.

Cezar lit some candles, then came over and lay next to Gedrec. "I couldn't let you go," he said. Cezar's deep voice resonated deliciously in Gedrec's gut; he felt warmth flood through his body. "But neither can I force love from you." He untied Gedrec's wrists.

Gedrec struggled to prop himself on his elbows, but fell back. "What's wrong with me?" he asked.

"Nothing that a few weeks of rest and good food won't cure," Cezar answered, "if that is what you wish."

"What do you mean?"

Cezar put his arm under Gedrec's shoulders and lifted him. "Here," Cezar said, pointing to Gedrec's inner thigh. Gedrec looked and saw a pair of puncture wounds. He turned to Cezar, who drew back with a wide grin. His teeth gleamed in the candlelight—including the two fangs that slowly emerged, like a snake's. He felt Cezar's cock stiffen as he caressed his wounded thigh. The fangs folded back as Cezar's lips covered his teeth.

Cezar cradled Gedrec's head on his arm and looked him in the eyes. He was gentle and sincere as he declaimed. "Thus far you have only served as a meal."

"A meal!" Gedrec felt hurt at being reduced to fodder. He tried for indignation, but he was too weak to manage more than a sickroom whine. "Is that all I have been?"

"Hush, now!" Cezar scolded, but his voice was no less loving. "No, not all. Only in terms of my feeding on you. And now it may end—if you wish—with your taking no further harm…" Here he stopped and drew closer, almost nose to nose, and his eyes glowed with excitement. "Or it can be a beginning. For you, for both of us. An adventure we will cherish forever."

Gedrec couldn't help but be intrigued at the prospect. "Tell me."

And so Cezar told all he knew from what Ivor had shared. The first feed, a meal. The second feed, within twenty-eight days of the first, would enslave Gedrec as a second-rate creature, a subpar vampire that would subsist on lower animals, half in the shadow of Cezar and the other in sunlight he would hate. The third would initiate him, and he would join Cezar as an equal—even to sharing feeds with him.

"But consider," Cezar cautioned, "Once done, this cannot be undone. I have resolved not to advise you." Cezar placed a hand on Gedrec's shoulder. "I love you, you love me. But your own good sense must prevail in this."

CHAPTER 9

Kurvat returned to Hemera just after dawn. She looked ungainly as she walked around the courtyard, but she moved with grace. She motioned to Kurvat to join her. "What did you discover?"

"Kirkland boarded the ship with Balanescu. Just after midnight."

"Where is the ship going?"

"New York. Then to England."

"You're certain?"

"First Mate told me himself," he replied, then lowered his voice, "after a bribe."

"They stayed on board?"

"Yes, Burgess. Watched it sail myself, right at dawn."

"A new nation has begun," Hemera mused.

She turned to Kurvat. "Come, my friend," she said kindly, stretching out her hand, "and bring me my book." He brought it to her, and she patted the arm he offered for support. "You are a good servant, Kurvat," she assured him. "But time may be short. We must notify our people."

She held out the book and gazed at it. *If only you were the Amaranth, I might fathom your wisdom and be grateful*, she thought, recalling the mythic tome her father told her of, beyond antiquity, on which Burgesses had relied for counsel until it had been lost long ago, or perhaps destroyed. Or maybe it was truly only a legend, invented to comfort those who shouldered the burden as she did, as her father did before her.

But it was just a book, and silent. Still, despite her doubts, she would honor tradition, and tell her child of the *Amaranth*, who would in turn take comfort in the knowledge of the many Burgesses who preceded them.

CHAPTER 10

After Cezar and Gedrec returned from Europe in December of 1857, having already pledged their immortal devotion, they had agreed: *Don't attract attention.* Scrutiny was something they couldn't afford. It was for that reason that Gedrec gave up his teaching post for reasons of health, so he said. Meanwhile, the local industry had definite use for Cezar's skills as an engineer for the railroad. So, after nearly six years in Baltimore, they were settled and respected, well-liked by their neighbors, despite their reclusiveness and odd habit of working at night.

If anyone guessed the nature of their relationship, nothing was mentioned. Rupert, their butler and valet, on the other hand, had full knowledge of his employers' peculiarities since they rescued him from starvation in England, and he was more than willing to return the favor. He was a robust, twenty-two-year-old, and they took enough of his blood to keep their excursions outside to a minimum. They did not kill or turn anyone—four feeds a week each seemed to sustain them very well.

At about noon on an overcast autumn day in 1863, Rupert opened the door to the grim, nondescript but impeccably dressed man who had knocked and insisted Cezar accompany him, refusing to disclose his name, purpose or destination. Cezar had been ready to decline until two strapping Federal soldiers appeared behind the stranger, arms crossed. He knew that Cezar—or he himself, for that matter—could disable any three humans of any size or skill with very little trouble. But they remembered their pledge: lay low, blend in. Besides, the trio looked ominously official—even more so, probably, to the neighbors passing by on the way home from the market. A blood bath, or even an easy escape, would be hard to explain.

Gedrec pulled out his pocket watch—which now held a miniature portrait of Cezar—and saw that it was now past ten o'clock, and the rain that pattered on the roof and windows echoed through the house, making it seem that much emptier.

***

Cezar was tense as he sat in the drafty warehouse. The two federal soldiers flanked him, watching closely, saying not a word and barely moving a muscle since he was brought there earlier in the day. Now it was dark and raining. He could have, of course, easily overtaken both of them—but to what end? He had lived as a fugitive once, and vowed never to do it again. Besides, he wouldn't take the slightest risk of putting Gedrec in harm's way.

Then a well-dressed man entered—a gentleman, surrounded by the cocky, stuffy air of a politician. The federal soldiers snapped to attention. The gentleman addressed them: "As you were." They assumed their stance, and the gentleman leveled a shrewd gaze at Cezar and said, "You've been recognized."

Cezar managed to look indignant and produce a cockiness of his own. "May I have your name, sir, and the reason why I've been abducted?"

The gentleman pulled over a chair and sat directly across from him. "My name is unimportant, as far as you're concerned. But yours is Cezar Balanescu. Still a subject of the Ottoman Empire, I believe."

Cezar felt stabs in his gut, first one of surprise, then of fear.

"And a traitor also, I'm told," the gentleman added.

Cezar, in a panic, scanned the room for obstacles and exits. He thought, *Four men. Even them I can handle, if I must.* To buy time, he asked, "Who told you this falsehood?"

"Oh, it's no lie, I'm certain of that. You've been observed for some time, enough to eliminate any question of who—and *what*—you are."

Once again Cezar was surprised—and wary. He listened closely as the gentleman continued.

"I mention this only as a means to offer you permanent asylum here. Even citizenship, if you wish, as this would in fact prove your loyalty. Gratitude from this great nation of ours." He paused. "On the other hand, if you refuse, the Sultan would be very grateful to know your location. Even if you escaped," he added with a smile, "your companion would not."

Cezar's mouth dropped open.

"Yes, indeed. At this very moment a contingent of soldiers surrounds your home. Your friend would be quite outmatched. No escape, I fear—except into the afterlife when the sun shines again." He leaned forward. "On the other hand, if you cooperate, your life as a couple will be both secure and prosperous." He leaned back and crossed his arms. "Well, sir. What is your response?"

Cezar bowed his head. "What must I do?"

Excitement crept into the gentleman's voice for the first time, and his voice was low. "A number of key Confederate officers must not live out the year. But no dying in battle, no heroics. Their deaths must appear by natural causes." He whispered in Cezar's ear. "A wasting disease, for instance? A fever, or flux, perhaps? We know you can slip past sentries like no spy ever could."

***

Gedrec heard the door open. He jumped up and bumped into Rupert, who was going to answer it, chewing, napkin in hand.

"I'll get the door, Rupert," Gedrec said. "Return to your meal. You'll need it." Tomorrow was the new moon—their turn with Rupert. And robust as he was, Rupert still needed all the nourishment he could get to sustain him during the feed.

Gedrec reached the front door just as Cezar hung up his coat.

"What happened?" Gedrec asked, trying to sound casual.

Cezar smiled at him—a tired, but genuine smile. "Nothing to be concerned about," he said.

"I was considering… perhaps we should return to England. After all, neither of us is a citizen…"

"No need for concern," Cezar replied, and he did not seem worried in the slightest. "It seems my services may be of benefit."

"To whom?"

"The Union."

"Thank Heaven for that," Gedrec commented. They both sided with the abolitionists. "I presume they need you for the railroad?"

Cezar answered, "I will have to travel."

"Travel where? For how long?"

Cezar looked distracted and said nothing.

Gedrec grabbed his arm. "Cezar? Did you hear?"

"Of course I did." He scolded him gently with mock-fierce eyes. "I would never leave you behind." He lifted Gedrec's hand to his lips and kissed it. "Those whom fate has brought together, let no war put asunder." Cezar grinned, and Gedrec chuckled. "We are quite safe now. Both of us. Rest assured."

Their concerns were put to rest by the next night when the last sliver of the waning moon vanished against the clear night sky. Rupert was already lying nude on the bed, his back propped against the headboard, when Cezar and Gedrec entered, arm-in-arm, stripped down to their drawers.

Rupert had never professed romantic interest for another man, even when surviving as best he could as a rent boy on the streets of London. Gedrec and Cezar understood that, and they gave back as much as they took, and more. After they fed, they apologized and assured him that he would be as fit as ever after a few weeks, putting him up with a room of his own at their hotel, tending to him like a long-lost brother. And when Rupert recovered, he was more than pleased to reciprocate in kind. Orphaned at birth, his new friends were as close to family he had ever known. Over the years that followed, while he had no desire to transform, Rupert still looked forward to each new moon phase with growing excitement.

Just like this one.

A ritual of lust—of blood.

But first, of flesh.

They flanked him, Gedrec kissing and licking one muscular pec, Cezar at the other, then nipping at Rupert's nipples. Rupert began to writhe and moan as his pleasure began to mount. Cezar stroked the soft skin of Rupert's throat, and with his gentle hand turned Rupert's face toward Gedrec, who had been nibbling on Rupert's ear. Gedrec planted a firm kiss on Rupert's mouth as Cezar's mouth opened wide. Hinged fangs, like a snake's, poked out. With subtle care Cezar punctured Rupert's throat and sucked gently.

Rupert mumbled a moan through Gedrec's kiss. Gedrec stroked Rupert's rock hard abs, tracing the ridges of muscle with his finger. His tongue soon followed, tracing the muscles down into the thick light brown pubic hair and over his stiffening uncut cock, running his tongue over it. He didn't linger, instead tonguing the ball sac, again only briefly. He went on to lick the muscular inner thigh, tasting the skin, then sank his own fangs into it. Gedrec sucked deeply for a full two minutes, at which point Rupert's body shook with a seizure, lasting only seconds and terminated in a huge orgasm—a half dozen spurts of thick cum flew everywhere. Rupert let out a long, satisfied sigh, and his body relaxed; his half-hard cock twitched.

Gedrec and Cezar lay next to Rupert on either side, hugging close to him, all sated in their own way, waiting until Rupert drifted off to sleep. He would slumber for the next eighteen hours or so, and awaken refreshed.

Rupert stayed with them for another five years, but only intermittently served as sustenance during that time—when Cezar was home. He was out in the field as often as not, performing whatever duties had been thrust upon him on that gray day back in 1863. What these duties were Cezar never volunteered to say, and answered Gedrec's questions only in the vaguest terms—something to do with national security, the railroad, or both. And lucrative though it was, he would have settled for less money and more Cezar, whose absence left him with an ache that he could barely stand.

Finally, though, to Gedrec's relief and joy, Cezar returned home—to stay.

It was the seventh of May 1865.

CHAPTER 11

President Lincoln's assassination shadowed Gedrec and Cezar's reunion, but in time they had reason to be optimistic again: Cezar accepted a post with the Pacific Railroad, which had been laying track across the Western territories. Almost at once they rented their house, to a certain Mrs. Burgess, a widow—lovely in a stately sort of way—with her handsome young son, Lemuel, who appeared taller and stronger than his nine years. Lemuel watched the couple in silence, with great interest, as the widow dickered with Cezar.

But saddest of all, with tears shed on all sides, was bidding goodbye to Rupert. He planned to return to England to seek his fortune, perhaps take a wife. With promises to keep in touch, he parted with spontaneous kisses and a generous severance.

One of Cezar's wartime associates, a tall, thin, middle-aged man named Fairfax, invited them to the Maryland Club for drinks and cigars on the night before their departure westward. They were advised to wear their best. Fairfax received them warmly, and paid special attention to Gedrec. "So we finally meet! You must be relieved," he said, "to be permanently reunited with your friend."

"Yes, I am indeed," Gedrec replied. "We have been most fortunate."

"Oh, more than fortunate. Much more!" Fairfax blurted out. "Your good fortune has been well earned. Cezar has been of great service to us. We would not be standing here, if not for him. But that you already know, I'm sure, being cut from the same cloth."

"I beg your pardon?"

"Come, no need to pretend now," Fairfax chided genially with a reassuring look. "You're among friends." He gave Gedrec a slow once-over, head to toe, and said in a low voice, "I can be an even better friend."

"Is that so?"

"Yes, indeed." Fairfax gave him another long look, this time lingering on his crotch, looked Gedrec right in the eye. "You're going west with your companion, yes?"

"That's right."

"Very dangerous road, so I've heard."

"Thank you for your concern. But we can take of ourselves."

"Of course you can," Fairfax chuckled. "Cezar is quite the traveler. And with both of you so fit," he commented, now frankly admiring Gedrec as though he were a prize stallion, "I'm certain that he can perform just as well in the wilderness as he did for us.

"Us?"

"The North, of course. I even suspected you might have had a hand in it. A meal is a meal, yes?" He gave Gedrec a gentle poke in the ribs. "A General's blood is as rich as any other man's. Well…maybe a *little* richer," he said with a wink. "Though from the reports, the Confederate ranks seemed thinner than battle could account for." He whispered in Gedrec's ear, "That's why I reckoned you might have lent a hand—or a tooth?"

"I don't know what you mean."

Fairfax snorted. "No? Well, I'm sure you know that you need a proper start to your journey."

"Proper start?"

"Unencumbered. So much rests on a man's reputation to secure his future. If anything unsavory were to come out…" He shrugged with feigned helplessness.

Gedrec said in an even voice, "He might be ruined."

"No question of that. But you could prevent it. You would do that for a friend, wouldn't you?"

"A 'better' friend? Like you?"

"To everyone concerned." Fairfax arched an eyebrow.

Gedrec saw Cezar make his way toward them through the throng. He pursed his lips. "Very well," he said in a chilly voice. "How exactly shall I satisfy?"

Fairfax wasn't put off by the chill in Gedrec's voice. He leaned over and whispered in Gedrec's ear. "I have rooms here. Come at midnight. You will be expected."

Cezar joined them. He was only partially able to conceal his alarm. "Is this a private conversation?"

"Not at all," replied Gedrec in a breezy tone. "Mr. Fairfax has been telling me how much he admired the way you discharged your duties and how... cooperative... you were. He also expressed his concern about our safety. And how important it was that we depart without..." He turned to Fairfax. "What was the word? Encumbrance?"

"It was indeed," replied Fairfax with a smile that froze Cezar's marrow. "Just as a friend," he added, turning to Cezar. "Considering our past association, you understand."

Gedrec's smile was glassy. "I was just about to reassure Mr. Fairfax that there was no need for his concern. I told him that I... that is, *we*... are quite handy with the unexpected." His smile turned warm as he gazed at Cezar, put his hand on his shoulder and gave it a squeeze. "Aren't we, Chuckaboo?"

Cezar was startled at Gedrec's using his private nickname in public; likewise, Cezar called Gedrec *Bricky* in their tenderer moments. He looked at still-smiling Gedrec, whose cold eyes were fixed on Fairfax. Clearly, something was up.

***

Gedrec presented to the Club at the time appointed by Fairfax. He was admitted by a plain, short, elf-like man, who said, without even looking up, "Hall on your left. Door at the end."

As dwarfish as the servant at the front door had been, the one attending the hall door was equally tall and burly, and had even less to say. Silent and looking through Gedrec as though he were invisible, Burly opened the door a quarter of the way.

Gedrec slipped in and found Fairfax, standing by a table, lighting a cigar, wearing a burgundy silk dressing gown that hung on his frame, making him seem taller and thinner than ever. Gedrec noted for the first time the specks of silver in his beard and hair. Fairfax offered a crooked, confident smile. "Very punctual. I like that. I like it when people do what they're told. Just like your Cezar. But then…" He paused to throw back the curtain at the foot of the canopy bed, "he didn't have much choice, did he?"

Gedrec realized the question was rhetorical.

"I assume that Cezar is the 'man' of the house, so-called?"

"Is that what he told you?"

"We never discussed your domestic arrangements. There was the war, after all." He paused, and continued with some tenderness in his voice. "He cares for you deeply, you know."

Yes, thought Gedrec, *I know.*

Earlier that evening, after he had told Cezar of Fairfax's "proposal," Cezar told him of Fairfax's ultimatum in the warehouse when he was taken in 1863, and the true nature of his involvement in the war. Gedrec was disappointed at first, thinking Cezar should have stood firm; they both strongly supported the Union cause, certainly, but had sworn to stay neutral, for practical reasons, when it came to the States' War. *"But Fairfax threatened us, my love,"* Cezar *said, his voice edged with desperation. "To separate us. Even kill us. For you I would face the noon sun with no regrets,"* he added tearfully, *"except I could never bear not seeing your face at every sundown."* So, taking into account that they both had been hemmed in by opportunism, even in the face of substantial reward, Gedrec conceded—and both agreed that they must make Fairfax pay for his scheming somehow.

"So you may repay Cezar's devotion in kind," Fairfax said, coming over to Gedrec and undoing his trousers and feeling up his buttocks. "We must all make sacrifices, yes?"

"Yes," Gedrec said as he groped Fairfax—who was surprisingly well endowed—and then gripped like a vise. "All of us." Just as Fairfax cried out, a hand came around from behind him and covered his mouth, muffling the sound. The hand jerked Fairfax's head to the side. First he saw the drapes fluttering in the breeze from the open window, then saw whose hand it was over his mouth—Cezar's, who whispered in Fairfax's ear, "Some of us more than others," then opened his mouth wide, and sank his fangs in, and none too gently.

The last thing Fairfax could recall was so terrifying, he wasn't certain it wasn't some sort of fever dream.

He was still in Cezar's grip, his neck stinging, his limbs flaccid. Gedrec was sitting in an armchair, naked from the waist down, his cock stiff and massive, standing straight up from his thicket of pubic hair and generous ball sac. He felt Cezar lift him as though he weighed nothing, lifting one leg wide, exposing his anus as he approached Gedrec, who held his cock in his hand, aiming as if to urinate. Fairfax's own cock was far from limp, but stuck straight out from his body, hovering over Gedrec's lap, the head brushing against Gedrec's lips. Fairfax ached to have his cock sucked—but the desire was ripped from his mind as his ass was pushed down hard, and

Gedrec's cock speared him. He screamed into Cezar's hand that firmly covered his mouth. "Not done yet, my man," Cezar whispered. Those were the last words Fairfax heard; the world was going gray, with spikes of fiery red, as Cezar rammed his own stiff cock, joining Gedrec's inside his already sore ass, reaming mercilessly, as Fairfax's world went from gray to black.

***

They had done the unconscious Fairfax a favor and put him to bed. As they shared the washbasin, rinsing and drying their privates, Gedrec said, "One thing." Gedrec broke the embrace and stepped back a full stride, fixing Cezar with a determined gaze. "No more secrets. And no more broken promises. We stand firm. Agreed?"

"That's two things." Cezar reached out and took Gedrec's hand. "And I agree to both." They left through the open window, pulling the drapes and closing the window behind them.

***

When Fairfax became fully conscious weeks later, his nightshirt and bedclothes soaked with sweat. He had awakened from a terrifying dream, so he said. A doctor was tending him, telling him he had been ill. Initially a rat-bite on his neck had been blamed, but it was finally decided food poisoning had been the culprit, though no one at the Maryland Club had taken ill that night, fortunately. The blood in his bowel movements disappeared by degrees. His staff exchanged fearful glances but said nothing.

CHAPTER 12

Cezar and Gedrec lived and worked out of hotels as they traveled, keeping nocturnal hours which few, colleagues or acquaintances, ever questioned. And if anyone speculated about his relationship with Gedrec, no one commented on it, at least to Cezar's knowledge.

Gedrec found a new diversion as they moved across the Western Frontier, the "Native Peoples," as he referred to them—the Cheyenne tribe in particular. The various Indian nations found Gedrec just as remarkable, referring to him as "Two-Spirit." They invited him to their most secret and sacred ceremonies, and even provided lodging. It was as though they understood the primal side of their guest and accepted it just as that—a natural, and as such, beautiful thing.

Cezar, for his part, wasn't surprised at Gedrec's interest, considering his fascination with cultural roots. In fact, he encouraged this interest, and was not at all resentful that Gedrec embraced their rituals even when Cezar was excluded, particularly since he was often too busy to take issue.

One Cheyenne warrior found Gedrec so intriguing that the young Indian watched from the shadows, so quiet that Gedrec was hardly aware of his presence at first. Eventually Gedrec tried in vain to engage the young man, and finally able to get what he assumed was the warrior's name, who said as he pointed to his chest—*Oh-Kahm-Ah-Keet.* Gedrec did the same, eliciting a sudden brief smile from the Indian. Later Gedrec discovered it was indeed the warrior's name: Chief Little Wolf.

Then one night when Gedrec became aware of his own growing hunger, the warrior became bolder, emerging from the shadows, standing next to him, gazing into his eyes. Still he said nothing, but patted the side of his neck.

Gedrec's appetite began to rise, like magma in his gut, and he became more aware of the Indian's powerful stature, and noticed for the first time he had a scant, even beard, black as his hair. Gedrec became aroused as his fangs began to protrude, but forced back his lust. After all, as an honored guest, wouldn't it be an insult to impose like this? He felt he should discourage the young man. "Chief Little Wolf," he began in a gently dismissive tone that he hoped didn't sound condescending.

A Tribe Elder trudged into the lamplight and announced, "My nephew wants to bond with you. In your way." His English was stilted but surprisingly good.

"I gathered that, sir," replied Gedrec respectfully. "But it would be improper. "

"He chooses. *Epp-eh-vah.*" Gedrec knew the phrase: *It is good.*

"*Heh-eh.*" This from Little Wolf himself. *Yes.*

Gedrec could see the pleading behind the pride on Little Wolf's face. It was clear that the real insult would be in refusing him. He addressed the Elder. "He will be ill for a time afterward. But he will recover. Does he understand?" He indicated Little Wolf.

A slight nod from the Elder, a second's hesitation, and Gedrec set to his task. He felt Little Wolf's body tense, then shake, his cock stiffening and then spewing his seed on the ground.

Chief Little Wolf did fall ill, but not so deeply and recovered quickly, in two days, seeming more robust than ever. In the weeks that followed, the warrior visited Gedrec and treated him as an equal. He felt warmth like the noonday sun flow from Little Wolf. At last, when Cezar's work took them farther westward, Chief Little Wolf presented Gedrec with a pipe he carved himself. A salute—outstretched hand, palm down—and a single tear marked the warrior's goodbye, after which he disappeared into the darkness without looking back.

Gedrec had trunks filled with notebooks, tossed in at random, documenting his experiences. He had come to love the subtle beauty of the open spaces of the prairies and the majestic panorama of the mountains, and he found himself heartbroken to leave them behind.

They finally settled in San Francisco's Bay Area, and purchased a house and adjacent properties on Castro Street. Cezar felt very much at home among a large contingent of Russian and Finnish immigrants.

They both kept busy. City planners consulted Cezar regarding a new public transport system called the "cable car," which fascinated him. Gedrec offered his services as a tutor, which were in high demand from students attending several of the new schools that had recently opened. He had little time to work on his own research, and thought he might take on an assistant or a protégé—but he had even less time to screen likely candidates.

They barely had time to feed, in fact. Fortunately for the pair, their neighborhood was perfectly located: near the docks and the Mission District, both of which had plenty of nighttime activity. San Francisco was still in the grips of "gold fever." Reckless prospectors roamed the streets with more money in their pockets than sense in their heads, and police officers were few and far between. So the pair fed carefully and followed a strict plan—prowling well-defined areas which they rotated every twenty-eight days, and keeping as much as possible to healthy men, who would recover quickly with no memory of the incident. From time to time they 9considered scouting for a permanent, willing participant as they had in Rupert.

Then in the autumn of 1899, providence heard their call—and answered it, but in a way neither Cezar nor Gedrec expected.

CHAPTER 13

While a fair number of men answered the newspaper advertisement for a domestic servant—no cooking required—none stayed for more than a few minutes. They offered a variety of excuses but they looked uniformly uncomfortable as they left.

"Maybe they realized that we were … together," Cezar suggested.

"Or that we're peckish. It's been more than a week. You do get that ravenous look," Gedrec commented.

Just then a knock came at the door.

"Did we see everyone?" asked Cezar.

"Everyone who inquired."

Gedrec shrugged and opened the door.

There stood a young woman, unusually tall and rather thin. A slightly tattered coat covered a wrinkled white blouse with a loosely tied black ribbon at the neck. The dark skirt was also wrinkled.

"I'm here to apply for the position." She lifted a newspaper, which had a grease stain at the fold.

The two men stood staring.

She cocked her head and quoted. "Domestic servant for two gentleman required immediately." After a pause, she rattled the paper. "No cooking, it says."

Cezar came to life. "Well … we were expecting a man."

"Doesn't say so here." She weaved to and fro on her feet, and put a hand to her forehead. She seemed on the brink of fainting.

Cezar took arm and steadied. "Come inside and rest a minute," he said as he brought her into the foyer and helped her down onto a settee.

Gedrec pulled Cezar aside. "Think she's faking?"

"I don't think so. Look at her."

They watched as she tried to collect herself. She was indeed quite pale, but they also saw she was uncommonly pretty in the gaslight, with thick, cider-colored hair.

"May I trouble you for some water?" she asked. "And perhaps a little something to eat? I haven't eaten in three days."

Gedrec avoided her pleading expression. "I'm not certain what we have in the pantry," he said. "We usually ... go out for dinner," he finished lamely.

"Oh, I'm sure we can find something," Cezar commented, then asked, "Would you care for some brandy?"

"That would be lovely."

Gedrec grabbed Cezar's arm. "May I have a word?"

"Certainly," Cezar answered, then turning to the woman. "I'll return presently with your brandy, Miss . . . ?"

"Call me Elspet," she said.

"Very well. Elspet," Cezar agreed as Gedrec led him out of the room into the library. Cezar went over to the breakfront and rummaged around inside.

"What do you think you're doing?" Gedrec asked.

"Looking for that brandy I got for Christmas."

"In the other cabinet. I mean, what are you doing about *her*?"

"Ah! Here it is." He snapped the seal on a bottle of brandy and poured a generous quantity into a small glass.

"We're hiring a servant, not running a home for itinerant drunkards."

Cezar strolled over to Gedrec. "Don't be so harsh. I like her, that's all. She reminds me of someone I met a long time ago."

"Oh? Who?"

"A certain lady who did me a kindness." He leaned over and kissed Gedrec. "Long before you and I met. In the old country," he finished with an exaggerated accent.

He pointed toward the hallway, then looked askance at Cezar. "You're not thinking of … I mean…" He pointed at his neck.

"Hell, no! Lucky to get a pint out of that poor creature. Hardly worth a jab!"

Gedrec shook his head, not knowing if Cezar was serious or not. But he had to admit, she looked as if she could use a good meal. "Perhaps offer her some money? That way—"

But Cezar breezed past, handing him the glass, and went toward the kitchen.

"Cezar!" Gedrec hissed.

Cezar returned almost immediately. "Here's something," he said, holding an unopened tin of water biscuits. "From last Christmas."

Gedrec's nose crinkled in mild disgust, but he said nothing; there didn't seem to be any point. They returned to the foyer, where Elspet sat, leaning back, fanning herself.

Gedrec handed her the brandy.

"Oh, thank you so much," she said, taking a sip.

"I don't know how good these are, but it's all we have," Cezar said. He pried at the tin; the lid popped off. He held out a flat, perforated biscuit; it was as gray as a tombstone.

She offered a weak, grateful smile. "Anything at all."

She tried to look dainty as she bit, but the hunger in her expression turned at once to a grimace. Her jaw clenched as she tried again and bit a piece off with a snap. She chewed gingerly, trying to manage a smile. She had rather a time trying to swallow, finally getting it down with the brandy, half the glass in a gulp.

Cezar looked at Gedrec, challenging him.

Gedrec let out a long sigh. "Well, well. How about a proper meal then?" he asked. "I believe the Baldwin is still serving."

***

The Baldwin Hotel dining room was nearly empty, to the relief of the men, but if she felt any embarrassment about either her shabby clothing or ravenous appetite, she didn't show it. And they were impressed when she made no comment when neither man took so much as an aperitif or breadstick. In the better light they could appreciate her unaffected manner—*frugal*, Gedrec thought. They found her guileless and candid, with a forthright, sensible charm. Her surname was Phillips, and Cezar mentioned her vaguely British accent.

"My mother was traveling abroad when she met my father in Leeds," she said, slathering butter on a roll.

"I was born in Leeds!" cried Gedrec.

She offered him with a slight smile, then continued.

"When I was a year old, my mother took us to Maine to meet her family. We docked in New York, and then …" At this point Elspet went quiet. She put down her utensils and bowed her head. When she looked up again there were tears in her eyes. "She fell ill and died." She paused, dabbing her eyes with her napkin. "Father hardly ever talked about it, but it was pretty clear that my mother's family blamed him for her illness. And her death." Evidently there was plenty of blame to be had, considering that he was a physician—a "gentleman" physician, having gone to Oxford, and had learned nothing about treating illness. "So finally," Elspet continued, "he blamed himself even more than my grandparents did. He vowed to do all he could for others what he couldn't do for mother." And so, no longer a gentleman, her father headed west with his daughter beside him, healing the sick, bringing them his own concoctions made of herbs and spices, learned from the locals—along with soup and bread he made himself. "

"America had many frontiers, father often said," Elspet mused.

"What happened to him?" Gedrec asked.

She fell solemn. "We were in Colorado. We had just helped some miners through a flu epidemic, when an Indian came to our lodgings one night, saying his young son was ill."

The illness was cholera, and though time seemed against him, the little boy survived. Elspet hung her head. "But father didn't," she whispered. She nursed him the best she could against his express wishes, fearing that she would become ill as well. "It wouldn't have mattered," she said. "I didn't know enough anyway. And besides," she added with a weak smile, "and I was scared of getting sick." She nodded. "I was a coward. Something father never was."

So finally she decided that the best solution for her fright was knowledge. She scraped up all her money and went to the university—one of the few women there. "I was thrifty, but my money only lasted two years. I tried contacting some distant relatives back in Yorkshire. When that came to naught, I tried to locate her mother's family in Maine—but ..."

As Elspet continued, Gedrec and Cezar learned that she had done her best to support herself in the city, pounding the pavements. She offered her services as a governess, but without references she was politely shown the door time and again. She tried sewing, but she was clumsy with a needle; it looked like she stitched with a fishhook. She was clumsier still during two stints as a waitress, or even washing dishes, always owing more than she earned by the time the cook yelled her off the premises.

There was, however, no shortage of offers for the role of a "left-handed wife." She had even briefly considered *that*—*if* it allowed her to complete her studies. But the risk of disease was a poor tradeoff for her sole remaining Victorian virtue— maidenhood.

Her last recourse, then, lay in discarded newspapers, then, and she saw the ad that brought her knocking on the door of her hosts.

Cezar gave Gedrec a questioning look; Gedrec nodded.

"Excuse us for a minute," Cezar said.

Elspet kept her eyes riveted on the men as they arose and moved a fair distance away from the table, whispering together. She had just sneaked the remaining bread into her pocket when they returned.

"We have decided to offer you the position," Gedrec said, obviously pleased.

"You will have your own room and a modicum of privacy for your personal needs," Cezar declaimed. "Your wage will be five hundred dollars per month, beginning today. Are you agreeable?"

Open-mouthed with surprise, she nodded.

"Very good. We will discuss your hours and duties in further detail tomorrow," standing and straightening his jacket. "As well as other options," he ended cryptically.

"You must be exhausted," Gedrec said to Elspet. "Shall we?"

She stood and slipped on the coat Cezar held out for her. While she buttoned up, he leaned over, and into her pocket slipped something loosely wrapped in a linen napkin. "Might as well take the butter, too," he whispered.

CHAPTER 14

Cezar opened the door to the Castro Street house and strode in, followed close on by Gedrec and Elspet. It was well into the evening of St. Valentine's Day, and the air throughout the house was fragrant with a bounty of two dozen long-stem roses—a gift to Elspet, and a generous one, more than a year after the Crash.

"Bet you never thought you'd be spending tonight at the talkies in San Francisco with the two of us, did you?" They had gone to the San Francisco premier of "Dracula."

Elspet smiled and then pressed a button on the wall. Mellow light flooded from the Tiffany lamps—Elspet's pride and joy—in the foyer and parlor. She was mad for Art Nouveau, which Cezar indulged and Gedrec disliked.

Cezar snatched a rose from a vase and held it out to Gedrec. "Well! What did you think of the picture?"

Gedrec gave him a wry smile. "I found the audience more amusing."

"True," replied Cezar. "Odd to see them shocked at the screen when the real thing was in their company, and so close to our meal time, too!" He turned to Elspet, as he lit candles around the parlor. "What did you think, my dear?"

"I thought Lugosi was charming. Very courtly," she replied.

"A little *too* courtly, I thought," Gedrec put in, "and too melodramatic. And the music was fitting, all those Romantic composers."

"Cynic," Cezar said to him, turning off the lamps; the parlor glowed amber candlelight.

"Will you stop!" cried Elspet, looking indignant. She had been busy at the mirror on the wall in the parlor, refreshing her lipstick. "I wasn't finished, thank you very much!"

Cezar offered a smooth retort. "You always look beautiful, my dear."

"Thank you very much again," she said. "But considering how much we spent wiring the house—" She pressed the light switch, the room glowed brightly again, and she finished putting on her lipstick.

Cezar pouted. "I *like* the candles. Natural light is so … elegant. And so much more flattering thatn electric light."

"Let's discuss it later," Gedrec said. "Who's hungry?"

Cezar licked his lips. "You know I am. That film spurred my appetite. Let's go."

Elspet grimaced and squared her shoulders, her face set with determination. Cezar noticed and prompted, "Remember that in the long run, we do no harm."

Elspet understood. "I know. But must we treat them like so much cattle?"

"Like so much *life*. The one you *chose* to live. A life, like any other, that takes as well as gives, my darling girl," Cezar countered.

And chose to live it, she had.

Cezar had suggested it first. She was bright and intuitive, patient and receptive, a perfect working partner for Gedrec, and when Cezar suggested the plan to turn Elspet for that purpose, he couldn't have been more pleased. And so together they proposed the idea to her.

For her own part, she had grown so fond of her benefactors that the prospect of an eternity with them, even without sunlight, was tremendously appealing. She had only one reservation—her aversion to blood that continually stymied her father's efforts to turn her into a nurse. Finally, though, the fondness for her friends trumped her fears. During a crescent moon, Cezar took his first taste of her.

"I realize you still aren't accustomed to this," he said in a kind voice, "but please remember that you are not alone. You are family, and we love you."

Gedrec had joined them; he looked concerned. "That's right, Pet," using his own soubriquet for her. She managed a smile when she heard the name and squeezed his hand. The crisis seemed over.

Looking much relieved, Cezar went over the map of the city and pointed out their properties, and where grown, healthy men could readily be found, bachelors in particular.

"Come feed with us tonight," Gedrec urged Elspet.

"Thank you, but no. It's time I tried going out on my own."

Cezar looked pleased. "I knew you were made of sterner stuff."

Yes, thought Elspet. *I do believe I am.* She suddenly had a brilliant idea. One that would satisfy both her thirst *and* her moral dilemma. She couldn't wait.

***

When Mario saw the woman with cider-colored hair enter the Bourbon & Branch, he thought, *What a looker! Real class!* He caught her eye and motioned to her to join him. She looked out of place in the loud speakeasy, with her stylish finger-waved coif and understated clothes, not to mention her graceful walk; she seemed to glide across the floor, as if walking on air. She couldn't have been more than twenty, but had the worldly wise finesse of a woman twice her age.

Mario speculated. *Maybe she's looking for someone. Long-lost brother or something.* For a moment he searched his memory among the many people he'd bumped off. Or some chump who went crazy or croaked from a batch of bad booze he'd hawked. Whatever it was, she'd get more than she bargained for, if she was as smart as she looked—with those beautiful dark eyes that seemed to see a bull's-eye on his forehead as she approached.

Suddenly Mario felt like some teenage kid on his first date. But as she grew closer, he felt himself relax. She slipped onto the chair next to him and whispered in his ear. "You look like the gentleman I need to see if I want to wet my whistle." She had a young voice that seemed at odds with her sophisticated looks. He had a sudden, strong urge to tell her everything about himself.

"You got that right, doll," he answered. His tongue felt thick. "What's your pleasure?"

"How about some privacy to start?"

He shot her a wicked smile and got to his feet and offered his hand. She stood and snuggled against him. He snapped his fingers; at once a waiter came over and handed him a bottle. Not once did he break his gaze from her eyes, even as they walked, arm-in-arm, toward the door marked "Office."

***

Cezar and Gedrec stood across from The Fremont apartment building they owned in North Beach. It was early morning and the street was deserted. They watched a strapping young man in his underclothes pace back and forth through a window on the second floor. He stopped in front of a mirror and scrutinized his face, turning his head first to one side then the other.

"Fetching, isn't he?" Cezar said. "Found him a few weeks ago, stripping at Finocchio's."

"What's that?"

"A new place on the Barbary Coast."

Gedrec glared at his lover, who returned a sidelong glance. "Yes. I partook. Delectable."

"You said you'd been busy while you were here. Now I know why." Gedrec turned to him with challenge in his eyes. "And I thought we all agreed—not to drink from anyone more than once."

That was true enough. Plenty of people around, both healthy and itinerant. Over the years, Gedrec had been infatuated more than once, saying nothing lest it hurt Cezar, who was almost ferociously devoted to their relationship, which made Gedrec intensely curious; he had to admit he was a little jealous of this young buck.

Cezar hugged him close and whispered, "No need to be envious, my dear."

Then a thought struck Gedrec, and he spun around. "Wait. Did you say a few weeks?" He spun around and faced Cezar nose-to-nose. "Are you daft? We can't have another go until…" He was going to say *twenty-nine days*, but no one knew that better than Cezar. His eyes went wide. "Unless you plan to…"

Cezar answered with a sly smile. "Come. Meet Alastar, our next *argat*."

Gedrec was astonished. "*Ours?*" he gasped. Sharing a meal, as they had with Rupert, one thing … but a servant, bonded for life? That was something else. He had never considered it, but then … why not? Cezar seemed to have every confidence.

He grinned and nodded. "Happy Valentine's Day," he said, then nuzzled Gedrec's neck.

Gedrec looked up. The young man went back to his pacing, but stopped dead and cocked his head, as if listening. He went to the window, peered down and spotted them watching. He held up his hand in greeting, grinning eagerly. Gedrec caught Cezar's eye, exchanged a ravenous look, followed him across the street, into the building, and sprinted up the stairs, where the youth known as Alastar leaned against the sill of the open door.

When Gedrec saw Alastar in brighter light, Gedrec could understand Cezar's fascination.

Alastar was unusually tall. He moved aside to admit them, closing the door behind them. He wore a sleeveless shirt, and his boxers tented out with his enormous erection. Without a word, he held out both hands toward his guests, and he pulled them toward the candlelit bedroom. The heavy shades were drawn—not out of modesty, Cezar knew, but in case they lingered after dawn. The room was bare except for a candle holder, high as a pulpit, holding a thick, beeswax candle and its flickering flame, shadows playing over the large mattress that lay on the floor.

With his hands still clinging to the two men, the youth moved onto the mattress and fell to his knees and lifted his face to the ceiling, as if expecting a benediction. Cezar moved in first, bending over and lifting an arm, licking the crook of the young man's armpit.

Gedrec had not been idle. With his tongue he glossed over the smooth flesh above Alastar's collarbone and kissed the moist area softly, tracing along the vein. He felt his fangs press against his tongue. He opened wide and pierced the vessel, lapping around the wound, not wasting a drop. Alastar's throat tensed as he groaned in exquisite pleasure.

Meanwhile, Cezar had turned his attention to servicing Alastar's cock, which had reared up while the two men sucked and lapped at his open vessels. Alastar, in his turn, had returned the favor. First he unzipped Cezar's fly and managed to pull the stone-hard cock through—no easy task. They intertwined into a supple union, mouth on flesh, shadows in the candlelight playing over the powerful muscles of the three men as they writhed with passion.

Then Cezar noticed Alastar's glazed eyes and gave Gedrec a warning poke and glare. Gedrec released Alastar's throat with a smack, licking up the dark red smears surrounding the wound, after which Alastar started to rouse. With a soft grunt he groped Gedrec, whose own cock pressed against his fly. Alastar took out Gedrec's cock with feverish intensity and stroked the thick shaft, as Gedrec leaned over and took Alastar's massive head deep into his throat, slowly sliding up with delicious suction as he worked his way to the crown, then licking it in a steady spiral before he mouthed the head, again and again. Finally, after a moment's eternity of sucking, Gedrec let up on Alastar's cock, which was drooling gobs of pre-cum.

Alastar fell forward on his knees, breathing heavily, open-mouthed. He was on all fours, looking back and forth at his partners, eyes pleading, nearly in tears. Cezar slid behind Alastar while Gedrec moved to the front. They kneeled and watched each other over the stretch of Alastar's strong back as they prepared to consummate the union and lay claim to Alastar's soul. Cezar spit into his hand, rubbing the bright pink drool over his cock. Alastar had already began sucking off Gedrec, every bit as lovingly as Gedrec had done for him; but when Cezar entered him with a steady, measured, implacable thrust, he crammed Gedrec's cock down into his throat, matching each thrust with a masterful stroke on the slicked up shaft.

Alastar felt one of the men take hold of his cock and start to pump, up and down, bringing him closer to a climax, then slowing, letting the cum settle back into his loins, then starting again. He felt something pierce the nape of his neck, and the world ebbed to a gray blur.

***

Alastar awakened the next day lying on the mattress among cold, sticky, nearly dried pools of blood and cum. As his head cleared, he recalled a brief blaze of consciousness in which he shot his cum—for hours, it seemed—from his aching cock, while Cezar and Gedrec had hovered over him, bare-chested, shoulder to shoulder, and watched him with kind, almost loving smiles.

Now, in the bright morning, he felt serene. Everything looked vivid and bright. He was hungry, too. He strode into the kitchen and saw the note on the table. He picked up the note and recognized Cezar's handwriting at once. *My dear friend Alastar*, it began, and as he read on, he realized the promise—and the price—of this new friendship.

The promise was that he could present himself as someone worthy in the eyes of his father, the General, and even more so, in the eyes of Lemuel, his older half-brother, in whose shadow he thought he might smother forever.

The price was that he would be indeed worthy of them—as an adversary.

CHAPTER 15

It was going on eight o'clock. Elspet came downstairs, went into the office and found Gedrec already at work at his desk. Cezar sat in an armchair, reading *The San Francisco Chronicle*, as he did every evening.

"Evening, gents," Elspet said, and went to her side of the partner's desk, sat down, and started leafing through papers.

"Good evening," Gedrec said, looking up with a smile. "Have you started cataloging the Neander digs?"

"Just about to," she answered, smiling in return.

"Some excitement down on Jones Street this morning," Cezar commented.

Elspet didn't look up. "What kind of excitement?"

"Found a local wise-guy dead at the Bourbon & Branch. Slumped over a couch in the back office."

"They play a dangerous game down there," she replied. "No wonder they get shot."

"He wasn't shot," Gedrec put in. "His moll came in this morning, saw him laid out, looking white as fog on the bay. She got scared and squealed. They're closing the place. Afraid maybe it's another flu epidemic."

Elspet shrugged and looked up. Her face was all innocence. "Maybe it is. No problem for us, right?"

"Depends."

"On what?"

"You know very well. On keeping a low profile. Blending in." He sauntered toward her, hands on his hips. "*Never* killing. Especially the *Cosa Nostra*, which takes a dim view of losing one of its own."

Elspet looked indignant. "Are you accusing me?"

Gedrec rose from his chair. "Cezar, do you honestly believe—"

Cezar cut him off, and focused on Elspet. His voice was kind, paternal. "You would do well to admit any involvement in the matter of this gangster. If only to prepare."

Elspet looked at her feet, then held her head high. "All right. Yes. I killed him."

Cezar took a deep breath. "Would you like to tell me why?"

"The woman who found him…the moll?"

Cezar nodded, and she continued. "Well, she has a child, a girl. His daughter." She paused, as if embarrassed.

"Go on," Cezar said.

"Only twelve years old. *Twelve.* And he was going to put her out on the street. His own *daughter!*" She seemed on the verge of tears.

Cezar crooked an eyebrow. "I never realized you had such a maternal bent."

"Why shouldn't she?" asked Gedrec in her defense. "It's natural enough."

"Nothing about us is natural enough," replied Cezar. "Certainly not enough to risk detection. Persecution. Or worse, putting our talents at these gangsters' mercy, of which I suspect they have very little, if any at all!"

He took some deep breaths. As much as he admired Elspet's motives, their safety came first. He went to her and hugged her like a father. "We'll say no more about this. But in the future," he said, cupping his hands under her chin, "you must be careful with applying your principles. After all, it puts us all at risk. Promise me."

"I promise," she muttered. "I'm sorry." She did seem contrite.

"No need to be sorry," Gedrec told her. "All is forgiven." He looked at Cezar. "Isn't that so?"

Cezar said, "Indeed. We are the only family we have, and must trust one another. Next time, when you have an attack of solicitude, talk to us first. Agreed?"

Elspet nodded.

Gedrec grinned. "Fine. Settled. Shall we get to work? Lots to do before we leave."

"Which reminds me," Cezar said. "Your tickets and itinerary are there." He pointed at a pile of papers and folders on Gedrec's desk. "You have your own rail car, of course," Cezar continued, "with plenty of room to work."

Gedrec opened the envelope and examined the contents. "A stay over in Chicago?"

"Yes," Cezar replied. "Fuel stop." That was their code for feeding when they traveled any major distance. "That should hold you until you reach New York."

Gedrec moped. "I don't see why you can't come with us." He had never been apart from Cezar for more than a few days.

"Someone must attend to matters here, you know that," Cezar replied. "And the German government threatened to close down your digs if you don't return. So what choice do we have? Besides," he said heartily, "your assistant will more than make up for my absence." He turned to Elspet with a smile. "Isn't that so?"

"Indeed," she answered. "We'll have plenty to keep us busy. Though you will be missed," she added, "by both of us."

Neither Gedrec nor Elspet had expected their perfunctory goodnight kiss to linger in their memories and had expected even less the amorous night they spent together. Even one night of fucking they could put down to curiosity, but one night led to another, and still another. By the time they reached Chicago, they fed together—like fast friends—on an indigent not far from the train tracks. When they rolled into New York, they felt like soulmates, then fed together again in the few days they had before boarding the ship. At this point they realized they couldn't bear to be apart. Friendship had blossomed into romance.

Neither mentioned anything to Cezar. But they were both stunned to realize their secrecy was not out of embarrassment or even guilt. They were so immersed in each other's company it simply didn't occur to them. "Mad about the boy," Elspet later referred to it, and Gedrec, admitting likewise, agreed there had to be some lunacy to their affair. Cezar had booked separate cabins on the RMS Olympic, but as time passed, they found each other irresistible; it seemed more practical to use one cabin for resting and the other for working.

And they "rested" more than they worked—all the way to Southampton and beyond, over the two years they explored the Neander Valley digs, working—and loving—side by side.

Or was it "loving"? Their passion was a ferocious predator nipping at their heels, relentlessly driving them—to what?

Cezar paid them one visit but seemed to suspect nothing. He had been concerned about the rising unrest in Europe as the vise of the Great Depression gripped even harder.

"The German Reich is no longer a safe place," he said. "You should consider coming home. *Soon*," he insisted.

"Of course," Gedrec said. "If you think it best, we will book passage at once."

"Already done," Cezar replied.

Elspet offered a tight smile and went about collecting their notes and artifacts. Once again they discussed telling him about their relationship. After all, Cezar was hardly a prude. But they always decided against it. Perhaps they couldn't face the pain of separation if Cezar demanded it, or maybe it was guilt after all.

They continued their trysts in secret, but they were infrequent—half a dozen times over the ensuing decades, always when Cezar traveled, and ceased without a word when he returned. They never mentioned it afterward, even to each other. But both realized that each time it was more difficult to part than the last.

CHAPTER 17

The Baltimore City Police had contacted Cezar in San Francisco regarding illegal activity at their property on Liberty Street, which had been vacant for a few years. Evidently, it had since become home to a number of squatters dealing in drugs and prostitution, which was only one of several disasters Cezar had to deal with that year—a minor one, compared to others. He was already entangled in a tragedy that centered on one of their local tenants, a law firm targeted by a man named Ferri who appeared on the premises with rifle in hand, killing eight persons and wounding six. To make matters worse, a number of properties owned by the trio along the banks of the Mississippi were drowning in what was already being called "The Great Flood of 1993." It was only July, and the river wasn't expected to crest for another few weeks at least. Cezar decided to deal with the insurance and restoration himself.

Meanwhile, since the Archeology Department at Johns Hopkins University had already invited Gedrec and Elspet to present their Neander Valley research, they would go early to Baltimore and attend to the squatter situation.

It turned out that much of the original furniture was missing, some obviously dragged in from the street as replacements. Despite its historic reputation, the neighborhood itself was no longer the quiet, respectable area they remembered, and the police said it was a sign of the times—an upswing in violent crime, especially there on Baltimore's East Side.

The squatters themselves had been carted off to jail; however, addicts and prostitutes still showed up at the door and left paler and a little worse for wear, but with more money in their pockets than memories of what happened, scratching at their bite wounds, and avoiding that block of Liberty Street afterward.

With somber mood they called Cezar and apprised him.

"What about the structure itself?" he asked.

"The outside is fine. Same old red brick. Inside, there's some damage, but it's mostly cosmetic," Gedrec said. "It seemed they didn't live here so much as work here."

"If you could call it work," Elspet called out, poking at a chink in the living room wall.

"There are mattresses laid out in the bedrooms upstairs and makeshift ashtrays, but doesn't look anyone set up housekeeping."

"I'm surprised they didn't install meters," Elspet muttered morosely.

Gedrec put a hand over the phone and mouthed, *Too expensive.* Elspet frowned and shrugged.

"I'll be stuck here for at least another six months," Cezar warned. "You can handle it, can't you?"

"Oh, yeah. Do what you have to do. We'll manage. Not as well *without* you, of course. I miss you. We both do." He motioned Elspet over, and she rushed over, sharing the earpiece. "Love you. Take care of yourself."

"You too. And have fun with the presentation."

"Best to Alastar," Gedrec said, smacked a kiss, and hung up. "Well," he said. "What's your pleasure? Sweep or mop?"

***

A week later the house was well on its way to ship-shape again.

In the upstairs bedroom, Elspet lay with her head on Gedrec's chest after a prolonged fuck—at least they thought it was fucking—especially perplexing because they could remember very little about the whole experience. They knew it was wonderful and told each other so but couldn't say exactly why, unless it was the singular vivid memory of a peculiar novelty—

feasting on each other's blood, evidenced by the similar bites on each other's groins, and more than just nips of passion—these were deep, *feeding* wounds.

However strange it was, though, for the first time they had felt truly serene. The furious need to be with each other had settled into an odd, relaxed contentment. They lay in each other's arms and looked out the window at the bright earthshine on the dark of the waxing crescent moon.

"Beautiful," Gedrec commented. "It puts me in mind of something special. Can't put my finger on it, though."

Elspet's brow creased as she thought. Then she cried out with delight. "I remember! The moon was just like when I—"

Gedrec's cut her off, his face deadpan. "When you were turned." It wasn't a question.

"That's right."

They agreed it was a happy coincidence, but didn't give it any more weight as they drifted off to sleep.

CHAPTER 18

Gedrec took Elspet's arm as they strolled across the quad at the university. The library had just closed, and Elspet demanded that he meet her there. The news had certainly been urgent—and distressing. There was no one around, but they whispered anyway. Gedrec was trying not to panic, but was confounded nonetheless.

"But how could it be?" he asked. "After all this time?"

"I have no idea. I thought *you* would know. Maybe Cezar would have said something."

"The subject never came up. What would be the point?"

Elspet racked her brain. "I don't know...curiosity, maybe?"

"Are you sure about...this?" Gedrec sounded desperate. "I mean, *really* certain?" He looked at her sloppy sweatshirt and tight jeans, the latest fashion craze. "You're not showing or any—"

Her expression was fierce as she grabbed his hand and placed it on her belly. He felt only the slightest bulge. Then his eyes went wide. He felt a vigorous squirming sensation. He didn't turn around as he felt around for the bench behind him, afraid he'd faint. He eased himself onto the bench.

Elspet remained standing. "It's not anyone else's business anyway," she commented. But her bravado sounded flat, and Gedrec said nothing.

They had set something in motion, and they both knew it. There was no getting around that, and there was no going back.

CHAPTER 19

The tall handsome woman arrived in East Baltimore, as instructed, just after sunset. She double parked on Hampden Avenue, blocking the way, but she wouldn't be there long. She knocked on the door of the whitewashed rowhome with brand-new windows, which looked out of place among the dirty brick or flagstone structures on the block, decorated with flags for the Fourth of July. She looked up at the sky; it would be a beautiful night for fireworks.

The door opened, and she was surprised to see Lemuel—the Burgess *himself*—standing there. *This must be important*, she thought.

"Rosamund," he said. "Right on time." He opened the door wide to let her pass into the foyer.

"Caleb said it was serious," she said.

"Momentous, possibly," he answered. "How is my cousin?"

"Well enough. Curious about what's going on, of course." She and Caleb, her partner, were in the midst of preparing for the annual Revel, which they were hosting this year at their compound in Maine. "As a matter of fact, Burgess, so am I. You mentioned something about fostering a child. No disrespect, but we've been so busy with—"

"With the Great Revel. I know. Fair enough. Which brings us to the case at hand."

He beckoned with his hand, and she followed him down the empty hall, and couldn't resist asking, "Did neither parent survive their bouts?" Death of a Vanator during bouts was extremely rare, but *both*? *Impossible*, she thought.

"You will understand," Lemuel said. "Right in here." He walked to the living room, which was large. The sheeted furniture reflected the candlelight. He pointed to an infant carry seat on the floor. In it was an extraordinarily pretty baby, with thick black hair and dark eyes that studied her for a moment before giving her a ghost of a smile.

Lemuel said, "Rosamund, this is Roi." He bent over the infant, and with his hands on his knees, said, "Roi, this is your Aunt Rosamund. She's going to look after you." Roi looked up at Lemuel with a solemn expression.

"Aunt? But I thought I'd be his…" She paused as a thought dawned on her. "You mean he's not one of us?"

Lemuel interrupted with a shake of his head. "Why do you think I insisted on meeting after sunset?"

She hesitated for a second, then looked at Lemuel in awe. "You don't mean to say…" She looked at Roi, then back at Lemuel. "You think he's …?" She looked back at Roi, her eyes popping wide.

"I'm not saying anything for certain. Not yet," Lemuel added, "Meanwhile …"

"I observe."

He nodded. "And protect." He put a hand on her shoulder. "You understand what that means?"

"Yes. Until …when we know for sure."

"That's right."

She paused. "One question. Why me?"

"Your education. Training. Temperament. You're the best choice."

She turned her attention to Roi. She knelt down and gave him an affectionate smile. "Hello, Roi, my love. We're going to have such good times. We have much to learn from each other."

Lemuel held out a cautionary palm. "Let's not rush it."

"Yes, I know. Play it safe. But you must admit, he's a very dear little boy. And so beautiful."

"That's right." He handed her a large manila envelope. "The deed to your new home—comfortable, safe, out of the way, nothing fancy. Also his birth certificate. Passport. The appropriate medical records. Money and credit cards. All the documents you'll need for a new life with your orphaned nephew."

She picked up the carry seat. "And what about Caleb? You know how he hates being kept in the dark."

Lemuel gave her a cryptic smile. "He's the last of your worries." A horn honked outside. "There's your cue." He opened the front door.

She walked past him and out into the street. An irate woman sat behind a junker. A cooler sat shotgun, and Old Glory decorated the antenna. "You wanna move it along, honey?" she yelled in a juicy Baltimore accent. "Some of us got things to do!"

Lemuel nodded in farewell; Rosamund returned the nod, then walked to the car with a conciliatory wave to the woman.

All they could do now was wait.

<<<◇>>>

CHAPTER 1

The man in cheap shoes wasn't expecting company, especially the slim, youngish woman who waited for him at the door of his third floor walkup. Not bad looking either. She looked familiar, and it took him a minute to place her. Then it hit him. *The chick at the blood bank!*

"I was just about to knock," the woman said.

He was out of breath as he mounted the landing. He nodded. "If you're lookin' for your money back, it's too late." He held up a bottle wrapped in a brown paper bag.

"You haven't been drinking today, have you?" the woman asked with a crease in her brow.

"Hell, no. Didn't even crack the bottle yet." He paused. "There's plenty to share, though."

"Actually," she replied quietly, "I've come to ask for another donation." She nodded toward the small cooler in her hand.

"Well, I don't know . . . "

She held up a wad of bills. "All I ask is that you keep it between us."

The man was silent for a second, then locked his eyes on hers. "Maybe I don't want cash."

The woman didn't answer or move a muscle.

Worth a try, he thought, then shrugged, ambled over and snatched the wad out of the woman's hand, then pulled out a door key.

CHAPTER 2

The flight had been packed, despite the early hour. The passengers deplaned at the International Terminal in Vancouver; daybreak was still hours away.

Rosamund saw her nephew before he saw her. The infant she had first laid eyes on years before had grown into a young man of average height, but certainly not average looks. His strong brows and high cheekbones were complemented by his three-day growth of beard, which was as black as his thick, straight hair. He peered around, searching among the milling people.

"Roi!" the woman called out.

The young man zeroed in on the sound and gave his aunt a broad smile. There was a spring in his step as he made his way toward her. His eyes, a beautiful, rich mahogany brown, sparkled even in the drab fluorescent light of the terminal. Rosamund herself wasn't immune to the arresting effect his gaze had on everyone else.

"Aunt Roz!"

She embraced him, and they exchanged kisses on the cheek and headed down the concourse.

"Good flight?" she asked.

"Flights, you mean. Two red-eyes in two days. How's working at the blood bank?"

She shrugged. "It's a job. Some junkies and drunks, but mostly nice folks needing a little cash. But I should get my license soon." She had applied for her nurse practitioner certification some days before.

His cheerful manner turned serious. "So you finally found a house?"

Rosamund was jubilant. "Signed the lease last night. Wait till you see it."

He offered a slight smile. "And the furniture?"

"On its way." She stopped and turned him around by his sleeve with a worried frown. "You're a little pasty."

He answered with a weak smile. "I'm okay. It's been about twelve hours."

"Don't worry. We'll fix that as soon as we get home."

She tucked his arm through hers as they walked toward Customs.

CHAPTER 3

Corey wasn't familiar with Vancouver. He'd forgotten to charge his phone, so he had no GPS. Now he couldn't remember the directions the convenient store attendant had given him not long before. It seemed as though they were going in circles as he whipped the moving van from lane to lane, making turns, peering at the street signs, swearing now and again.

"You should have written them down," commented his partner, Jake.

It was a suggestion only. Jake was an easy-going, laid-back guy, at odds with his strapping six-foot-three powerful frame, earning him nicknames like "Moose" and (less often) "Bubba" from total strangers, which he took in stride.

Corey, on the other hand, was short, wiry and energetic, with a hot temper that cooled as quickly as it heated up. He was baffled at the schedule they were given earlier by Nicole, the dispatcher at Mack Power Movers, chewing gum as she handed over the schedule.

"They want the stuff there when this lady picks up her nephew at the airport."

"Shit! The plane lands at fucking 3:00 a.m.!" Corey complained as he read. "We're supposed to just sit around in the dark and wait?"

Nicole's tone was weary. "What's it to you? You're on the clock, right? She's loaded. Paid in cash. And you'll probably get a decent tip," she added, with a fish-eye, "IF you don't have an attitude."

And he was trying his damnedest not to have one, running into one dead end after another. *Good thing I have Jake on this run*, thought Corey. Jake was strong, cheerful, never shirked, and never *ever* complained—and *smart*, but not showy about it.

"How fucking hard is it to find 99? I used to know Vancouver inside and out," Corey mused bitterly.

"It can't be far. Let's get our bearings." Jake pointed to a wide alleyway, wide as a street. "Pull in there."

Corey pulled in and turned off the engine. Jake pulled out his phone and started poking at the screen. "I'll give Nicole a call. She'll be pissed, but—"

A sudden pounding on the driver's side window startled them. A pale young man with a wide smile greeted them from outside. He made a gesture to Corey to roll down his window. But ever-cautious Corey turned to Jake for quick advice. "This is Shaughnessy, right? A nice neighborhood?"

"So I heard."

"Safe enough then," Corey said, rolling down the window and facing the man. "What's up?" he asked. "You okay?"

"My friend needs help," the young man said in a thick accent.

"Oh, yeah? What kind of—"

At that moment, with surprising strength and speed, the young man grabbed Corey by the lapels and yanked him halfway through the open window. Corey began to kick, and Jake barely managed to dodge a flailing work boot.

Jake opened the passenger door and bolted out, but he was distracted by a *very* tall man, taller than himself, and broad-shouldered, elegantly dressed—leaning casually on a gleaming black SUV that blocked the entrance to the alleyway. He was clearly older than the young man assaulting Corey, but beyond that it was hard to guess his age—thirties, or perhaps early forties.

Jake divided his pop-eyed attention between Corey and the tall man. His mouth gaped, as if trying to decide between a question and a scream, but he was unable to do either. Before he knew it, the younger man gave way as he yanked open the driver's side door and pulled Corey to the ground, straddling him. He clamped his mouth on Corey's neck with greedy grunts and slurping sounds which drowned out Corey's groans, which to Jake sounded more of pleasure than pain.

Meanwhile, the taller man leaped over to Jake in a single stride, so that when Jake turned back they were nose to nose. Jake was mesmerized, paralyzed, scrutinized.

"Maestru?" asked Corey's attacker. "You promised." He pointed to Corey. "My own *sclav*?"

The Maestru nodded. "Of course, Kostin."

With terrifying glee Kostin drew back and gazed down at the barely conscious man, raised a thumb, bared his canine and nicked it. Dark red blood welled from the wound. With his other hand he jacked open Corey's mouth and held his dripping thumb over it. Crimson drops trickled into Corey's mouth, and Kostin patted his cheek before rising and joining the other two men. He looked into Jake's eyes and said, "Your friend's future is decided."

A deep voice echoed down the alley. "Hey! What's going on there?"

At the far end of the alley stood a figure, straining to see the ruckus. Momentarily, the figure started toward them.

Jake's eyes widened in hope of rescue, but he remained frozen, riveted on the pair.

Kostin started toward Corey. "No time for your quarry, I'm afraid," the Maestru said with some regret. "Bring this one instead. He's the better man."

Jake couldn't cry out; his vocal cords were frozen with fear. Kostin's mouth tightened with disappointment, and he pulled out black rope and bound Jake, face forward, with almost no effort, stuffed a cloth in his mouth, and lifted him as though he were made of cotton and tossed him into the back of the van. Then the Maestru climbed in and sat next to him while Kostin moved into the driver's side, started the van and drove off. All this in a matter of seconds.

Jake's eyebrows knotted with confusion. His breath came fast and loud through his nose. But he was even more puzzled by his persistent erection, which Cezar was shaping and gently squeezing through his coveralls. "Impressive," he commented.

Kostin drove. Before long they turned into a curving driveway next to a vast, meticulously landscaped lawn toward a sprawling house set back among some trees. They were only blocks from where Jake had been abducted, in the heart of the Shaughnessy district, one of the richest in the province.

As they approached the garage he heard a *click* and the second of four garage doors opened. The van slowed, rolling into the huge, empty garage, whose windows were painted black. He pulled in and turned off the van, amazed to find that both of his passengers had disembarked in seconds. Kostin opened the door and pulled him out with surprising strength, slamming the car door and pushing him against it. Kostin got right in Jake's face and bared his teeth. *Holy crap, there they are,* thought Jake as he saw the pointed canines—*Just like in the movies.* He closed his eyes and waited to join Corey in the hereafter.

CHAPTER 4

Hope it's nicer on the inside, thought Roi.

The house Rosamund had chosen was anything but imposing on the outside. That was no accident. Nestled a good distance from the road in a quiet Richmond suburb not far from downtown, it suited their needs perfectly. The weather was overcast, the stars hidden behind the clouds. Aunt and nephew stood on the porch, facing the front door. Roi was all anticipation.

"It's bigger inside. You'll see," Rosamund remarked. "And you'll love your studio," she added brightly. "That's why I picked this place." Abruptly, she scowled. "And where is that truck? They were supposed to be here by now. I'll be damned if we're sleeping on the floor."

She took out her phone and poked at the screen. Her voice was sharp with irritation, punctuating each syllable. "This is Rosamund Phillips. We're at the residence and waiting for you to arrive. Call me right away. You have the number." She put the phone away and addressed Roi. "Let's at least get our stuff from the car."

It didn't take long, but he seemed to be struggling with her overnight bag—large, to be sure, but bulky rather than heavy. He followed his aunt up the stairs, hauling the suitcases into the living room, but with less vitality, Rosamund noticed, than only minutes before. He dropped the suitcases, and stood still, head drooping, arms hanging limp at his side. Rosamund rushed over and lifted his chin, pushing up his brow and examining his eyes.

"Your mucous membranes are white," she said, adding with an angry hiss, "Where the *fuck* are those guys with our stuff?" But to Roi she said, "No worries, dear. We still have the cooler in the back."

"I'll get it," he answered.

"You'll do no such thing," she commanded, and headed out to the car before he could protest. She had seen him in this crisis twice before in his twenty-two years, and both times she had averted the need for a visit to the hospital. She climbed into the back of the SUV and rummaged through the cooler, feeling around the two units of blood.

Then her stomach sank.

Not a single transfusion needle.

Fortunately, the blood bank was a local one. Half an hour, there and back, tops. To save time, she ran up to the door, opened it and yelled in that she'd be back soon, not to worry.

But he *was* worried. He reached in his pocket, took out a silver pocket watch and opened it, as he always did when he was nervous or frightened or lonely. He was never without it, like a good luck charm. He gazed at the photo nestled inside the cover; the image of the dark-haired man—as dark as his own—with deep-set eyes always cheered or comforted him as the occasion demanded. He was still gazing at it forty-five minutes later when the world around him seemed to implode, its colors bleeding away into an encroaching dark gray frame. He grabbed his phone and dialed 9-1-1 just as the blackness engulfed him.

CHAPTER 5

Adam Giroux strode into the ER cubicle with his usual easy confidence. The first thing he noticed was the young man lying on the gurney, bleary and alarmed, looking around. Then, standing next to the gurney he saw the pudgy form of Baxter, the ER nurse in attendance, whose plain but not unpleasant face sported a thick mustache atop a gap-toothed smile, a firm hand on the man's bare forearm. An IV of plasma was running.

"Just relax," Baxter said in his high-pitched, soothing voice, "you're in Vancouver General Hospital." Baxter removed his hand, a red handprint like a bad sunburn was clearly outlined on the white skin, which Adam was quick to notice.

With a friendly nod Adam joined Baxter at bedside, the nurse's comforting smile broadening as he did so.

Adam Giroux had a vitalizing effect on everyone he met. Cheerful, direct yet diplomatic, self-confident yet considerate, he inspired the same in others. He looked every bit the athlete he was. He was more than an excellent clinician; he never forgot he was a human being first and treated everyone, colleagues and patients alike, with due respect. And he *listened.* Yet, as many admirers as he had, they also sensed a certain aloofness, even with his fiancée, Merit. Most people put it down to simple professional conduct.

"Thanks, Baxter. That's it for now."

"Okay, doc." Baxter patted the youth's leg and bounced out.

Adam inspected the IV bag, then perused the chart hanging nearby as he donned latex gloves. Without looking at his patient, he asked, "Mr. Kirkland?" He had a sensuous, almost lazy, baritone drawl, like distant thunder, typical of the Deep South.

"Roi. Call me Roi."

"Okay, then. Roi. I'm Doctor Giroux."

Beaming a programmed, professional smile, he inquired, "What happened here?" He looked at the reddened flesh, and his brow arched with concern.

Then he looked at the young man full on for the first time, and his voice faltered.

One look at the young man lying there brought him to a standstill. For a few long seconds, they gazed at each other, intent, neither moving a muscle, their expressions frozen in mutual appraisal. Adam was caught by surprise and barely resisted the strong temptation to run his fingers through Roi's coal-black hair. He placed his hand on the wall instead.

Roi was just as mesmerized as he locked onto Adam's seafoam-green eyes, which enhanced his ruddy complexion and thick chestnut-colored hair, streaked light by the sun. Adam drew back and stood tall, never taking his eyes off his patient. He felt himself instinctively flexing his bicep, his deep chest thrust out, as if to demonstrate his prowess.

Roi, for his part, had no words, awkward with banter at the best of times, much less in the presence of such an imposing figure. He stared at the ceiling. But with a sidelong glance he noted the considerable bulge in Adam's pants.

With some effort Roi propped himself up and shifted position to cover his own erection while offering his hand to shake. Still, their eyes were locked. Adam took Roi's hand and was startled at the strength in its long, graceful form. Adam thought Roi might be a pianist.

Roi wasn't so much surprised at the strength of Adam's hand as he was at the soothing warmth of his firm skin, even through the glove. *This is the hand of a healer*, he thought. Roi had never before felt as safe as he had at that moment, just from a simple handshake. Not even the years of trust and familial affection he had shared with his Aunt Roz compared with this.

He looked deep into Roi's eyes, leaned close and whispered, simply, with a slight smile, "'Adam,' please. Now let's have a look at your arm," stretching Roi's arm out.

But the redness was gone.

Slightly startled, Adam said, "Must have been the pressure." He continued in a light, jovial tone. "Didn't think Baxter had it in him."

He let go of Roi's arm, and Roi fell back, breathing easier, but still a bit labored. He felt a little stronger now, but he felt a pang of fear at Adam's look of concern. He pulled down the cloth and hesitated for just a second at the sight of Roi's smooth, well-defined chest, as if he were drinking in the sight. He caught Roi watching him as he huffed on the chest piece of his stethoscope. Adam was used to a certain amount of adoration from his patients, but Roi's caught him between abashed and gratified.

"Just warming it up for you," he said, with a quick grin, placing it on his chest.

CHAPTER 6

Inspector Devan Olsen had parked across the entrance to the alleyway, blocking it. He had been ready to leave for work when the call came in. There had been a lot of call-offs—could he go to a crime scene in Shaughnessy? It took less than half an hour to reach the scene, and now the traffic on the street was becoming heavy with early morning commuters. The patrol officers had already put out cones around the abandoned moving van and asked the witness to remain.

Devan interviewed the middle-aged man who had been on his way to work when he happened upon two male figures assaulting the driver of the moving van and his partner, whose ID he had found in the cab.

It was too dark to make any useful identification, except that one man was tall, well over six feet, and that they were both white.

"Two Caucasian males?" Devan asked as he wrote.

"Well, yeah, I guess," replied the witness. "But what I meant was that they were pale. Like lit from inside, almost."

Of more interest to Devan was that the witness took notice of the vehicle itself and its unmistakable emblem. From the description by the witness, Devan recognized the model right away. He knew the price tag—the mid-six figures—and considering the prohibitive cost, also knew relatively few would be sold. It would be easy to narrow the search. Otherwise, the robbery itself appeared to be a routine one—the door to the cargo hold was left ajar.

Routine, that is, until the witness pointed to the body of one of the victims—"Corey," according to the name patch on his overalls. The witness agreed to remain until the M.E. arrived on the scene.

Devan got the number for Mack Power Movers and called to inform the company and garner the necessary information for the report.

***

Rosamund, purse over her shoulder and holding a plastic bag, burst into the lobby of the ER and rushed over to the reception desk. The nurse behind it greeted her.

"May I—" she began, but Rosamund cut her off, as politely as her worry would allow.

"I'm Roi Kirkland's aunt. I understand he was brought here."

The nurse was unruffled as she pecked at her keyboard. "Yes, that's right."

A male nurse joined her behind the desk. "Baxter, this is the aunt of the gentleman in number 9."

"How is he?" Rosamund asked anxiously.

Baxter reassured her with a warm smile. "Stable. He's with the doctor now."

"Where is he? May I see him?"

"Ma'am, I can assure you that—"

But Rosamund didn't wait. She marched into the ward, poked in her head, one cubicle after another, until she found Roi. The fixed smile on her face belied the worry that roiled in her gut. Roi lay on the gurney, his expression peaceful as he watched the doctor take his vital signs.

She took a quick look at the doctor. For a moment she was struck by Adam's good looks and powerful physique, evident even through his blue scrubs, which heightened his rich tan and accented his green eyes. She tried to control her fretfulness with a grin but succeeded only minimally.

"I'm Rosamund Phillips. Roi's aunt."

"Adam Giroux. A pleasure." He offered his hand.

She shoved the plastic bag she was carrying onto Adam's outstretched arm, like a purse. His expression of surprise mixed with confusion was lost on Rosamund, who kissed Roi's forehead.

"I'm sorry, sweetie," she said. "The traffic was terrible, and it took forever."

Adam pointedly cleared his throat. He had opened the bag and was holding up the item inside—a transfusion spike in its sterile packing. "Thank you, Ms. Phillips, but—"

"Rosamund."

"Not to worry, Rosamund. We have plenty of these in stock."

Roi laughed out loud. He didn't laugh often, and Rosamund often said that was a shame. His laugh had a lilting, gutsy quality that made Adam want to join in, but instead he managed a wry grin and offered his hand to her again.

Rosamund never took her nephew's health lightly, and she didn't intend to let *any* physician compromise that. But she liked Adam's calm, professional manner and took his hand.

"I left the extra spikes with our stuff being moved in a van. But I work at a blood bank—"

Adam nodded. "I know. The Lifebank. Roi told me."

"I'm sorry I worried you, Aunt Roz," Roi said. "But it happened so fast this time."

"Shush," she replied, stroking his forehead, "you're okay. That's what counts."

With a smile, Adam gently wedged between Roi and his aunt. "Excuse me, Rosamund. Just want to finish up."

"Of course."

Adam placed a reassuring hand on Roi's shoulder, unable to resist squeezing it gently, massaging the firm muscles beneath. He tried to distract himself from his half-hard cock, uncomfortably aware that it was pressing against his scrubs, stretching them.

"Roi brought me up to speed," Adam continued. "and the support you've given him . . . well, I must say I'm impressed. No physician could have done better. But now I hope we can take some of that burden from you. Give you a little break. And as one colleague to another, please call me 'Adam'." His tone was conciliatory.

Roi piped in. "Give you a break. That's a great idea, don't you think, Aunt Roz?"

There was no denying the sense in that, so Rosamund found herself reconciled, at least for the moment. "Maybe," she answered.

Adam continued, "Roi tells me his main concerns are his aplastic anemia and porphyria."

"Yes. It's congenital."

"Hereditary?"

Rosamund paused, avoiding Roi's interested expression. "Undetermined," she mumbled.

"He should have an alert bracelet."

Rosamund said nothing. A technician wheeled in a transfusion stand with a bag of blood hanging, checked Roi's wristband, and started preparing the transfusion.

Adam turned to Rosamund. "The EMT gave him a unit of plasma on his way here. We'll try one unit of whole blood for now and see how it goes." He phrased it as half a question, as though checking with her, and was a bit startled at her almost casual attitude. Rosamund was distracted, and curious as to why Roi had rallied, even partially, considering the severity of the crisis, but she dismissed it, not wanting to tempt providence.

Rosamund's cell phone rang. She nodded as she spoke into the mouthpiece and left the examining area. "Hello? . . . Yes, this is she."

She turned to Roi. "I have to take this," she said.

"Is it the movers?" Roi asked.

Rosamund shook her head. "Don't you worry about that. Just get squared away here." She turned to the doctor. "Excuse me, doctor . . . Adam. It was a pleasure."

"Likewise," Adam replied.

She nodded to Adam as she spoke into the phone. "Could you hold on a moment while I go outside for a better connection?" She put her hand over the mouthpiece and addressed Roi. "I'll be right outside."

***

Rosamund settled into a chair in the lobby as far away from the hubbub as she could get, and spoke into her phone. "Okay. Go ahead."

"Ms. Phillips, this is Inspector Devan Olsen of the Vancouver Police Department. Did you engage the services of Mack Power Movers?"

"I did. Is there a problem?"

"My colleague and I are investigating a moving van abandoned in an alley. The driver and his partner were not in the vehicle. The clerk at Mack Power said the van contained your belongings and gave us your contact information."

"I see. And what about our things?"

"There was evidence of some rummaging, but not much. The manifest will show if anything was taken."

Rosamund let out a long, loud sigh. "So, when can we expect our delivery?"

"Ordinarily you would discuss that with the moving company," Olsen said. "But I'm afraid we'll have to impound the truck and its contents, at least for the time being."

"And why is that?" cried Rosamund. "Can't the moving company get someone else to finish delivery?"

Devan didn't mention the discovery of the corpse, per department policy. "It's still a crime scene and needs investigation. The truck must be processed. It will be towed to the impound and be quite safe there. We will contact you with any further developments."

Rosamund fell silent, considering.

"Ms. Phillips, are you still there?"

"Yes. How long do you expect this to take?"

"Depends on what we find."

Of course, Rosamund thought, but said aloud, "Thank you, Inspector. But if you'll excuse me, my nephew has a medical issue that needs my immediate attention. You have my number."

"Yes, ma'am. And you have ours."

Rosamund slumped back into a chair and sighed as she thought: *Great. No fucking furniture.*

***

Meanwhile, Devan poked at his phone. The woman who answered had a strong, voice, confident and authoritative. "Forensics. May I help you?"

"Hello, Sadie. Devan here."

"Well, as I live and breathe. What's cookin', tiger?"

"The usual. Missing you, of course."

"Too bad, that ship done sailed, sonny boy." Devan laughed. Through her mirth, she asked, "What can I do for you, stud muffin?"

"Possible homicide. Need a photographer down here, pronto. Who's up?" He heard a page flip, then another.

"Looks like it's yo' girlfriend."

"Chavi? No way! She's still on probation."

"People out today. Damn bug goin' around."

His tone was pleading. "Any contractors?"

"Sorry."

Not as sorry as he was. "Ah, shit."

"Now, don't be so overprotective. She'll do fine, baby. Just give her a chance."

"Sure," he said, not at all convinced. "Eno will be here, if I'm not. You better give Chavi the bad news. Thanks again, Sadie."

"You got it," she said, and hung up.

Devan would have to do most, if not all, of his own legwork, but he didn't mind. He knew it would be done right, and most of the other inspectors felt the same way. He felt bad for his girlfriend, but if she wanted a career in law enforcement, even as a civilian, she had to be ready for anything.

Adam pulled over a chair and sat with his face close to Roi's. "Now, back to business," he said. "I know you can't go out in direct sunlight. I'm guessing that why you moved to Vancouver."

"Overcast sixty percent of the year, right?" countered Roi.

"Yes," answered Adam.

"Also because Vancouver has one of the few hospitals that specializes in treating erythro . . ." Roi paused, trying to remember the rest of the phrase.

"Erythropoietic protoporphyria. 'EPP' for short," said Adam.

Roi smiled. "I rest my case."

"I've only run into one other case since I've worked here. But you're in good hands. I'll make all the necessary referrals. You have a job?"

"Freelance artist. Sculptor."

"Maybe I could see your work sometime," he said with genuine interest.

Roi shrugged. "Maybe I could show it to you."

Adam smiled. "Maybe you should."

At that moment the technician reappeared, and with impressive efficiency removed the port and bandaged the site. Adam continued, careful not to stand, since his cock was still at full attention. "You look a hundred percent better." True enough; the ashen hue had disappeared from Roi's face. Though still pale, his full lips had regained their usual pale rose color.

"For now, I want to see you again within the next three days. Just for a follow-up." He looked Roi straight in the eye as he clasped his shoulder again, squeezing gently; his already stiff cock reared up again; his balls began to throb with a delicious ache. He had to get out of there.

He sighed with relief as the technician left the cube, wheeling the stand behind him. He stood up; there it was—a sizable tent at his crotch—and to his amazement, embarrassment—he felt insanely proud—and possessive. "Ready to go?"

Roi slipped off the gurney and stood next to him, a little unsteady on his feet. Adam supported him with a strong arm wrapped around his back and shoulder, pressing Roi's lean, muscular body against his own.

He looked down.

Roi had a nice-sized tent as well. Their gazes met and locked once again. They inched closer, almost nose to nose.

A voice piped up behind the curtain.

"Doc? You in there?"

Adam cleared his throat, but his gaze didn't waver. "Yes, Baxter."

"Could you come over to number twelve? A high school kid with a dislocation."

"Be right there," he called out. "Remember," he whispered to Roi, "follow up in three days. *Three*. No more." It was more a command, albeit a gentle one, than a request. Roi answered with a smile.

"Thanks, doc," Roi answered, trying to be casual.

"You're welcome. And call me 'Adam.'"

He followed Roi's retreat as he removed his latex gloves and tossed them in the repository nearby.

CHAPTER 8

Chavi couldn't believe what she was hearing. But Sadie was emphatic when she delivered the message from her boss, that she was to go and photograph the crime scene.

"Can't Steve go?" asked Chavi, a plaintive whine, rife with desperation. She loved photography, and she was good at it. But thus far her photographs were, in her mother's words, "artsy-fartsy"—meaning *unprofitable*.

"No. He's sick, too." Though Sadie's considerable patience was waning, she felt for the fledgling technician. "Look, honey, I know how you feel. I've seen it a hundred times. But it's not that bad. And the M.E. says the scene isn't messy at all." She put a reassuring hand on Chavi's arm. "You'll be fine. Don't think about it. Just take your notes, take the photos, and it'll be over before you know it."

***

The Medical Examiner was standing next to the body when Chavi arrived, wearing her badge. Her mouth was a tight line of determination.

"What happened to Steve?" the doctor asked.

"Sick," she said in a meek voice. She held out a hand. "Chavi Kapur. I started last month."

He stood, taking her hand. "Inocente Velazquez. Call me Eno." He scrutinized her, taking note of her perfect brown skin and apprehensive expression. "First crime scene?"

She nodded, looking sidelong at the corpse at their feet as she took out numbered evidence markers, placing them around the body with a shaky hand.

"Relax," Eno said with a sympathetic smile. "Most people freak a little on their first assignment."

Chavi nodded again and started taking photos of the corpse at various angles, stopping now and again to adjust the lenses. Eno opened Corey's mouth with a latex-gloved finger. Chavi adjusted for a close-up and snapped the photo.

"Hmm," he said, holding up a burgundy-stained finger. "He may have bitten his tongue."

He crinkled his brow as he smeared the blood over the glove. "Odd. No coagulation. And still bright red." He held it out to Chavi, who jerked back instinctively, then continued to take photos.

Then he undid the top of the overalls. He inspected Corey's arms. "No track marks or scars." He lifted a hand and examined the fingers. "Some staining on the fingers. Maybe freebasing." He inspected the body, pressing here, poking there, turning the head to one side and then the other, pushing the torso on its side, pulling over the jockey shorts and inspecting the buttocks. "No rigor. Bizarre," he commented.

He stood up. "There. See? No blood pooling. Weird."

He lifted his hand to shield his eyes from the sun, which had come out from behind a cloud a moment before.

A mist seemed to come out of nowhere.

Except it was no mist.

"Eno?" Chavi asked, pointing at the body, fear in her voice.

He looked down at the body. The cracking skin billowed smoke, and Corey's eyes popped open. He reached out first to Chavi, then Eno, then to Chavi again, pleading, as his body burst into flame, mouth gaping open in a muted scream. Eno instinctively jumped on his body, hugged and rolled around, extinguishing the flames.

After several rolls he found himself atop Corey's flat overalls, the smoke dissipating. He held up the garment, noticing first the charred edges and spots on the fabric, then the name patch, soiled the same color as the gray ash that poured from the empty sleeves and pant legs. Chavi looked on, incredulous. He dropped the overalls into the pile of ash that the breeze had already started to scatter away.

Astonished but composed, Eno brushed himself off as he turned to Chavi, who was frozen with shock. "Welcome to Forensics," he said with a wry smile. "At least the van didn't combust."

She offered a weak grin as she faced the vehicle, camera at the ready.

Adam was just about halfway through his shift, which was a busier one than usual. He went to the nurses' station and announced he was going on break. "Be back in a few." He rushed to the nearest bathroom, almost colliding with a patient in a wheelchair pushed by an attendant, who scowled and clicked his tongue.

"Sorry," mumbled Adam as he bolted in and locked the door.

He stood and leaned with one arm against the wall, facing the toilet, shucked down his blue scrubs and frantically pulled down his briefs, his cock jutting out, rock-hard, his testicles swelling inside their sac. He stroked himself, easing the ache somewhat. His rod angled upward to steel-hard stiffness as Roi's face, like sculpted ivory, filled his mind's eye. Although he tried his damnedest to think of Merit, his fiancée, as he had many times before, he had no success. Her face gave way to a very few split-second images that flashed through his mind like a slide-show gone wild, highlighting his occasional but extraordinary conquests: a beautiful Asian graduate student; the lovely dirty-blonde, whipcord-thin competing marathon runner who came close to besting him; then, suddenly, the strongest image of all, and the one most persistent—his very first sexual encounter: the occasional mutual jerk-off sessions with the one guy in his past, a fellow wrestler on the high school varsity team, every bit as hot as himself, but which—until now—he put down to a phase.

But that was before. He was mesmerized as he recalled Roi's deep-set eyes—haunted, hungry, pleading with him in such a way that compelled Adam to reach out and pull him close, penetrating and banishing all the other images. Adam stroked his cock, now so thick he could barely get his large hand around it. He looked down at his massive member with new appreciation; a new intimacy suffused him as he savored the image of Roi, recollecting the long, lean musculature he felt as he squeezed the young man's shoulder.

He imagined Roi sitting on his haunches, reaching out to him, pulling down his scrubs, those eager, bright dark-brown eyes, filled with adoration, looking up into his as he stroked the doctor's cock, licking, circling the head, and lovingly swiping the sweet spot with his tongue. His heart swelled with pride as he imagined Roi taking the massive head between those pale rose-colored lips and beginning to slick up his shaft, when Adam pumped himself over the top. He looked down, wanting to stave off the delicious moment, but clearly too far gone to dam the flood from his aching loins. Generous pre-cum oozed out, followed by thick spurts of semen as he heard himself saying, "Roi . . . yeah, take it . . . it's all yours." The vision of Roi's face, still full of joy and adoration, faded with the white noise in Adam's head, through which man's voice from outside the bathroom door piped up after a few loud knocks.

"Hey, you just about done in there?"

He took some deep breaths, orienting himself. He was still stroking his semi-hard cock, squeezing out the few remaining pearls.

"Holy shit," Adam whispered, breathing heavily, looking at the streams of cum on the walls, toilet seat, floor, fist. The voice piped up again. "Hello? You okay in there?"

Adam eased onto the toilet seat, spent, still trying to catch his breath, looking around. "Got an issue," Adam called back. The words were hoarse and wavering. He cleared his throat and steadied his voice. "There's another bathroom down the hall, on your left."

"Feel better, man," was the answer.

Adam turned on the faucet and rinsed his hand, then took paper towels to task, puzzled by this new feeling. When he was finished, he realized he felt as he did a few hours after a marathon, peaceful or empowered. But there was something about this that was brand-new, unique, and somehow profound.

Then, suddenly, as Roi's face reappeared in his mind's eye, he knew the word for it, but didn't know why.

Eureka.

CHAPTER 10

Rosamund was silent as they drove home. She sneaked sidelong glances in Roi's direction, baiting him. Normally he would first pretend indifference, then demur. Not this time. He was in his own world. But she was burning with curiosity, so she charged in.

"I saw you two in there. Something was going on. And it was more than playing doctor."

After a long moment Roi answered. "You answer my question and I'll answer yours."

Rosamund had heard this demand before, but never with such finality. She dodged his question often enough, but lately Roi had become more persistent, not wanting to drop it, immune to all the distractions that worked in the past. *But he's not a kid anymore,* she reminded herself.

But how could she tell him *everything* about his parents, before the proper time?

The answer was, she couldn't. Not yet. Roi took her silence as retreat. They shared a couple of somber glances and then the matter was dropped. For the time being, at least.

***

Chavi clicked on the desk lamp in her office and closed the door behind her. The office was tiny, but it was hers—the symbol of her promotion to forensic photographer, which she didn't really want and definitely didn't feel ready for, after a *very* brief internship and swift departure of her mentor in the wake of some scandal.

Now she was left with a disgruntled boss who clearly had no more faith in her than she did herself, when all she really wanted was to take advanced photography courses and have the department pay for it—which it did—then quietly retire from her civilian post as documentarian and become the next Diane Arbus.

Karma's a bitch, she thought, lighting a cone of sandalwood incense and placing it in the elaborate brass holder, which was a gift from her mother to remind her, for the zillionth time, that she was a direct descendant of an ancient Vedic. Chavi didn't buy into the mysticism—it was the twenty-first century after all—but the history and culture fascinated her, as did some of the rituals, like *yajna*—ritual fire—of which incense burning was a small part. Not to ward off evil, as far as Chavi was concerned, but as aromatherapy. At first she thought the pungent fragrance might bother her coworkers, but no one had mentioned it so far. And at least she didn't chant mantras.

She plugged the digital camera into her computer, and with a few clicks the images popped up like mosaics. She labeled the images methodically, starting with the cab of the van, moving to the cargo area, where the pillaging seemed to be perfunctory at best. What did interest Chavi was the padlock, which lay on the concrete at the rear of the van. The shackle was snapped with its ends bent at an angle, as though it had been twisted and yanked off.

But the next series of photographs were as perplexing as the padlock had been interesting. She had taken at least a dozen photos of Corey as he lay dead, yet not one contained a solid image of his remains. His image was transparent, the cement underneath showing through in one photo after another with all the cracks and roughness clearly visible through Corey's ghost-like body.

At that point, to her surprise, her boss, Steve, appeared at the door, leaning against the jamb.

"I thought you were sick," she said. In truth he looked it, pale gray and exhausted, his casual outfit disheveled, as if he just got up from napping on the couch.

He ignored the question. "You got the photos?"

"Yes." Then, in a cautionary tone, "I should tell you though, some of the images are faded. Maybe the camera—"

"Just send it along." He leaned in and sniffed the air. "What is that smell?" he asked.

"Incense. Sandalwood."

His expression brightened a little. "Got any more?"

* * *

Evidently the incense burning in an ashtray on Steve's desk hadn't improved his mood. He didn't even have enough strength to change expression from exhaustion to impatience. He gave Chavi the evil eye as she stood at his desk.

"What the fuck is this?" He made no attempt to hide his annoyance.

She shrugged. "I told you. Like I started to say, maybe it's the camera. But half an image is better than none, right?"

"I'm not in the mood for jokes, little miss."

"Sorry." And she was. Mostly for herself.

He gave her an ugly squint. "Get the fuck over here."

As she peered over her boss' shoulder, and her jaw went slack at what she saw on the computer screen. The half-images had vanished. She checked the file labels. Yes, they were the exact same ones.

Steve took her silence as retreat. "Do you have any notion of the bind you put us in?" His words were flat and measured, heavy with accusation. He put his head in his hands and coughed several times before taking a deep breath. "I know you didn't want field assignments," he said wearily, "but you know I had no choice. And then to pull a stunt like this." He looked away, at a loss for words.

"Steve, I saved those images. They were there when I stored them. I swear!"

"Swear all you want, doesn't change anything. You know the rules. If you don't have photos, it didn't happen. Take a few days off while I try to fix this. I'll fight for you, best I can."

He laid his head on the desk, face down, as though the effort sapped his last strength. Despite her dismay and the hurt she felt by Steve's disappointment, she was concerned. His skin was as pale as paper.

"Steve, are you all right?"

He waved her away with a listless hand, without comment or looking up. She left, knowing full well the "few days" might be more than a few. After all, she was still on probation. Though she believed him when he said he would fight for her, it was still *in spite of*. He didn't really buy her story. But she saw what she saw, and knew that, in the end, the real battle was hers alone.

The doorbell was so loud in the near-empty house that it broke Roi's concentration as he roughed out the clay model for a new sculpture. But his curiosity trumped his inspiration, and he bounded down the stairs. He met Rosamund in the hallway. She was wiping her hands on a towel.

They saw a woman standing on the porch—late forties, Rosamund guessed, or maybe early fifties. Her attire was rakish, however, colorful and casual—and expensive looking.

Roi gave Rosamund a sidelong glance. "Fashion Forward. In the extreme."

Even in the grey midday light the woman's rosy tan glowed. She wore a bright smile, and waved cheerily when she saw Roi and Rosamund.

"Welcome wagon?" Rosamund guessed.

Roi shrugged. "One way to find out."

Rosamund opened the door. The woman's attitude was as flashy as her clothing. Moving a bit closer to the screen door separating them, the woman started right in.

"Hello there!" She pealed in a strident, youthful voice, not unpleasant to listen to, and slightly accented—maybe Western European.

"Hello," said Rosamund. "How can we help you?"

"I'm Imogen Fuchs. I live next door."

Rosamund remembered her manners and opened the door. "Won't you please come in?"

Imogen strode in. She peered around the empty room and offered her hand. "So happy to meet you," she chirped.

Rosamund took Imogen's hand, while Roi backed away when it came his turn, as politely as he was able, holding out clay-caked hands.

"Sorry," Roi mumbled. "You caught me working. As a matter of fact, I should get back."

Imogen's grin showed friendly interest. "A sculptor?"

"Yes."

"Then please," Imogen added, "return to your creation." She reached out and gave Roi's bare forearm a quick pat. He pulled away as fast as good manners would allow, then retreated up the stairs, two at a time, mumbling "Nice to meet you," as he went. Out of sight, he winced and fanned the burn on his forearm.

Rosamund gave Imogen a warm grin. "Coffee? Tea?"

***

Adam had no trouble finding Roi Kirkland's website. But it was "under construction" and contained a hyperlink for the White Cube gallery in London, which in turn had links to recent exhibits. He clicked on Roi's name and was treated to photos of two dozen or so pieces: birds in flight, a series of heads with assorted expressions ranging from joy to grief, a figure on a pedestal, kneeling as if trying to get down. The last was another male figure—looking much like Roi himself—with his hands pressed against what looked like blown glass formed around him like an aura. It was then Adam realized that all the sculptures were enclosed in this way.

But what especially caught his eye was the photo insert of Roi himself. It seemed that he was caught off guard, in the throes of contemplation—perhaps considering his next project. Adam sensed enormous strength behind that dreamy-eyed visage, and all at once his heart broke, as intense as the image that came to mind during his lusty release in the bathroom. As it had been a *eureka* moment then, now serenity flooded over him and tears filled his eyes. He felt a different desire altogether: to get as close to Roi as he possibly could—mind, body and heart.

He felt transparent, like blown-glass bubbles encasing Roi's sculptures—and it frightened him more than he liked to admit.

By the time Roi took a break and made his way downstairs in his clay-streaked smock, it was full dark. Imogen lounged on the hurriedly purchased inflatable sectional, while Rosamund relaxed in the matching armchair. They sipped on red wine. Roi was impressed with the faux furniture; it didn't look inflatable in the least.

"There he is!" Rosamund said.

"I have a suggestion, young man," Imogen commented, lifting her glass, "one which I hope you will approve of."

Roi looked at Rosamund, whose eyes were bright with delight. The suggestion, it turned out, was studio space at the coveted Beaumont Studios.

"Studio 16," added Imogen with a certain civic pride. A studio centrally located on the first floor and, evidently, a shrine to the prestige and prosperity of previous tenants. Roi was as grateful as he was stunned at the generosity of his neighbor on such short notice.

"I've seen your work," Imogen said, and for the first time Roi noticed, sitting in her lap, the portfolio of photos from a show several years before. Roi must have smiled in gratitude, since the others raised their glasses in a toast.

***

The first sliver of morning light seeped around the drawn curtains into Roi's bedroom. He awoke to find himself sitting up in bed, feeling more gratified than he ever had. He stretched and turned over and over on the inflatable mattress for a moment, then threw off the downy comforter.

He trudged over to the window and pulled back the heavy blind, a housewarming gift of sorts, left by the previous owners. Edging away from the patch of sunlight streaming in, closed the blind again, diffusing the light in his room into pale gray shadow. He caught his reflection in the full-length mirror on the back of the closed door. He slowly turned and stretched to scrutinize his body, as though it belonged to someone else.

His hairless torso was lean, and his stomach was flat, smooth and firm. His trim waist gave way to strong thighs and a pair of firm buttocks, thanks to mountain biking and ice skating. He watched his fingers trace the black downy trail from his navel into silky coal-black pubic hair surrounding a generous-sized penis. He saw he was still half-hard as he recalled Adam's strong fingers stroking through his hair, the timbre of the doctor's voice melting him, even in recollection, as he commanded Roi to follow up: *Three days. Three. No more.*

For a few seconds afterward, the arms of Adam's ghost seemed to remain as Roi opened his eyes and gazed at his reflection. His expression reflected the pure contentment he had never felt before and had always assumed was the stuff of fiction.

CHAPTER 13

Adam sat in the doctor's lounge, sipping on tomato juice, an untouched sandwich before him. He looked at his watch again. He had been edgy for a few days, ever since he had met Roi for the first time.

Adam's fiancée Merit had also noticed how preoccupied he seemed since dinner the other night. He had dismissed her concern, citing fatigue from double shifts, which was true enough. Adam had been taking extra shifts when offered, especially on the weekends. He had hoped the extra work would distract him from his obsession with Roi. Unfortunately, it wasn't working. His fatigue, in fact, only intensified his longing for the young man.

He also found himself in the unfamiliar habit of daydreaming, usually about Roi. He imagined himself supine, the young man straddling him, watching him with eyes filled with desire as Roi massaged his chest, shoulders, then lying down prone next to him, his expert hands exploring, stroking his cock to hardness as Roi whispered softly in his ear. Meanwhile, he would not be unmindful of Roi's firm ass and its delicate, inviting curves. Usually at that point Adam would awaken from his reverie, stiff inside his scrubs, trying his best to dispel the exciting image from his mind while, with some difficulty, he would will his cock to slacken before he stood up.

He looked at his watch. One thirty-five.

With some irritation he wondered when Roi would show. He thought he made himself clear. *Three days. No more.* Then, unbidden, another thought crowded in: *I'm going to have a talk with that guy.* His fierce possessiveness first surprised him, then perplexed him. The fact that he couldn't shake the feeling, despite his best efforts, surprised him even more.

***

Roi descended the stairs at a brisk pace, skipping a step now and then with his typical peculiar grace. He strode down the hallway into the kitchen, calling out a cheerful "Good morning!" in his strong tenor voice.

He looked around in surprise. Rosamund was nowhere to be seen. Then abruptly the door at the far end of the kitchen opened and out popped his aunt, yanking the chain to the overhead light. The room behind—the "mud room," Roi recalled with some amusement—plunged into darkness. He gave her a curious glance.

"What were you doing in there?" he asked.

"I thought I heard something outside," she replied. Did he hear a nervous quiver in her voice? "Thought I'd check it out."

"But why close the door?"

"Oh . . . habit, I guess."

"So what was out there? I hope to God it wasn't another stray," implying that once fed, it would never leave. She had a habit of rescuing itinerant cats and dogs. Not that he blamed her, but he wished they liked him better. Even as a young child, his occasional pets always seemed comfortable enough around him yet shied away from his touch, however gentle, and there was no indication that would every change. Roi was always a little sad and more than a little hurt when the poor creature crept away, looking back at him with something like regret.

"No, as a matter of fact," she replied. "And so what if it was a stray? We have enough room. And it's hardly morning, young man. It's nearly three o'clock, in case you didn't know." She handed him a smoothie.

Roi was not entirely convinced of her argument, but his stomach was gurgling, so he decided to let it go for the moment. He held up a palm, indicating surrender as he guzzled down half of the delicious concoction in a few gulps.

"So what was it?" Roi asked.

"What was what?"

"The sound you heard."

"My imagination, probably."

She seemed relieved to hear the doorbell ring and rushed off to answer it. Roi was grateful for the time alone to contemplate if the mud room warranted further exploration. He heard Rosamund's voice as she welcomed Imogen, who echoed her delight. They visited together often now, at least once a day.

Meanwhile, Roi reflected on Rosamund's uneasiness when he entered the kitchen, and that made him even more curious.

He looked at the closed door to the mud room and wondered.

He turned his head to hear the conversation in the front. Rosamund invited her back for coffee. As the days passed she had lost some of her natural reserve when it came to Imogen; she chatted easily as Imogen followed her into the kitchen.

Imogen carried a large paper bag, and the rich aroma of good coffee filled the room at once. She held it out to Roi. "Look what our thoughtful neighbor brought."

He took the coffee and inhaled it; it was fresh and sweet.

Imogen beamed a great smile. "I was shopping at my favorite bakery and couldn't pass up sharing these scrumptious goodies."

She produced a small tray of croissants, which held no magic for Roi. A good thing, since Rosamund had already taken the tray and was picking at the pastries.

"'Goodies' is right," Rosamund commented. "I suppose I can indulge," she added, as she glanced at Roi, a guilty look on her face.

"And how about you, my dear?" Imogen asked Roi. She reached out to him, and he jumped back in panic.

After momentary surprise, Imogen smoothed over the awkwardness. "Of course," Imogen said. "Your aunt explained everything. Never mind. I have another treat for you. The prospect of . . ." She paused for dramatic effect; "an exhibition at the Beaumont Studio!"

Roi, taken by surprise, recovered quickly enough. He thought that someday he might have another exhibition, but he knew the few pieces he had didn't merit one at present. "Well," he said sheepishly, "I am working on a new series. So as soon as we're settled . . ." He glanced at Rosamund, hoping she'd chime in, but all he received was a pleased, noncommittal smile in reply.

Imogen smiled. "Then let's consider that a commitment."

The subject changed to the local social scene. Their neighbor, it turned out, was actually from the area. She had moved from the bustling, urbane center of Vancouver to a smaller home in this more sedate neighborhood which afforded more rest and relaxation.

While Imogen and his aunt chatted about the local merchants and the best deals, Roi's mind wandered back to speculate about the mud room, until he realized Rosamund was addressing him. "Excuse me?"

"I said, I'm going out with Imogen. I figured you want to get back to work?"

"Oh. Yes, of course," he answered with a bright smile. "Enjoy."

Later, Roi stood in the middle of the mud room, dark despite the small filthy window on the far wall. He felt around for the hanging chain and pulled.

The dim overhead bulb wasn't enough to completely eliminate the deep shadows, and he saw little of interest among the mostly empty shelves: a few cans of vegetables and several cartons of beef stock; a couple of bottles of avocado oil.

He sighed with disappointment and reached for the light chain. He was about to pull, when he noticed a white box sitting on the floor in the corner, tucked under the bottom shelf almost out of view. He pulled it out; it was a large plastic cooler with a blue lid, snapped shut but not locked. He reached down and put his hand on the snap.

Then the sharp ring on his cellphone made him jump. He heaved out a frustrated breath, hauled out the phone and looked at the display, his lip raised in a snarl of irritation which then went slack.

The display read, "Doctor."

Roi steadied himself as he tried to quiet the embers of excitement in his gut, then answered, hoping his put-on nonchalance sounded genuine. "Hello?"

"Roi? This is Adam Giroux."

"How are you?" he said, certain that the thrill in his voice broke through.

Roi noticed a slight hesitation.

"Well enough, thanks. How about you?"

"Good, thanks. I mean…you know, considering."

"Yes, I know. I'm calling to remind you to schedule your follow-up. I don't mean to be a pest, but—"

"No, not at all."

"Adam."

"Yes. Adam. I do apologize. It slipped my mind, trying to get settled and all. Plus our moving van got impounded."

"Why is that?"

"Some sort of crime. I think somebody got hurt. Looks like they may keep it for a while."

After a short pause, Adam said, "If there's anything I can do to help . . ." Roi heard a frantic voice in the background.

"Hold on," Adam said. Roi heard a brief, muffled conversation, then Adam came back on. "Roi, I've got to go. Make time for that follow-up, okay?"

"I will."

"And don't forget, you promised to show me your sculptures. I hold you to that."

"Sure. Whenever you're ready. But I don't have much right now, aside from my portfolio and some clippings."

"That's fine. Let's do it soon. 'Bye."

Adam hung up befgore Roi had a chance to reply.

CHAPTER 14

Chavi had gotten Rosamund Phillips' address from the police report. She was determined to follow up, and her fortitude flagged just a bit before she realized she had nothing better to do. She pulled into the driveway. No car.

Maybe nobody's home, she thought with sneaky relief, and thought about turning tail, then cursed herself for her cowardice. Finally, with feigned confidence, she marched up to the door and knocked. She took a deep, involuntary breath as she saw a young man approach, tall and lean, with strong brows and high cheekbones.

When he opened the door, she held up her ID badge and said, as authoritatively as she could, "Vancouver Police." She told herself that she wasn't *exactly* impersonating an officer. And it looked like the dude was buying it.

He backed away from the door.

"Come in."

She stepped into the foyer, squaring her shoulders. She had no idea what she would ask Ms. Phillips or the handsome young man standing before her. But she had to start somewhere. Even casual conversation might shed some light on the events surrounding the strange man known as "Corey," that first baffled her, then betrayed her. She began the interview, recalling the few 'ride-alongs' with Devan and trying to mimic his style.

"Good afternoon. I'm Chavi Kapur."

"Roi Kirkland," he replied.

"I'm looking for Rosamund Phillips."

"That's my aunt. Any progress with the van?"

"That's why I'm here."

Roi raised an eyebrow. For the first time Chavi could break away from Roi's gaze.

"I thought maybe Ms. Phillips could lend a hand. Or perhaps you could," she said.

Roi's smile was kind as he answered. "I'd be happy to do what I can. Both of us would." The young man had a beautiful voice, lyrical and soft.

"Do you know anyone named 'Corey'?"

"No. We're new to the area. We don't know anyone yet."

"Any history of being stalked? A disgruntled ex, maybe?" As soon as the words were out of her mouth, she regretted them.

To her surprise, Roi chuckled. "No. Not to my knowledge, anyway."

Chavi pondered a minute. "Maybe theft, then? According to the police report the perpetrator didn't steal anything. Is there any object of value the perpetrator might have been looking for that wasn't in the manifest?"

Roi pursed his lips as he thought, then another shake of his head. "No. We brought a few things with us in the car, mostly personal items. Everything else we own was on the truck."

Chavi racked her brain for something she might have missed. A few seconds ticked by.

"My aunt is out right now, but she'll be back later, if you want to speak to her." She considered that, but if he called the station and mentioned her visit, she could get into even worse trouble.

"No, that's okay. I appreciate your time."

Ping! A text message from Devan: *Just heard about suspension. You OK?* She typed, *Yes. Lunch later?*

"Hope you don't mind showing yourself out," Roi said, backing away from the sunlight that had begun streaming through the window.

"Not at all. Thanks again."

She left, and he stood reflecting on Chavi's warm and easy manner, even in disappointment. Something wasn't jiving, but he couldn't pinpoint what it could be. But he didn't care. He liked her. And he felt serene. The undercurrent of anxiety he had felt, like a persistent low-grade fever, had vanished. Then it occurred to him that he wanted to do . . . what? He couldn't remember. It seemed like it might be important. It was right on the edge of his memory but would go no further.

CHAPTER 15

Adam's concern grew as he examined "Jane Doe 27" lying supine on the table. She had just been brought into the ER unconscious by a frantic middle-aged man, and then triaged as "serious." She was a robust young woman, whom he judged to be in her early twenties, six feet tall, her body firmly muscled and well proportioned. The comatose state of the woman concerned him nearly as much as the arrow piercing her right thigh.

Not far away, Devan interviewed a man whose voice, high-pitched and querulous with shock and guilt, didn't match his burly frame.

"And you're sure she was conscious when you hit her?"

"Yeah!" answered the man. "I was going round a curve, and she kinda stumbled out onto the road. But then I was right up on her, too late to stop."

Devan scratched his pen in his notebook as the man peered around, trying to catch a glimpse of the woman he had struck. The man chattered on.

"Yeah, I was enjoying the scenery. You know how nice it is out there on Crown Mountain."

Devan did know. He'd hiked the trail many times.

"Then, BAM! There she was! Good thing I was going slow. I stopped and checked her out." He grabbed Devan's arm and asked, wild-eyed, "Did you get a load of that stick shot through her leg?" He didn't wait for an answer. "She was still breathing pretty good, so I loaded her into my truck. No easy task, man. That chick is an Amazon! Brought her straight here. Good thing the traffic was light."

Devan reassured the man and sent him off, telling him not to worry too much; clearly it was an accident. Then he joined the doctor. He could see why the driver was so impressed despite his panic. Jane Doe 27 was a beauty.

Meanwhile Adam had carefully removed the arrow, inspecting it. Underneath the surprisingly little blood stain, he admired the beauty of the shaft, with its wide array of grain, brown to gold, smooth and glistening. The arrowhead was a bullet point made of some sort of black metal with a high gloss. The trine fletching was made with feathers of brilliant cobalt blue alternating with black and white stripes—a startling contrast to the deep rich wood of the shaft. He was deep in admiration until Baxter broke the spell.

"Doctor?" Baxter stared at him anxiously. "Are you all right?"

"Sorry." He held up the fletching. "Beautiful, isn't it?"

Baxter gave a noncommittal shrug and nod. "Gorgeous."

Adam placed the arrow on the tray and covered the woman up to her neck. "Did we get a panel?"

"Drew blood when she came in," Baxter replied.

"Okay. Let's get her to Imaging." Adam wrote on the clipboard and hung it on the gurney. He left the woman to Baxter and walked toward the nurses' station, racking his brain, trying to pin down why the woman looked so familiar to him.

***

Cezar's one-story house in Shaughnessy was large and sprawled over an acre of landscaped lawn. The rear of the house was surrounded by woods.

Inside, in the sparsely furnished living room, logs crackled in the fireplace. It was the only light in the room, the windows were covered with thick shades to block the daylight. Two armchairs flanked an end table. Cezar Balanescu lounged in one, his long legs stretched out before him. He studied Jake, who stood before him, back straight, tall, long-haired, deep-chested, bulging biceps evident, even through the long sleeves of his work shirt. His hands were large, rough and strong. He seemed ready to spring into action, and his bright eyes were alert and wary as he regarded Cezar. "What am I doing here?" he asked, his tone as wary as his visage.

"You're in no danger."

"Where's the guy I was with?"

"At the moment, I have no idea. But certainly in no need of your assistance in any event." Cezar straightened in his chair. "But to answer your first question, you are here because you are quite exceptional. A young man among many. Very many."

"What does that mean?"

Cezar paused again with a lazy smile. "Jake . . . " He pointed to the name patch. "May I call you Jake?" Cezar took Jake's stoic silence for assent. "Tell me your story."

Jake's tone was cautious. "Nothing to tell. I'm a furniture mover. Or was. Probably fired by now. Can't see how that makes me special."

Cezar had used time and local influence to good advantage. He stared off into space as he recollected, declaiming as though from a dossier. "Abandoned to the devices of social service agencies at three months, but never adopted. Still managed to excel on the athletic field as well as in the classroom. 'Never says much. Never lets us down,' according to one of your coaches. Always dependable, but there was something about you that both attracted and repelled people. Went to college on a wrestling scholarship but dropped out in your junior year. That was five years ago. Drifting from one job to another ever since."

Jake barely moved a muscle during the recitation, never taking his eyes off Cezar. There was a hint of insolence as he replied, "You seem to know my story already. Why bother asking?"

"Your self-control is impressive," Cezar remarked. "There are precious few who can resist my voice for more than a minute. This alone stands you above thousands. But you are correct. I didn't bring you here merely to catalog your underachievements."

He rose and approached Jake, who stood and faced him, unafraid. "You've been hiding. Yes. All your life. What's more, you still are. Certainly not from lack of courage, we both know that very well."

Jake stood steady as Cezar drew closer and ran a long, pale finger along the soft brown stubble on Jake's neck. "I can feel restiveness of the soul," he said, then stretched his jaws open, wide as a tiger's, with fangs just as formidable, adding, "*Your* soul, Jake."

Jake's jaw dropped in wonder.

Cezar put his arm around Jake's shoulder, his voice low and confidential. "We believe in the hierarchy imposed on us by nature. She ferrets out the weak, eliminating them, refining, always seeking the champion, that which stands towering and triumphant. Like you, Jake. She has no use for compromise, or those who venture to subdue us and undermine all we stand for."

Cezar pressed his body against Jake's and whispered in his ear. "Here, with us, you will find a vessel for all your strength and resolve." Cezar grew closer. "Here, at last, you will find your just reward."

***

The lunch crowd at Lucy's had started to thin when Devan and Chavi arrived. Their food came quickly, but that didn't alleviate the stern look on Devan's face. "You're going to get your ass canned, if you're not careful." He took a bite of his sandwich. Chavi picked at her salad.

"So you fucked up," he continued. "Think you're the first one?"

"I didn't fuck up!"

"Well, *something* got fucked, and you're left holding the bag. It happens."

"You don't get it. It's more than just the photos. Something else is going on. Eno thinks so, too." She paused, musing. "I wish he'd tell me what."

"Oh, no you don't!" he burst out. "Listen. You leave it be. You're in enough trouble. Ride it out."

She said nothing. He scrutinized her to make sure his advice hit home. She caught the scrutiny and said, "Maybe you're right."

Satisfied, Devan took a large bite of his lobster roll, eye-smiled, reached over and squeezed her hand, and she squeezed his.

***

Devan had been right. It had taken no time at all to narrow down the registrations on the DMV database that matched the dozen or so SUVs to the one described by the witness. He decided to start searching close to the crime scene—in Shaughnessy. Not only because of its proximity, but the likelihood that residents of that neighborhood were among the few who could afford such a vehicle.

The first stop was a large house, set back behind a semi-circular driveway. The grounds were well tended and there was wooded acreage all around. Even though the day was overcast he put on his shades. He got out and readied his badge and notebook.

A short, well-built man promptly answered the door. "May I help you?" he asked in a thick accent.

"Inspector Devan Olsen, Vancouver Police Department. Is . . . " he squinted at his notebook, parsing out the syllables, "Cesar Balanescu available?"

"'*Say-zahr*," the man corrected. "He is at home, Inspector." He moved aside to admit Devan. "Won't you come in?"

The man's grin reminded him of a shark about to feed, and Devan suddenly felt uneasy. But he had a job to do. He ignored the strong urge to turn tail and run. "Thank you. Appreciate it," Devan said, and walked inside.

***

It must be my day for defiance, thought Chavi as she pulled in next to Eno's official car. But this time she didn't hesitate. She went into the building, flipped her badge at the clerk and kept on walking. She went down the hallway until she stopped at an open door and recognized Eno's solid, compact form standing at an examining table.

Eno looked up, pleasantly surprised. "Well, hello. To what do I owe the pleasure?"

"Curiosity, mainly," she said. "I had an idea about what happened at the moving van."

"Well, hello. What are you doing here? Steve filed the report already. Said you were off the case."

Chavi countered with a little courage. "Actually, I've been . . . suspended."

He gave her a sly smile. "You've got a real fire in your gut, don't you? I like that." His smile broadened and he waved to her. "C'mon. Let me show you something."

Chavi joined him. He held the arrowhead taken from Jane Doe 27 under the magnifying glass. He nodded. "Take a look."

She peered through the glass and saw a shiny black surface. "What am I looking at?"

"A *Triquetra*."

"A what?"

"Look again."

She bent over and looked more closely. It wasn't easy to see the three interconnected leaf-like projections. "You mean those scratches?"

"They're not scratches. They're carvings."

"What do they mean?"

Eno was nonplussed. "Could mean a lot of things. It's a very old icon. But there is someone who may know for sure."

"Who?"

"Gaige Sutton. Friend of mine from grad school. He may point us in the right direction. He's on his way."

He faced her, his expression open and curious. "So, you have an idea about the van. I'm up for any theory, crazy or not. Shoot."

"Well . . . " She looked around, as though someone might overhear, then lowered her voice. "What about spontaneous combustion?"

Eno was momentarily surprised, but stared into space as he considered it, then nodded. His tone was reasonable. "Okay," he replied with a note of caution, adding, "but all the cases I've heard about, they all involved living persons." He shrugged. "But hey, who knows? Let me look into it. It's better than what we have. Good thinking!"

CHAPTER 16

When Chavi awoke she was surprised to see Devan sleeping beside her. He was nearly always awake before she was, and usually made breakfast after his morning run. Now here he was, dead to the world.

She sat up and poked him in the back. "Hey. It's after eight. Are you working today?"

He didn't stir. She shook his shoulder. He groaned and swatted her hands away.

"Devan? Aren't you going to be late?"

She was about to shake him again, when he turned over and faced her. He looked ashen, and there was a bluish tinge to his lips. His eyes were sunken and glassy.

"You look terrible!" she said. "How do you feel?"

"Like shit," he mumbled.

"You gonna call in sick?"

Another groan, which she interpreted as a 'yes.'

"Do you want me to call for you?"

He nodded. She got out of bed and shot him a worried look as she picked up her phone. She called in and got an abrupt 'thank you' from Sadie, who then ended the call with a sincere wish for his speedy recovery.

She went over and knelt next to him. "You want something to eat?"

From the curt rebuff and look of disgust on his face, one would think she had offered to shit in his shoes. "Fine," she said, trying not to feel hurt, remembering that this strain of flu going around was, by all accounts, particularly nasty. "Let me know if you need anything."

Normally Chavi didn't fret or nag, but she had a helpless feeling as she heard him toss and turn, refusing any kind of comfort she had to offer. After lunch she decided she had a bad case of cabin fever, and would start snapping at Devan if she didn't get outside for a bit. Besides, she was bothered by the symbol Eno had shown her. She was sure she had seen it before, but for the life of her she couldn't remember where. Worse than that, she couldn't shake the feeling that it was somehow important. She decided to go to her parents and check out some of her old portfolios. Maybe have some tea. Darjeeling always seemed to help center her thoughts.

"I'm going out," she whispered in Devan's ear.

He looked half asleep, and said through his dry mouth, "Fine. Be careful on the road."

"Do you want anything?"

He shook his head and waved her off, closing his eyes.

She noticed an odd smell about him, like soil after a rain.

Must be from the fever, sweat and all, she thought, picking up her keys.

CHAPTER 17

The last thing Eno expected to see when he arrived at work the next morning was an unfamiliar car parked next to the official vehicles. When he approached the car he was surprised but delighted to see Gaige Sutton behind the wheel, fast asleep. He savored the feeling of deep affection he had for his old friend before he tapped on the glass.

Gaige woke with a start, bleary at first, then delighted as well. Eno stepped back as Gaige opened the door and hopped out of the car, alert and full of energy. He was very tall and lanky. And agile. They shared a tight hug.

"You're early," said Eno. "I'm not complaining, but I thought you said this weekend." He paused, his smile slackening. "Why didn't you call?"

Gaige adjusted his glasses and combed his long brown hair with his hand. "Didn't want to wake you. May I see that arrow of yours?" Gaige asked in his tony British accent, his voice tight with barely suppressed excitement, almost demanding.

"Right this minute?"

"Right now."

Eno was startled. In the years he had known Gaige, he found his friend the most circumspect person he knew. With a note of incredulity, he asked while taking out his keys, "Even before coffee?"

Gaige's excitement didn't wane one bit, but he mustered a little more patience. "If you insist."

***

At her parents' house Chavi sat in her old bedroom leafing through her portfolios. Mementos of a happy childhood surrounded her. Ajay, her father, had been a journalist from

Punjab in his youth. He had joined a group whose platform espousing human rights, unpopular at first with the oppressive theocratic regime, became so dangerous as to drive the group underground. His story had fascinated Chavi for as long as she could remember, and at her insistence he made a meticulous sketch of the compound where the group had hidden for months. She had it framed and mounted on the wall, along with the photos she was proudest of. Underneath, in a clear plastic coin case, rested a supposedly thousand-year-old amulet given to her by Myra, her mother. Myra said the amulet was a precious heirloom of the Joshi, her own family.

Chavi thought back when she'd first asked how her parents met. There was little romance to it, unless it was the radical kind of romance reserved for the displaced. Ajay had barely escaped to England and met Myra, a graduate student at the University of London. They clung to each other as much out of comfort as love. They emigrated to Canada, settled in British Columbia, became teachers, and when the time was right, had a daughter.

A stew of nostalgia simmered in her gut, punctuated with unexpected jolts of joy as she recalled fond memories of her parents, classmates, and adventures with the camera.

Her mood was interrupted by her ringing phone. Her mother. She felt a sharp fear; her mother never called during working hours.

"Hello? Mother?"

"Yes! It's good to hear your voice, Chavi." She sounded relieved.

"Good to hear yours, too. How are you?"

"I'm fine."

"How is Dad?" That was at the core of her worry.

"He's doing well also. But how about you? Are you well?" There was an urgency to her voice.

That startled Chavi, and she wanted to reassure her. "Yes, Mom, I'm fine. Really."

"I just had this feeling . . ." Myra's voice was apologetic. "Never mind. It's just that we haven't spoken in a while." She paused. "How is Devan?" Her voice took on a tentative quality. Her parents liked Devan, despite the fact that her father disliked police in general. But marriage, they said, is a different thing—cultural tradition must be respected. "Especially considering your background," her mother added, alluding to her mystic ancestors, which Devan found to be *total* nonsense—Chavi herself, only half.

"He's not too good today. It's the flu that's going around."

"And your job? Why aren't you at work?"

Chavi was glad her mother couldn't see her pained expression. "Researching a case. I need to find some old photos of mine. As a matter of fact, I'm home right now. I mean at your house, looking through my old portfolios."

"Then why not stay for dinner? Your father would love to see you!" Her mother sounded delighted. She found herself wanting to see her father as well. And her mother's cooking was always welcome. "Okay. Sure. I'll see you when you get home."

"I won't be late. See you then. Love you."

"Love you, too."

She hung up and returned to her photos. As she browsed through them, she thought with frustration, *where's that damn three-leaf thing?*

Adam lay on the living room couch with Merit snuggled next to him. He was watching television—the latest medical drama. He loved debunking the popular myths assigned to emergency medicine, but also giving credit where credit was due in the few instances where they got it right. But tonight he used the show as subterfuge, feigning interest while he obsessed about Roi, whose face drifted unbidden into his mind at inopportune times, as it had now. Adam felt the fire in his belly and then his cock stiffening, and felt inexplicably embarrassed as he positioned his legs to hide it.

Meanwhile Merit watched the screen, her thoughts as distant as Adam's. While Adam was more affable and outgoing, confident among a crowd, Merit preferred to stand back and observe, chiming in with intelligent questions when appropriate. As a couple they were, in many respects, perfectly complementary, tuned into the ebb and flow of each other's psyches. They were quietly competitive with each other without antagonism.

Tonight, once again, Merit noticed Adam's remoteness. For several days his detachment had found its way into the bedroom. In the words of her favorite author, Gertrude Stein, "There is no *there* there."

Later that evening, after what felt to her like perfunctory lovemaking, she came to a decision. She concluded that Adam needed some space.

"Adam?"

He *humphed* in reply.

"Eno called today."

"What did he want?"

"Some help with a blood anomaly that popped up."

"You gonna take it on?"

"I think I'd better." She frowned. "It's only verifying some samples. Just in case the CDC might have to get involved." Her frown deepened. "And since we were thinking about starting a family . . . well, it might take some time down the road." She didn't add that Eno had already sent over a case of slides for review.

"No. You're right. It's smart to think ahead. Help him out."

***

It was sundown by the time Chavi got home, carrying a plate of food along with her parents' wishes for Devan's quick recovery. She was astonished to find Devan, not only up and around, but dressed for work.

"You're feeling better, I see," she said, her surprise obvious.

"Considerably," he replied and even sounded a little cheerful. To Chavi he still looked pale and washed out, but acted more robust and energetic than ever.

"Mother and Dad send their regards. Along with this." She offered him the plate. He backed off a little with a look of mild disgust, then noticed her surprise. "Stomach's still not all there," he said with a ghost of a smile.

"Are you sure you should go into work? Why not wait until tomorrow? Get a good night's sleep."

"Already behind on a case. Just for a few hours. Some fresh air and activity will do me good."

"Take this with you," she said, offering the plate again. "Just in case you get hungry later." She went into the kitchen. "I'll pack it up for you."

He fought back a grimace, and forced out a grin, in case she appeared unexpectedly.

CHAPTER 19

After Jake was brought to Cezar's home, he saw no one except for Kostin and his host. Yet he thought he heard other voices, echoing through the empty rooms, soft laughter, groans of pleasure or, sometimes, shrieks of surprise—or terror. He grew lonely, cloistered, and restless.

One late afternoon he ambled from the house onto the estate grounds. The sun was low in the sky, but there were still long shadows, and he thought he had a good hour or so before darkness set in. He had unintentionally wandered off the well-mowed lawn into the surrounding woods. Only then did he fully understand the meaning of the phrase "pitch black." He literally could not see his hand two inches from his face as he hunted around in the dark. He had just reconciled himself to spending a cold night outside, sleeping against a tree until daylight when he felt a strong hand grip his arm and guide him through the trees and out onto the smooth green near the house, which was candlelit from inside.

His rescuer was Kostin, who stood there with his arms crossed and a smirk on his face, giving Jake the once-over.

It turned out Jake wasn't more than twenty yards away from the house. Kostin's cornsilk hair seemed to shimmer, even though there was no moon that night.

"I hope that taught you," he said in his thick accent, "not to wander around outside at night." His tone was chiding, with a touch of malice, but he clapped Jake amiably enough on the shoulder and nudged him back toward the house.

They passed the living room, and Jake caught sight of Cezar sitting in his armchair, scrutinizing a tall youth standing before him. The youth stood, his posture in a slight slump, short blond-on-black hair spiked in all directions, clothes disheveled.

Jake paused at the door, fascinated by the youth, who offered Jake a wicked grin and narrowed eyes. Jake couldn't seem to break his gaze.

With a nod from Cezar, Kostin pulled the door closed, commenting cryptically, "You'll see him again quite soon, I should think. Yes, quite soon."

***

Later that night, Jake swam up from a deep sleep to the echoing sound of soft slurps and smacking lips. His room was bathed in candlelight. He felt an exquisite friction on his cock; the white sheet bobbed up and down with the assiduous effort.

Jake pulled back the sheet, and ran his hand over the muscular back of a man nursing on his cock, up and around the nape of his neck, then ran his hand over the man's spiky black hair, frosted blond on top. Spurred on by this, the man lifted up, never taking his mouth off Jake's cock, and lay by his side so that his own erection was inches away from Jake's mouth, the young man looking down.

It was the youth Cezar had been scolding earlier that evening.

Jake took the invitation and gently grabbed the man's stiff member, stroking it slowly, then licking the head, opening wide to take the shaft, taking it deeper down his throat, closing his mouth around the column of hard, hot flesh, pressing his face against the man's pubic hair as he sucked deeply, edging the man to greater passion, as he himself approached the delicious moment. He felt the man's salty pre-cum leak onto his tongue, and he pulled back and slowed down, waiting for the man's lust to ebb, just a little, before he started in again, slowly at first.

The man, however, continued to suck steadily, hungrily—and expertly. For a quick moment, with a gasp and groan, Jake ceased sucking as his loins roared toward orgasm, trying to stave off the mounting explosion of pleasure. But the man was almost *too* skilled. Fortunately, even though he was edging quickly to climax, Jake was able to steel his resolve. He lifted his body, pulling his cock, jutting out and throbbing, from the man's mouth. With amazing strength, he grabbed the man's arm and pulled him close, grabbing the brush of hair and pulled the man's head, face up, and over the mattress, the nape of the man's neck pressed against the edge. The room was dusk-lit, and deep shadows outlined the powerful muscles of Jake's thighs.

The young man understood at once what was required of him. He opened his mouth just in time as Jake crouched slightly. As he did so, he grasped the young man's nipples, kneading them. He paused for a few seconds, steadying his stance before ramming his cock down the man's throat in a series of mighty thrusts, then reaching out and stroked the man's rock-hard member in sync with the movement over the man's blood-gorged pole. In short order, a dozen thrusts or so were enough to put them both over into a glorious abyss. One final, deep throat fuck, and with a mighty shout Jake blasted a huge load down the man's eager throat, just as the man's jizz spurted before flowing over Jake's hand like a pearl river.

Jake leaned on the bed and took deep breaths as he hovered over the man for a moment. He felt lightheaded at first, then felt engulfed by a peculiar stupor. Jake saw the young man pull back with a bright, cold gaze, his mouth stained with the blood oozing from the wound on Jake's thigh.

Then the young man spoke, and the sound of his voice was like a tightening fist in Jake's gut. But it seemed to come from another world, which he barely caught as he sank into oblivion.

"My name is Lorik," he said.

CHAPTER 20

Roi glanced back and forth on the sketch pinned to the easel as he carefully applied the red clay to the armature, pausing, glancing back and forth between each slab, joining them with gentle pressure. He stood back, standing dead still, as if in a trance, as he looked at the sketch again.

The doorbell rang.

Roi paused for a moment, wondering if he should answer it. *Maybe it's Jehovah's Witnesses*, he thought with sudden hope. Or better yet, a uniform pair of Mormon missionaries. From some unaccountable, wicked center of his being, nothing pleased him more than squaring off with the sanctimonious. Especially dressed as he was, barefoot, in a T-shirt and his favorite flannel pajama bottoms, worn to threadbare in several spots.

But he was itching to get back to the clay and keep its momentum. As he debated, the doorbell rang again, and the urge to answer it was almost irresistible.

No, he decided. It *was* irresistible. He gave into the impulse to run to the front door, afraid he'd miss the visitor. His heart quickened when he saw whom he thought it was, and for a moment he held his breath as the strapping man standing at the front door came into full view.

It was Adam.

Roi took a long moment to look over his guest. The doctor would look stunning in any light, but he looked especially good in the late afternoon sunshine.

He was dressed for jogging in warm weather. He wore running shorts that were snug around his tree-trunk thighs. His sleeveless T-shirt was soaked here and there with sweat and clung around his biceps, and his bronze skin glistened. Roi's gaze lingered on the sturdy neck joining his strong, square jaw. His yellow tee opened to a "V" that shaped his solid pecs and rode above his powerful biceps, the right one flexing as he lifted a fist and knocked, tenuously at first, and then pounding as his eyes narrowed, his mouth set with determination.

Roi was so dazzled by the sight of Adam that he had trouble finding his voice for a moment. He looked down and hoped his erection wasn't too obvious. A little obvious, maybe, but there was nothing for it.

"Door's open!" Roi hollered.

Adam pulled open the door and entered, a little hesitantly at first, then seeing Roi, approached him with a smile that was almost shy.

For a moment, Roi thought Adam was going to take him in his arms, but Adam stopped at arm's length. They looked deep into each other's eyes, never moving as they spoke. Roi was close enough to hear Adam's heartbeat—a bit fast, but strong and steady, matching his deep breaths.

Adam's eyes were still fixed on Roi. "When the weather's nice I jog in the park nearby sometimes." He was still breathing heavy from the effort. "Thought I'd drop by and make a house call, just like a country doctor."

Roi was tongue-tied, awed by Adam's vigor, but he was saved by his manners. "Want some water?"

"Sure."

"Come on in."

Adam followed Roi into the kitchen, and Roi stood and watched as Adam helped himself to a tumbler of tap water.

"Thanks," Adam said when finished. "You promised to show me your sculptures. So I thought, while I'm here . . ."

Roi paused, as if considering, but his loins exploded into fire. "I'm working on a piece right now. My studio's upstairs."

"Perfect. Lead the way."

Adam followed Roi up the stairs, so distracted by Roi's firm ass undulating through his pajama bottoms that he almost stumbled—more than once. Adam licked his lips involuntarily, and then as if he had heard, Roi turned his head and gave Adam a quick, very charming smile.

They reached the top of the stairs and made their way toward the front of the house and Roi's studio.

Bright diffuse light flooded the studio through white shades covering the window. Roi stood by, allowing Adam to take in the organized chaos. A large sketch pad rested on an easel next to a shapeless mass of red clay at the far wall. Adam stepped over to the sketch, peering at it, slack-jawed. After a moment he turned to Roi and said in a low voice, "I'm flattered."

It was a beautifully rendered study in charcoal of Adam himself. Roi moved closer next to Adam, but still an arm's length away, indicating the red clay on the armature. "That will be the three-dimensional model."

"If it's only half as gorgeous as this sketch. . . " Adam shrugged, at a loss for words. "You have any more?" Casually he flipped up the page to the next sketch, and heard Roi gasp behind him.

"Wait!" Roi cried. Adam saw nothing but a blur as Roi whizzed past, and grabbed at the page, knocking over the easel. Roi lost his footing and started to fall.

But he never hit the floor. Adam had reached out and caught Roi's wrist in a firm grasp, gently pulling him to his feet. Adam didn't let go. He was fixated on Roi's incredulous expression as he gazed at his hand, still wrapped around Roi's wrist. He let go, but Roi was still focused on his wrist, his eye's still wide, then faced Adam in disbelief.

But Adam wasn't looking at Roi—only at the sketch Roi had been so desperate to hide.

It was a sketch of Adam himself, a full nude in which he was aroused. Its accuracy was astounding. "Damn close," Adam whispered, his voice soft with wonder. He looked over at Roi, whose mouth parted as though trying to speak, and whose eyes were wide with longing.

Or was it fear? Adam couldn't tell.

Not knowing what else to do, Adam went into professional mode. "Let's have a look at that wrist. I gripped it pretty hard." He gently took Roi's hand and felt around Roi's wrist. He looked up at Roi and started to speak, but the sight of Roi's cheeks glistening with tears silenced him. He cradled Roi's chiseled jaw in his hand and tenderly wiped away the tears with his thumb. "Did I do something wrong?" he asked.

Roi held up his arm, pressing as if to test if it was solid. "You don't understand," he said, his voice filled with wonder. "You touched me," he stammered, "on my bare skin."

"Yes. So?"

"And it's not . . ."

Adam gripped Roi's hand, gently this time. "It's not what?" With his other hand around the back of Roi's neck, pulled him close. They looked deeply in each other's eyes.

"I'll explain later," Roi whispered.

Their lips touched, at first gingerly, then with mounting passion as they sank to their knees, exploring each other's bodies.

After a few moments, Roi stood and led Adam into the hallway, down to Roi's bedroom. The heavy shades were still drawn; the room glowed cool in faux twilight. Still in each other's arms, they sank onto the rumpled bed.

Roi's eyes were wide and shining, almost trance like, as he slipped his hand under Adam's shirt, kneading his firm pecs and tweaking his nipples. Adam was entranced himself by Roi's fervor. When Roi lay back supine and pulled Adam on top to straddle him, he was astounded at Roi's strength. Lust glimmered bright in Roi's eyes—the look of a starving man who had just sat down to a hearty meal.

Roi pressed his groin against Adam's with his cock at full-mast. Adam caressed Roi's smooth, flat belly, slipping his hand under Roi's pants, skirting his erect cock. Roi was not unmindful of the impressive bulge in Adam's running shorts.

Adam fondled Roi's balls, pressing deeply into his scrotum, massaging firmly, before moving up to circle the base of Roi's erection. He felt the heat in his own gut spread to his loins as he gazed at the expression of naked awe on Roi's face. Adam was used to this reaction in his conquests, and for sure, he felt the usual surge of pride; but now he also felt a flood of tenderness, of unity, that he had never experienced before.

Roi's eyes glimmered—lust tinged with fear.

Then Adam realized that Roi felt defenseless.

And knowing that, his sense of triumph was bolstered along with his urge to hold Roi close, to protect him from . . .

. . . *What?*

Adam sensed the answer was there. Buried deep under layers from years of virtual isolation? Perhaps, but at the moment his mounting desire crushed his curiosity. He felt drawn to

Roi as irresistibly and naturally as an orbiting planet to its sun. He knew deep down that Roi needed him, no longer as a doctor, but a healer of a different kind, and someone much more than a mere friend.

He now realized the feeling had begun the moment he saw Roi on the emergency room gurney for the first time, cool and collected. Adam reflected on that moment, time and again, remembering Roi's beautiful, dark eyes, haunted, as if witnessing some catastrophic event from within. Adam recognized that he himself was at one of those crucial crossroads in his own life, one he would always look back on with joy or regret.

He looked down. He towered over Roi, who looked up, vulnerable, adoring, yet in a way so pleading and distant that Adam felt an overwhelming protective tenderness that brought tears to his eyes. He leaned down and covered Roi's mouth with his own, his tongue exploring deeply. After a few seconds' resistance, Roi reciprocated with a force that baffled him. Now both were evenly matched, at the mercy of their shared passion.

Adam felt Roi's hand on his crotch, exploring and teasing, so that his cock, as it stiffened to a raging hard-on, swelled against his gym shorts. With amazing urgency Roi groped with a quick motion, and slid his hand over Adam's cock, encircling the head, smooth and firm like ripe fruit, then slid down the thick, steel-hard pole, pumping with slow, perfect friction. Still locked in a passionate kiss, Adam's lustful, baritone growl echoed in his throat.

Then as if on cue, Roi broke away and dived down onto Adam's cock, pausing for a moment to take in its beauty, then licking slowly, around the head, sucking briefly, then running his tongue down the vein-laced shaft, making it slick for the pleasuring to come. Adam started to pull off his shirt, pausing a second or two as he groaned with pleasure, then taking it off in one frantic motion, tossing it aside.

Roi stopped for a moment, looking up to admire his partner. Adam looked down at him with primal fire in his eyes. No words needed to be said; Roi knew what to do. Roi's mouth traced every inch of Adam's torso, softly licking and kissing, moving up to his chest, sucking and biting his nipples, groping every muscled curve, while Adam eased down to a lying position.

Roi was eager to pay tribute, and Adam was more than ready to receive it. He felt Roi's tongue snaking along the underside of his ball sac, skirt around the inside of his thigh. He winced as he felt a sting, and then a hot flush spread to his groin, bringing a delicious burn. He felt Roi suck on his skin.

Adam looked down and saw Roi draw back, lick his lips. In one quick motion, Roi reared up his head and kissed Adam—a deep, long kiss, in one quick motion, then returned to the business at hand.

With incredible skill, Roi wrapped his lips around Adam's blood-gorged pole and sucked—first in gentle, steady motions, then increasing as he felt Adam swell to even more incredible hardness. He tasted the sweet-salt of Adam's pre-cum and increased the strokes and suction, teasing out the jizz.

A minute passed, then two, and Adam began to thrust in time with Roi's skillful throat fuck. With a loud gasp, Adam let loose no less than a dozen, pencil-thick spurts of cum. He fell back, panting in satisfaction, eyes on the ceiling, kneading Roi's shoulder.

"What about you?" Adam asked, still breathing heavy.

Roi's back was turned to him.

He pulled Roi against his chest in a tight embrace, then reached around and caressed Roi's thighs and stomach. He gasped in surprise.

"Yes," Roi whispered. "I came when you did." He turned to face Adam. He was licking all around his lips in a predatory way, as a dog or cat might. Adam thought it odd, but decided it was a compliment.

With sweet command in his voice, Adam said, "Come here."

CHAPTER 21

Chavi arrived at the lab with takeout from Lucy's to find Eno chatting with a tall, bespectacled man, introduced to her as Gaige, who kept his arms crossed as he peered at her. Not rude, exactly, more like curiosity. Still, she felt a little put off until he joined them at the table and started with meet-and-greet small talk. Soon enough they were finished with the food and got down to business.

Eno turned to Chavi. "Gaige here doesn't think Corey died of spontaneous combustion." He spoke in an odd, flat, skeptical, almost dismissive tone.

"Not a bad theory," Gaige quickly put in. "But none of the commonalities were present. Especially the ashes, which should have had a greasy texture accompanied by an unmistakable stench."

Evidently Gaige was, among other things, an evolutionary biologist. His pet project over two decades involved something special. "A subspecies," he said. "Actually, *three* of them." He described the trail he followed from the Nile Basin to the German Neander Valley.

"And that," Gaige announced, "is where I found this."

He carefully opened a pouch and brought out a cylinder, black and shiny, shaped like a rolling pin with a seam running lengthwise. At the middle of the seam was what appeared to be a brooch made of glass, or maybe crystal. Gaige's voice was soft with wonder. "According to carbon dating this object is approximately fifteen thousand years old."

Eno coughed pointedly, with an incredulous expression.

"What is it?" Chavi asked, hypnotized by the crystal, peering at it.

"A canister."

She ran her fingers over the smooth, glistening black surface. "What's it made of?"

"That's what I hope to find out," answered Gaige, with a sidelong look at Eno. "With the help of our friend Eno here."

Eno squinted an eye in suspicion.

"What's inside is the *real* mystery," added Gaige. He paused a few seconds for dramatic effect.

"There's no drum roll, if that's what you're waiting for," Eno said drily.

"No sense of style, this one," Gaige confided in Chavi. "Never had one."

But Chavi was getting a little impatient herself. "What's in it?"

"Open it and see."

With some reluctance, she picked up the canister. It was heavy for its size, with a seam running long ways, apparently latched with some sort of crystal or gem, clear and colorless. She looked at Gaige, who nodded, *Go ahead.* She snapped open the latch and opened the canister. She felt her spine shiver and her head go light with intense *déjà vu.* Inside was a loosely rolled parchment.

"This scroll," he announced, "is made up of some type of fiber, very tough."

"Papyrus?" asked Eno.

"From the same family, I'm guessing."

Chavi asked, "What does it say?"

"I'm not certain. I believe it may be some sort of Punjabi dialect. Possibly Malwai," continued Gaige, "I'll have it translated when I consult a colleague at the university."

Chavi wanted to ask more about the language, but Eno piped up first. "And what about these so-called subspecies? What are . . . I mean, what *were* they?" Again, to Chavi it sounded more like a teacher baiting a foolish student.

"Ah!" Gaige said with a smile. "Not *were*. I think they may still be among us."

"How's that?"

"About five hundred thousand years ago there existed a common ancestor to both the Cro-Magnon and the Neanderthals. But *my* research . . ." Gaige's eyes grew bright. ". . . has suggested the emergence of a *third* type of hominid. More advanced and with greater adaptability than its contemporaries."

Eno was nonplussed. "But there should be more proof."

"And there is. Oral tradition, stories set down on stone and paper throughout the ages all support my research. Not to mention DNA evidence. But there must be something, a common thread, that ties it all together."

He held up the cylinder. "I'm hoping the text within, once translated, is that common thread. And confirms my theory."

"Which is?" asked Eno with a hint of irritation.

"That this third type of human is still among us. Hidden, perhaps in plain view, with a history and future of its own. And we may find ourselves in the middle of it."

CHAPTER 22

Adam and Roi had been dozing on and off, when the sun began to set. They awoke, stretched, and laid in each other's arms for several minutes, wordlessly, kissing tenderly, before they rose and went into the shower. They spent what seemed like an hour under the nozzle, taking time to explore each other's bodies as they soaped up each other, with tender kissing that contrasted the lustful, almost animal grappling in the bedroom hours before.

The hot water streamed over them, emphasizing the lean curves as the light played over their bodies. Their soapy, semi-erect cocks fenced under the spray of water, and they shared a deep, hard kiss, nipping each other with mounting abandon, easing down, Adam sitting, legs spread, Roi crouched over Adam's groin. Adam reached under and lifted slightly, playing with Roi's ass, his fingers exploring, then gently stretching, the soft firm curves of his buttocks. He probed slowly, then more insistently as Roi writhed with excitement.

Roi groped Adam's muscular thighs and stroked his cock, rocking his ass against the hard flesh. Adam grew bolder, slipping first one soapy finger, then two, into Roi's anus, gingerly at first, eliciting a groan of pleasure from Roi as he steadied his hands on Adam's biceps, locked his mouth onto Adam's, tongue poking, teeth nipping.

He pulled back and sank to his knees, nuzzling Adam's thick pubic hair, tonguing his upper thigh, nipping more passionately as he went. He opened his eyes to gaze at his quarry, when—

Roi caught his breath and staggered to his feet, backing against the wall.

Adam was startled by Roi's terrified expression.

Roi followed the watery crimson trail from Adam's face, down his neck, encircling his pec and snaking down his torso into his groin, joining another red trail onto the floor of the bathtub.

The river of milky suds mixed with the deep pink that circled the drain. Adam looked down at the trail of blood. The blood had already slowed; the water streaming was already clear. Roi said, "Adam! I'm sorry!" He looked confused and sounded aghast, standing there, as if in a trance, as the water beat down on him.

Adam, for his part, was startled but not upset after he inspected the wound and found two negligible nicks which had already stopped seeping blood.

For Adam it had already been a strange week, one that had carried him into the chasm of his own desires that he had kept hidden for so long, but which had not allowed much room for contemplation so far.

At the moment all he wanted to do was console Roi—but was it personal or professional? Oddly enough, at this point he didn't care. What he did care about is the look of shock on Roi's face, an unaccountable fear that seemed to Adam to border on panic.

Suddenly Roi seemed to snap out of it and jumped out of the shower and started drying off frantically. Adam got out, too, and placed a placating hand on Roi's shoulder. Roi jumped away as if burned by Adam's touch.

"Hey," he said. "What going on?"

Roi paused, eyes focused in the distance. Adam was shocked to see terror on Roi's face.

"I hurt you," Roi said in a terrified whisper as he rushed out the door.

Adam stepped into the hallway, calling after him.

"No. You just nibbled a little too hard, that's all." He gave a sudden grin. "You didn't hear me complain, did you?"

But there was no grin from Roi as he made his quick way down the hall and into his room, at what looked to Adam like inhumanly long strides. He felt a strange jab of fear at the sight of this, but his concern conquered that, and he rushed to follow him.

He found Roi standing with his back to him, dead still as if hypnotized, in the middle of the room. Adam approached Roi with measured steps, coming behind him and placed his hand on his shoulder.

"I'm okay, really," he insisted. Then, after a pause, with a look of alarm. "Are you?"

Roi turned his head and gave a soft chuckle; he looked to be himself again.

"Yeah," he said. "I'm sorry. Just freaked out a little."

Adam turned him gently around, with a little smile, wiping off the smudge of blood under Roi's lip. "Open wide," he said.

"No, I'm fine, really," Roi managed a weak smile.

"Don't be a baby. You might have bitten yourself. I just want to check for a laceration."

With a sigh of resignation, Roi obeyed. With a professional squint and frown, Adam poked around with a finger, then finished with a grin.

"You're fine."

As Adam leaned over for a kiss, his cellphone buzzed in the pocket of his pants.

"That's your cue," Roi said, disengaging. "Better get dressed."

He started to don his own clothes, while Adam pulled out the phone.

"Hello?" Then after a pause, "Hang in there. Give me half an hour." He put the phone away. After dressing he went over to Roi and hugged him again. "Gotta go," he said.

Roi nodded with a quick grin.

"I'll call you," Adam said after a peck on Roi's cheek. "I want a look at that sculpture when you're finished." He gave Roi his no-nonsense look. "Promise?"

Roi nodded. "I promise."

"I'll let myself out," Adam said and forced out a parting grin. *Why is it so hard*, he wondered silently, *to reconcile myself to my first experience with another man that goes beyond gratuitous fucking?* He was walking through the front door, lost in this thought, when he literally bumped into a surprised Rosamund, a bag of groceries in one arm, keys in the other.

"Well, hello, Adam," she said, drawn by the scent of his strong, spicy cologne.

"Hello, Rosamund. How are you?"

"Just fine, thanks. So, is Roi okay? Nothing's wrong, is there?"

"No, no. Just came to check things out. Been a while since I made a house call. I'm out of practice."

Relieved, she gave a good-natured chuckle.

He continued, "If you'll excuse me, duty calls."

"Of course."

"Have a good evening," he called out over his shoulder as he made for his vehicle.

"Thanks. Same to you." She watched him with a speculative eye as his SUV roared to life. He waved. She waved back and went into the kitchen and put away the groceries. *Something's up*, she thought, and headed for the stairs.

***

Rosamund paused in the hallway a short distance from Roi's open bedroom door. "Are you decent?" she called out.

"Just a second," Roi called back. She thought his voice sounded odd; there was a subtle, serene elation to it.

"Okay," he called out.

She walked in and saw him sitting on the bed in the same shirt and sweatpants he had on when she left. She tried to appear nonchalant. "I saw Doctor . . . Adam . . . on his way out."

"Doctor . . . Adam?" he mimicked with a jovial smirk.

But Rosamund wasn't in a jovial mood. *Something's definitely up,* she thought again. "Are you okay?"

"How do I look?" he said, then unspoken, *None of your fucking business.*

But unspoken or not, Rosamund picked up on it.

"Wise-ass. I'm worried, that's all." She was hurt, but she had to admit that he looked better than he ever had, so she relaxed a bit.

"Sorry," he replied, and meant it. "How was the outing?"

"Wonderful." She pouted a little. "I invited Imogen for dinner tomorrow. To thank her."

He stood up, went over and hugged her. "I really am sorry. I know I can be a douche at times."

She hugged back in earnest. She got a whiff of his cologne, spicy, robust, rugged— and familiar. "You smell nice," she commented. "Hungry?" she asked.

"Starving."

"Give me a few minutes and we'll share a smoothie."

"You're on."

As she walked down the hall toward the stairwell, she stopped dead.

She suddenly recognized the aroma of the cologne.

It wasn't Roi's.

It was Adam's.

***

Adam had much to think about as he drove downtown. He mulled over the sex he had with Roi in the shower, steamy and satisfying in a way he had never experienced before, surprising and elusive.

But what surprised him even more was Roi's jarring change of mood after the inadvertent bite on his thigh. Adam was no stranger to fuck-driven bites and scratches, even those which drew a little blood from time to time. And he assumed Roi wasn't either, judging from his impressive sexual skills and the depth of his passion.

And yet, on reflection, Adam couldn't shake the feeling that the raw intensity they shared was as novel to Roi as it was to him.

As for any blood-borne diseases, Adam had no concerns at all. Although there were a few oddities in Roi's blood panel—which was not so mystifying, considering his condition—there were no contagions present in the baseline. And the laboratory was extremely diligent in pinning down harmful organisms.

No, thought Adam, *his eyes were haunted. There's something else going on with that guy.*

Adam was also certain that Roi had joined him at the crossroads, and that there was purpose behind it, a journey they were meant to take together.

But whom would they meet? And whom had they left behind? Of that, he was not certain at all. He wondered if Roi felt as uncertain as he did.

CHAPTER 23

Despite Eno's status as M.E. and hinting that they expedite matters, the hospital records room had taken hours to release the arrow taken from Jane Doe. Quite rightly they had insisted on completing all the proper forms, but Eno could have sworn they invented a brace of new ones.

Gaige, who had accompanied him, did not seem much put out. But then, Gaige almost never seemed put out, even when they were told that "Jane" was still out cold and could receive no visitors, even though her vital signs were stronger than ever and her EEG showed that she was very much alive—and probably aware. Gaige's quiet optimism was as unquenchable as it was inexhaustible.

Gaige could barely contain his excitement as he inspected the arrow as best he could in the evidence bag, feeling the shaft with gentle fingers, whistling with astonishment as he noticed the tip, its high gloss glistening even through the translucent bag.

Ever since they returned to the Eno's office, Gaige had been holed up in one corner, alternating between peering at the arrow under his magnifying glass and jotting in his notebook; every once in a while, he uttered a gasp of surprise. Eventually, curiosity got the best of Eno.

"What's going on? Did you find something?"

Gaige replied with an empty, lemony smile and muttered cryptically, "No questions yet. Not until I'm certain." So definite was the dismissal that Eno withdrew, trying not to feel hurt, and buried himself in his own work. And while the hurt went away, his curiosity only heightened. For added distraction he decided to call Chavi and invite her along to check on the status of Jane Doe 27 the next day.

***

Chavi was delighted to hear from Eno, glad to be of some help, however unofficially. They next day they were delighted to discover that Jane Doe 27 had regained consciousness during the night, but little good her recovery did for the hospital staff trying to treat her and wheedle *any* information, even a name, from the strapping young woman. Jane merely sat, arms crossed, alert, wary—and mute, just as the first-shift nurse had found her, the tubes in her arms removed, the fluids draining on the floor.

The medical staff, however, was more forthcoming. In fact, they were as astounded as Jane was mute. In a matter of hours, they said, Jane's wound had healed, a process that normally would have taken days. The tube ports were healed completely. "Let's see what the blood work tells us," they said, grateful that they had gotten any blood at all. While awake, Jane rebuffed all attempts at examination, to the point of almost crushing a technician's forearm, for which she was put in four-point restraints. Through it all, she had remained silent. "Nothing for us here," Eno remarked.

Chavi left with Eno, who returned to work. Gaige had since left for the university to evaluate the information he had gleaned, Eno assumed. Chavi called Devan and invited him to lunch. One thing she knew for certain: however aggressive and silently stubborn, Jane Doe was neither disabled nor clinically disturbed. She shared this impression with Devan later as they ate at their favorite burger joint, an out-of-the-way shack that sacrificed ambience for good food and generous portions. Devan looked a little better, but he still picked at his food.

"That's one tough lady," Chavi mused.

Devan nodded in agreement as he nibbled at his burger. "She'll come around," he said through a mouthful. "Give it a day or two."

"I'm being impatient?"

"A little, maybe. It's not like you."

He was right. There was something about Jane that was getting under her skin.

**

Adam knelt next to the police officer sitting propped against the wall next to the door to Jane Doe's room, taking his pulse. A nurse stood by. A patch of gauze covered a cut on the cop's buzzed scalp. A chair lay on its side nearby. The nurse supervisor rushed over. "What's going on?" she asked.

"Jane Doe went AMA," answered the orderly.

The supervisor groaned. *That bitch*, she said to herself. Leaving against medical advice—without getting the patient's signature on the proper form, no less—meant weeks of documenting and testifying.

The officer spoke up, his voice thick. "Didn't hear a thing. I stood up to stretch my legs, my back to the door. Then . . . " There was a tinge of shame in his voice.

Adam shone a penlight in the cop's eyes, back and forth, several times. "You're fine," he said, holding out his hand. The cop grabbed it and Adam hoisted him up. "You know the drill," Adam continued, "Take a day off and rest. And if you get dizzy, start puking—"

"Report it immediately," finished the officer, which Adam confirmed with a nod and walked off, trying once again to shake the eerie feeling that he had seen Jane Doe somewhere before, then doubting it in the next moment. Someone like Jane didn't slip one's mind.

The nurse supervisor felt a twinge of sympathy for the hulking policeman, who was gingerly rubbing his head. Clearly his ego was bruised as much as his head. She tried a note of commiseration in her question. "When did this happen?"

"Early morning. Maybe two."

The supervisor didn't press further. She gave the cop's hand a little squeeze and headed toward her office, pecking at her cellphone. "Inspector Olsen? We have a situation. With our Jane Doe."

CHAPTER 24

The afternoon was waning, and Roi and Rosamund were absorbed in their individual labors.

Roi was in his studio. He scrutinized Adam's sculpted forms, head and body, and wondered why they weren't his personal best, considering the fevered pitch with which he worked. His brow creased in frustration. He couldn't pinpoint why the figure wasn't quite right.

How could he convey Adam's inner strength?

He turned the base of the armature a quarter turn and inspected what should have been the perfect proportions of his powerful torso. He snatched away his apron and tossed it over the sculpture and paced.

Meanwhile, in the kitchen Rosamund smiled at her efforts. Imogen was far from a snob, but she was obviously refined, despite her quirkiness. And Rosamund wanted to thank their neighbor for her generosity by way of a truly impressive meal.

Roi sauntered in. He had a flat, distracted expression that Rosamund called his "creative squint" and long since learned not to take offense at any backlashes. As sweetly as she could, while laying out spears of asparagus, she pointed to the mud room. "Get me some olive oil on the shelf, please?"

With a sour look, he pulled open the mud room door and snapped on the overhead bulb's pull chain. He went over to the shelf, reached for the bottle of oil and knocked a bag of lentils onto the small cooler used to hold his transfusion supplies.

"Crikey," he grumbled, and stooped to pick it up.

He noticed a flap of plastic baggie caught outside the closed lid. He pulled out the cooler and lifted the lid, stuffing the baggie inside.

Then he paused as he stared at the contents of the cooler. Something was wrong, but it took a few seconds for him to figure out what it was.

The chest contained one transfusion bag, a corner of the O-NEG label peeling away from the label underneath.

Roi thought, *What the bloody hell?*

He picked up the bag and noticed that the seal was broken. A delicious, irresistible aroma wafted toward him. Wide-eyed and ravenous, he ripped off the cap and sucked out every drop of blood, licking his lips. Promptly his slight, satisfied smile was wiped out by a stunned expression as he looked at the now-empty vial in disbelief.

Rosamund appeared the doorway, and asked, "Hey, you get lost?"

But the smirk died on her lips as she saw her nephew, his unblinking eyes fixed on her.

She opened her mouth to speak—

The doorbell rang. For a long moment neither moved. The doorbell rang again. Rosamund's face was a study in guilt as she dropped her head and headed toward the front door, Roi's angry stare following her.

CHAPTER 25

Burgess filled out his Saville Row suit admirably. He sat behind the mahogany desk and surveyed the young woman before him.

"So *that's* where you've been. We thought you quit the Revel to set up the Manitoba camp early. But the hospital? That was sloppy, kid."

The woman bristled. "I'm not a kid!"

"You're sure as hell no adult when you pull a stunt like this," he barked. He thought for a second before belting out a hearty laugh. "Jane Doe, huh? That's you, Sabine. A *doe*." He indulged another peal of laughter before he cleared his throat and continued, more calmly. "I'm more worried about the dude who hit you. Okay, let's see the damage."

She pulled down her jeans to her knees, pointing at the light pink scar, now barely visible on the smooth, firm flesh.

He peered closer. "Just about healed up. What's it been? Two days?"

"Three."

He frowned as he considered. "That's about right. So you got jabbed. You're alive, aren't you? Worse things could happen. Welcome back." He returned to the stock reports on his computer screen.

She stayed put.

"Something else?"

She gritted her teeth. "They have the arrow. At the hospital."

His face went grim. "That's a little more serious. We'll have to handle that. Anything more?"

Once again Sabine was silent. Burgess assumed the worst was yet to come.

"Just who shot me." She lightened her tone, trying to minimize the words.

Burgess furrowed his brow and squinted an eye. "Well?"

She pursed her lips, and her voice became a whisper. "It was *him.*"

Burgess went very still. "You mean . . . ?"

She nodded.

He sank slowly into his chair. His steel-gray eyes went blank. "Oh. Shit." He shot her an accusing glance. "I told you letting that . . . *boy* . . . participate in our hunt was a risky idea." He clenched his jaw as he considered. "I'll take care of it." His tone was dismissive.

"Burgess . . . *please.* Let me fix it."

"Not a chance. This is no game. You stay away from that kid. In fact, go to Manitoba now. Set up the camp."

She had never seen him so angry, so cold. But she stood her ground. "I have a few DJ gigs yet."

He looked down. Was he counting to ten? "Fine. Finish those up. Then off with you. Now get out of here and let me think this through."

She left, but with a few thoughts of her own.

CHAPTER 26

Adam sat in the bubble of his dream world, oblivious of the hustle around him. He first felt his arms wrap around Roi as he nipped at Roi's ear, and then felt Roi's hand encircle his ball sac and cradle it with a soft, gentle squeeze. Then Roi's tongue swiped across his throat—warm and slick. He wanted Roi's amazing mouth on his cock. "Down there," Adam whispered.

He heard a faraway voice—not Roi's, but a high, strident tenor.

"Doctor?"

Adam bolted out of his reverie, back to the brightly lit ER where a patient lay before him on a gurney: a scruffy, bearded wreck of a man with gray pallor. The two large track marks on his neck were the greatest concern, having bled the man almost to death.

Baxter, whose voice had interrupted his waking dream, was at his side, asking, "Adam, are you all right?" a look of consternation on his face.

"Yeah, Baxter, thanks. I am."

"What next?"

"Naltrexone, and then—"

"Did that already."

For a quick second Adam was nonplussed. "Right. Let's type and cross for two units."

Baxter was so worried he decided to speak his mind. "You look exhausted, Adam. And when was the last time you had a decent meal?"

"Oh, gee, mom, let's see. Breakfast?" But if memory served, he had only picked at his breakfast.

Meanwhile, Baxter was having none of it. In his opinion, Adam didn't look much better than the patient they just treated. "Get some rest is all I'm saying."

Adam was touched by Baxter's concern and was sorry he had been so flippant. "You're right, Bax," he said. "I will. Promise." He looked at his watch. His shift was over five minutes ago. "Right now, in fact." He gave Baxter an affectionate slap on the shoulder. Baxter rewarded him with a gratified grin.

Adam went to the physician's changing room and trudged over to the bathroom. He locked the door behind him and washed his hands.

He reached down and pulled on his stiff, aching cock, trying to ease its thwarted appetite. He bowed his head, concentrating, trying to quiet the urgent feeling in his gut.

He stood in front of the full-length mirror on the door and appraised himself. Then he understood Baxter's alarm. The eyes looking back at him were those of someone he'd never seen before: pensive, wary, deeply ravenous. His growling stomach reminded him that his body was even hungrier, despite his lack of appetite.

Suddenly he saw Roi's smiling reflection in the mirror, behind him. He felt his heart thud as he spun around—and saw only the gleaming-clean, empty bathroom. *What the fuck is the matter with me?* Had his fantasies descended into hallucinations?

***

Roi stared at his aunt, aghast.

They were sitting in the living room, after a fairly lively meal, owing mostly to Imogen's irrepressible—and exhausting—good humor.

"A vampire." He made the statement leaden, hoping she got the message that he wasn't buying whatever goods she was selling. Yet his qualms were laced with confusion; this was very unlike the aunt he knew. Her sense of humor was invariably dry and pragmatic. And Rosamund was clearly standing her ground. Not a hint of amusement piqued her brow or caused a smirk. It was then that Roi realized she was serious.

"A vampire. Yes." She took a deep breath and waited for Roi to ask questions, exclaim, declaim—whatever. But Roi was too baffled for any of that. The silence hung thick in the air for a moment or two. Rosamund decided to break it.

"Your parents are vampires as well."

***

Adam needed to get out into the open air. He went to his locker and took out a jogging outfit, burying his face into the fabric and giving it a good whiff. It was relatively clean. He needed a good run. He pocketed his keys, cellphone and a few bills, slammed shut the locker and left.

***

She has snapped, Roi thought. "Right. My folks are still around? Fine. Where are they?" He couldn't keep the contempt—or hurt, maybe—out of his voice. He stood up and paced. "Yeah. So these two undead people fucked and had an undead kid, but never bothered to show up on birthdays. Or even Halloween." His voice was frankly mocking. "That the gist of it?"

"Don't talk like that!"

"How the hell should I talk?" He was shouting now. "No phone calls, no cards, nothing. Just a couple of photos. Without a fucking word from you. And now you spring this insanity on me?"

***

Gaige was on his way back to Eno's lab when, out of the corner of his eye he saw the canister inside the open leather case move, as if an animal trapped inside was trying to escape.

The canister rolled until the clasp appeared, its gem glinting in the sunlight. *Did I hit a bump in the road?* But ever since Chavi had picked it up in the lab, it seemed watchful—to have become . . . almost alive.

Ridiculous! he scolded himself, and dismissed the thought.

***

Adam jogged out onto the street, making his way through downtown, mulling over the events of the past week. Jogging always helped him think. The last time he had had any appetite—a ravenous one, if memory served—was evoked by his tryst with Roi.

There was Roi again, staking another claim in his routine, his life. First his imagination, then his loins, now his stomach. This dude was eating him alive, but he couldn't resist the exciting anticipation Roi continued to bring into his life.

***

Rosamund stood up and stayed very straight and still, her face blank. Her voice was soft and calm, the rational Rosamund he thought he knew and loved. "There was no way to know when the right time would be to tell you. But you want proof? You've already found it for yourself."

"What do you mean?"

"When you were in the mud room, what did you do?" Again, here was the Rosamund he trusted—rational, sensible, and for the first time in Roi's eyes, intensely frightening.

"What are you talking about?"

"You drank it right down, didn't you, Roi?" She went over to him. "Like it was second nature, right? Did you give it one second's thought?"

They stared each other down for a few moments. Then, feeling as though he'd burst with hurt and confusion, Roi grabbed the car keys and rushed out the front door, Rosamund following close behind. She remained in the doorway as he ran to the SUV, yanked the door open, jumped in, jammed in the key, and brought the engine to roaring life.

***

Turning a corner, Adam jogged toward Lucy's, his favorite all-night diner, downtown, not far from Vancouver General. He felt a strong desire to hear Roi's voice. But would that be prying, clingy? He wrestled with the idea for a moment, then pulled out his cellphone.

***

Roi sat for a moment, trying to control his rage and collect his thoughts.

Then he felt the poke on both sides of his inner lip.

He ran his tongue over his teeth and felt the unnatural sharpness on either side. Frantic, he looked in the rear-view mirror and bared his teeth, cocking his head sideways to get a better view—and saw the extended canines.

Hadn't he also felt them in the shower with Adam only days before? He had thought so then, but put it down to the imagination of a repressed young man whose passion, until that time, had poured out in clay, metal, or stone.

He listened to the purr of the engine and watched Rosamund's still, backlit form, slightly bent over with anxiety.

So it's true, he thought.

Oddly enough, he felt serene. Grounded. The world seemed, for the first time in his life, close to him, ordered and sensible. Like he finally belonged.

But a pang of fury stabbed through his new-found tranquility.

Why had Rosamund—more than family, but his open, closest friend—been so secretive, so untrusting of him when he trusted her implicitly? He had to know. He got out and stood behind the open car door, his voice hoarse with hurt. "Why didn't you tell me?"

"For your own good," she replied, hoping it didn't sound as lame to him as it did to her.

Roi's voice was clear and even above the engine's rumble. "I need to find my own way, Rosamund. Alone."

Even in the dark—his vision better now, too—he could see her stricken look, her mouth a rictus of grief.

"Roi, please! Don't leave! There's so much more I have to tell you!"

He shook his head. "I've got enough to think over. It's time one of us goes." His tone was firm, but not cruel. Maybe a little sad. They both knew this day had to come. He got back into the vehicle, threw it into gear and drove off. He looked in the mirror and saw Rosamund still standing in the doorway, arms hanging at her side, defeated. At that moment Roi fully realized how deeply he loved his aunt.

His cellphone rang. He was on the verge of tears when he answered, hearing a familiar voice.

"Roi, it's Adam. We've got to talk."

CHAPTER 27

It was just after sunset, beginning the night of a new moon. Kostin opened the door to the tall, muscular man who seemed, if he took a deep breath, that he might snap off the buttons of his expensive dress shirt. A bright smile blazed in his ruddy face. The light played on his thick, iron-colored hair. "Hello, Kostin. How've you been?"

Kostin bowed and averted his eyes. "Well enough, sir, thank you. Maestru is expecting you."

Burgess strolled in and surveyed the near-empty foyer, nodding as he caressed the rich dark wood paneling. "Understated, I'll say that," he commented.

An effusive voice piped from the shadows. "Burgess! Hello, my friend," Cezar said as he took Burgess's hand.

"You look the same as ever, Cezar. It's good to see you again," Burgess replied. They shook hands, slow and long, cool but friendly, appraising each other.

Cezar led him into the adjoining study, offering him a seat. Burgess noticed the dank smell of well-worn leather as he eased into the easy chair opposite Cezar.

"Sorry our reunion couldn't be under better circumstances." Burgess' smile was full of regret.

"Yes, and I'm prepared to discuss my son's transgression. Has the young woman recovered?"

"Sabine? Oh, yeah, a chip off the old block. Ego took a hit. But she'll get past it. Anyway, that's why I'm here. To check on young Lorik. See what he's up to. Smooth some ruffled feathers."

"I quite understand. Often enough I have discouraged Lorik from participating in your . . . games?" He looked at Burgess for approval of the word; Burgess nodded. "But he is quite impetuous."

"Impetuous!" Burgess chuckled. "Yes, no arguing that! But we must share some responsibility, too. Shouldn't have let him compete, but Sabine has a soft spot for the kid. Or did. Now some of us are up in arms, but I've got a handle on it." He leaned forward and looked Cezar in the eye, all business. "Now. Right to the chase. What can I expect?"

Cezar grinned with confidence. "The situation is already being addressed, even as we speak. Soon my son's cavalier attitude will be reined in and channeled properly."

Awestruck, Burgess whispered, "You finally found someone? Never thought you would."

"Even now he embraces us."

"Good to hear."

"May I assume, then, that the arrangement among our nations remains intact?"

"Yeah, sure." Burgess paused, his shrewd gaze fixed on Cezar. "But . . . there is, maybe, one thing." His offhand tone was forced. "The arrow has been taken. We should get it back."

"That may take a great deal of effort."

"Well, they're not easy to make. Heirlooms, you might say. But between us, just a small gesture of good faith, that's all."

Cezar considered. He didn't feel the effort was worth whatever risk it entailed, and he was very much in favor of one more dangerous arrow safely locked away. And, hopefully, forgotten. On the other hand, he depended on Vanator good will and neutrality, or possibly some future ally. He sought middle ground. "I will see what I can do. As you said, in *bona fide.*"

"That's all I can ask," Burgess said with finality, rising from his chair and extending his hand. Cezar took it, and Burgess pulled him close, whispering in his ear. "I know you've been away from the area for quite a while, and there's fresh game. I get that. But tell your group to lighten up. Cops are getting a little too interested, I hear. Just saying, as a friend."

"Yes, I have considered the local police to be a concern, too. I have already addressed the issue." Cezar assured Burgess with a warm smile and an affectionate squeeze on his meaty forearm.

Burgess rewarded Cezar with a gratified smile of his own and said, "I'll see myself out."

***

Soon after Burgess left, Kostin came to stand beside the bed, where a man lay. A man who had once been an itinerant furniture mover named Jake, and now began to awaken. Not just out of his deep slumber, but into what Cezar and his kind referred to as "hyperlife."

"I know this place," the man said. "But who am I?"

"*Yago* is your name now," answered Kostin, taking both hands and pulling the man to his feet.

Yago.

With that single word, Yago shed his old name with no effort, like so much snakeskin, as easily as the sheet fell from his nude body to the floor.

Kostin stood back, watching him stand tall, stock still. He had seen this many times before, this transformation from one life to another. Yago's muscular body had lost what little body fat it had the day before. Now it was more defined, muscles ripped, shoulders to calves, as he stepped forward, at first a little stiff and awkward, then with incredible grace as he relaxed and gained more assurance. Yago felt as if he were walking on the moon.

Kostin watched in silence. He knew that Yago's hyperlife was working its way inward: first the body, then the mind. At present Yago was operating on instinct—shaking out the cobwebs, as it were, of his former life. His mind had yet to fully awaken, but when it did it would be keener than ever. In the meantime, Yago's body arched taller with an awesome new power. His height had always dwarfed Kostin's; now Yago simply towered over him.

Yago noticed the twin bite marks on his groin, then stroked it lovingly. "What are these?" he asked Kostin.

"A sign that you are ready to begin your journey with your young master," Kostin said with some deference. Without being told, Yago knew he had been somehow conjoined by will to Lorik, predestined by their common benefactor, Cezar.

"Follow me," Kostin said, and as Kostin left the room, Yago did his bidding.

When they reached the cavernous carport, Yago's newly acquired night vision allowed him to see as he never had, even in the near-pitch black. There was another person there, with a head of thick blond hair atop the form of a youth, late teens or maybe early twenties.

Yago couldn't decide which was more ravenous, his stomach or his loins; he opted momentarily for the former. The youth was blind in the dark and couldn't have seen Yago approach him, wrapping him up in his arms, crushing the warm, young body against his own.

But the blonde youth did see Yago's deep-socketed eyes, blazing with enormous appetite, licking behind his ear before gently sinking his sharp fangs into the soft flesh beneath. At once, as though he had been waiting all his life for the embrace, the boy clung desperately to Yago, who drank deeply and released him only just short of death.

CHAPTER 28

Adam saw Roi standing outside Lucy's looking through the plate glass storefront. Adam couldn't tell if Roi was more interested in the customers or the shiny Fifties decor with its starburst wall clock and checkerboard linoleum. It was crowded, even at one o'clock in the morning, and the patrons were an eclectic mix: everyday people and upscale alike, students, senior citizens, and a sprinkling of the bohemian.

Roi saw his approach and smiled—a sad smile, Adam thought.

"Thanks again for coming out," Adam said. "Now let me treat you to the best coffee in the province."

There were two spots next to each other at the counter, near the end, affording them decent privacy. As they scooted around the tables Adam signaled a waitress with an established shorthand that assuredly meant "two coffees," and he and Roi slid onto the stools.

They took a long look at each other.

Roi seemed pensive and distant, and his shy smile seemed to have slipped a notch. But for some reason Adam felt closer to him than ever, more so even than their recent time in bed. He felt a tug from deep inside his core, an irresistible yearning. He moved closer. As though picking on the thought, Roi covered Adam's hand with his own with a strong, heartening pressure.

Adam sat and contemplated thin air for a while. Roi joined him in silence, giving him time to collect his thoughts. Meanwhile he sipped his coffee. After a short while Adam came back to life. His face was mobile and expressive. " I did it a few times with guys in the shower. After practice. You know?"

He looked up at Roi, expecting an answer. Roi didn't know, but he understood just the same, fascinated. "We got our rocks off," Adam went on, "but that was all it ever meant to me." It almost sounded like an apology, and Roi wore an uncertain, expectant expression. Adam's eyes blurred with tears, and his voice was rife with fascination. "But now, it's just you. Your voice. The way you look at me," he heard himself say. "It's in my head. All the time."

Adam released Roi's hand and grabbed him by the shoulder, his other hand on Roi's thigh, and squeezed hard. Though his voice was quiet, his facial expression was fierce. But then Adam broke into his usual engaging grin.

Once again Adam was struck speechless with wonder at the young man's handsome face, the high cheekbones, and eyes that were now wide with concern. He found his voice again. "Are you okay?"

"Are you?" Roi countered.

"Oh, yeah." He managed a light, reassuring laugh. "Yes. I am." He felt good in Roi's presence, looking to prolong it as much as possible. "I thought we'd talk. Get to know each other better. That's all." He looked intently at Roi. "It's so damn good to see you," he said with quiet conviction.

"Same here. And your invitation was dead on. I was heading out anyway."

Alarm crossed Adam's face. "Did I spoil your plans? If I—"

"No, not at all!" Roi was quick to reply. "Just going for a drive. I needed to get out for a while." Roi looked as though he'd cry.

"Something wrong?"

Roi said, "Just a lot to think about. You know."

Adam offered his gentle smile again. "Yeah, I do. For both of us." Then after a second, "How's Rosamund?"

Adam noted Roi's dismay, and the forced smile that followed. "She's . . . okay."

Adam cradled Roi's chin in his hand and whispered, "Bullshit."

"Okay, then," Roi conceded. "We had an argument."

"What about?"

Adam noticed Roi's hesitation as he worked out the reply in his mind.

"Being on my own, mostly."

Adam leaned back, his voice quiet, as if not to disturb old memories. "I know just what you mean. I was born and raised in the Deep South. The *Old* South, if you listen to my mother and Mawmaw. Generations of plantation owners who lost everything to the carpetbaggers. But we had a name. And a history that went with it. I went to college through ROTC. Not just for the free education. I wanted to be an officer and bring back some pride to our family."

Then he laughed, but Roi thought it sounded bitter.

"I loved being a soldier. But I loved science more. And when I took the MCATs . . . " He trailed off.

"MCATs?"

"Medical college admission test."

"That's great." Roi put his hand on Adam's shoulder and leaned forward. "Bet you did well."

Adam's crooked smile was fully of irony. "Spectacular! Only one problem."

"What's that?"

"My family. All staunch Christian Scientists."

"Oh," Roi said in a very small voice, after momentary confusion. "Right."

"Only my baby sister Zelie understood. We still talk. But I haven't been back home since . . . " He trailed off again and shook his head. "Then I met my fiancée in medical school. She's from here, in Vancouver. Beautiful and smart. I thought, 'new country, new life.' After my deployment in Afghanistan, I applied for residency at Vancouver General. With a name like 'Giroux' and my passable French, here I am. Naturalized." He spread his arms. "So, don't I get some applause? Or at least a pot shot?"

Roi slid off the stool and embraced him, laying his head on Adam's shoulder. "Lucky for me," he said, "that you wound up here."

Adam eyed the ceiling as he thought. "You know the saying about 'one flesh'?"

"In the Bible? Yeah."

"I'm not saying I believe all that. But what we have is damn close."

The server came over to them with a friendly smile. "If you guys plan on takin' this any further, you'd better get a room."

Adam and Roi looked at each other and shared a smile.

***

Cezar watched from the shadows as the blond runaway fell to his knees in supplication before Yago, barely breathing, nuzzling his crotch, the rivulets from the bites on the blonde's throat already drying to dark brown. He noted with interest that Yago managed neither to ravage or kill his victim; unusual control for one so new to hyperlife.

And on a first feed, yet.

Cezar smiled and said to Yago, "*Bun venit la noaptea.*"

To which Yago intended to reply, "I embrace it," but to his astonishment heard instead, in his own voice, "*Am imbratisa.*"

But wait. Hadn't his host's question been, *Welcome to the night*?

In English?

Cezar applauded. "Excellent!" He put his arm around Yago's shoulder.

Kostin, who had stood by, hoisted the youth over his shoulder as he grabbed the boy's backpack.

"You've absorbed our language already. Now. Questions, yes?" Cezar said kindly to Yago, who nodded, dumbfounded.

Cezar's smile was almost kind. " Sharpen your wits. Channel your strength. Hone your resolve. The struggle is at hand."

CHAPTER 29

Eno had just finished an autopsy that had taken the better part of the afternoon. He went into his office. Gaige had not yet returned yet from the university where he was researching with a colleague. A loud clatter made him jump, and he spun around, scanning the room. He saw that the canister had fallen out of the leather pouch, and now rolled lazily on the floor beside Gaige's workspace, resting with the crystal latch face up. The damn thing gave him the shivers, and he scolded himself for bending even slightly to Gaige's ridiculous superstitions, if that's what they were. He strode over and replaced the canister in its open case. He went to his own desk to prepare the postmortem report, forcing himself to dismiss the feeling that someone was watching him.

Someone was.

Chavi stood in the doorway.

Eno took a deep breath. "You startled me."

"Sorry. Is Gaige around?"

"Nope. Still at the university. He should be back soon, though. Have a seat." He motioned to a nearby chair, then held out an open bakery box. "Want a donut?"

"No, thanks. Eno, may I ask you something?"

"Fire away."

"You said that Gaige is your closest friend. But when it comes to his work, you treat him like a crackpot."

Eno looked sheepish. "We go way back, as undergrads. I love the guy and stand by him, always will, no matter how wild his theories get. He's brilliant. One of the best researchers ever,

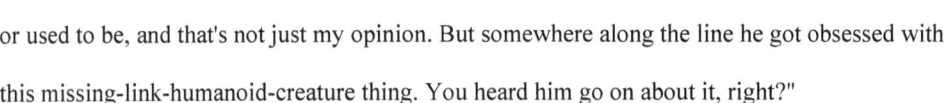

or used to be, and that's not just my opinion. But somewhere along the line he got obsessed with this missing-link-humanoid-creature thing. You heard him go on about it, right?"

"Of course."

"So, it got to the point that . . . well, he was accused of tampering with specimens. Never proven, mind you, but it was enough to cast serious doubt on his research. In the end he backed down and kept his teaching post, and as long as he does his own thing on sabbaticals they leave him alone." He paused, squinting as he looked into thin air. "But what the hell, it's his time and money. And you're right. He is my best friend, and I stand by him. I owe him that, even if I do give him tons of grief." He offered the box again. "Sure you don't want a donut?"

CHAPTER 30

It was dark in the motel room when Adam awoke. Roi was still nestled against him, and he lifted himself on his elbow to gaze at his sleeping lover, whose skin gleamed from the bathroom light, casting soft shadows against Roi's refined features.

Adam must have been lost in admiration for several long moments, when the silence was broken by rustling bedsheets as Roi arched his back, pressing Adam's hot, stiffening cock into the groove between his buttocks. Adam responded with a long, soft growl as he cupped his nutsac and guided his erection deeper in, reaching around to find Roi, who was just as aroused, a slight, slow smile curving his lips as he awoke.

Roi's smile turned lusty, and he turned around to face Adam. He pulled Adam closer, their hungry mouths locking on each other, their tongues searching and tasting. They indulged themselves with little grunts of pleasure as they groped each other's bodies. Passion mounted as they explored urgently every curve and bulge, every flex of muscle, every stretch of firm flesh.

Adam could stand it no longer. He traced a path, alternately licking and kissing Roi's strong graceful neck, moving down to his chest, making a loving circle around his pec, moving over to his nipple, now licking, biting, sucking. Roi writhed with fervor under Adam's deliberate ministrations, licking with love bites until he stopped, nibbling on Roi's lip before deep kissing with husky grunts, driving Roi, groaning, into peaks of joy.

Roi, his eyes bright with wonder, lifted his head to find Adam watching him as he worked his magic, seducing him to complete surrender. His desire to share this feeling welled up, matching his own desire to possess Adam completely. With both hands, he ran his fingers through Adam's hair, somehow finding the strength to pull away—even for a moment it was torture—and treat Adam to his own oral talents, eagerly pressing his mouth on Adam's neck, tongue tracing around and behind his ear. Adam let out a long, deep-throated groan, mounting to nearly a wail as Roi sucked on the side of his neck.

Adam lay back and abandoned himself as Roi kneaded the man's incredible bicep, powerful pecs and cobblestone abs, eagerly caressing the trail into the thick down of Adam's pubic hair. Roi's fingers massaged Adam's firm skin underneath, moving to one side to grasp Adam's muscular thigh with his long graceful hand, tenderly, as if in awe. With sudden eagerness, he squeezed Adam's ball sac, gingerly, lovingly.

Adam was not idle for long. He propped himself up on his elbow, and he gazed with admiration at Roi's flat firm stomach and dark-haired love trail. As he caressed the smooth ivory flesh and maneuvered south, he leaned over and once again covered Roi's full-lipped mouth with his own.

They found themselves stroking each other's cocks in mutual desire. They kissed even more deeply than before, as if their mutual ardor opened yet another passage to their souls, an ardor neither had experienced ever. Their lips parted and they drew back to gaze once more at each other again, as if to lay claim to an unsure reality.

It was one of those rare moments of perfect knowledge—symbiosis of shared bodies and minds. And certainly, if only a hint, of a common future, full of adventure. This realization struck them, together, and all at once. Time seemed to spin and then halt. They embraced once again, but now it was beyond passion. This time there was a mutual confidence in each other that neither had felt on their own. With silent consent and no wasted motion and in perfect synch, they lay facing each other in opposite directions. Gone was the fever of passion, but not its potency, gathering to critical mass. As they began to make love, they knew, with special certitude, that it was a commitment to love and look after each other.

Adam knew from experience that his endowment usually proved a formidable challenge to those few confident enough to try to please him. But there was only a hint of that from Roi, to whom sucking Adam was a little daunting at first, but the warmth of their new revelation seemed to relax his throat. After a few seconds, Adam's hardness slid implacably down Roi's throat. With his lips pressed firmly against Adam's pubes, he slowly—but expertly—pulled back, increasing the suction as his tongue slid, inch by inch, over the undersurface of Adam's shaft, stopping to pay all due attention at the sweet spot, circling and swiping with the tip of his tongue. Roi had been a fast learner, and in his lustful partner he had found boundless inspiration, so that now Adam was reaping its full benefit. Roi teased deliciously; firm sucking followed a series of light love nips over the head and shaft, in turn followed by spiraling licks over the head and shaft, bringing Adam's cock to iron hardness under his hot, veined, velvet flesh.

With Roi's loving attention, Adam felt an exquisite orgasm gather in his groin, now driven to a new height of desire, one outside himself, fostering an overwhelming desire to lift Roi to the same heights. He arched his body, gently dislodging Roi's incredibly talented mouth.

But as much as he wanted to please Roi, Adam's few experiences with men years ago, despite their ardor, had been conventional, even routine, but enjoyable in a perfunctory sort of way. Adam had only his own desires and deep affection to propel whatever talent he may have at cocksucking. Still, his passion for Roi had already passed the point of no return. He felt compelled to act, and with confidence that Roi would appreciate the effort, regardless of skill, he bent down, first kissing the head of Roi's cock, then taking it full into his mouth.

Adam need not have worried. Hearing Roi's clear voice groaning with pleasure erased all his uncertainty and bolstered his confidence. Adam began to experiment, taking cues from Roi, running his tongue up, down and around the shaft, just as Roi had done. Another revelation for

Adam: his deep devotion for Roi fostered all the innate skill he needed to show the depth of his affection. Encouraged, he bent over Roi's cock and took it all the way.

Roi watched as Adam took him, abandoning himself to the wellspring of desire brought forth by his lover. He reached over and ran both hands up Adam's muscular back to the nape of his neck, pressing down, his cock sliding down Adam's throat. It was then he felt his sharp teeth poke the corners of his own lower lip.

Brazen instinct began to conquer Roi as he opened his mouth incredibly wide, like a tiger ready to spring, bending over toward the soft flesh at the junction of shoulder and neck. Roi could hear the blood pumping through the distended artery as Adam sucked him off with incredible finesse.

Whether it was love or the desire to conquer and possess the man as much as he wanted to be possessed himself, Roi couldn't tell. But he did know that as he approached Adam's neck, he was driven to almost insane hunger—a longing of the soul, mustering fast to match the lust in his groin. All he knew was that he must have Adam for his own, stake his claim on him beyond any doubt, for all time. As he bent toward Adam's neck, he slid his hand under the powerful arms, around the muscular torso. Searching for the thick shaft of Adam's cock, he moved his hand up to feel the pre-cum over the massive head. He spread the creamy wetness down the shaft as he closed a firm, gentle hand around Adam's cock and began to pump, eliciting a deep, thundering growl from Adam as he sucked Roi's cock with greater fervor; now it was Roi's turn to groan, and he arched back.

Adam had felt Roi bending over behind him and the passionate breathing on his back. He swore he could actually feel Roi's lust, like waves of baking warmth soaking from his lover's body into his own. The hot breath moved from his back, slowing ascending to his neck, as if savoring every inch. When Roi started jerking him off, he felt his orgasm seethe in his loins. He felt Roi tense and pull away from his neck, knowing that his lover was as close to the divine moment as he was himself.

Suddenly Adam was seized with the need for Roi's mouth—Roi's incredible mouth—on his own. He arched back, replacing his mouth with a gentle fist around Roi's cock, facing up toward the ceiling, only to find that Roi had the same idea. Without a wasted movement they kissed deeply as they shot, Adam beating Roi by seconds, offering each other his tribute of cum. They broke their kiss and embraced tightly, as if to join their bodies.

They slowly relaxed their embrace, but still clung together, neither wanting to break completely. They kissed again, now searching each other's spent bodies with mouth and hands: cheeks, nipples, neck, ears. They became aroused again as they explored each other; but the desperate urgency had subsided. No longer was it rushed or galvanizing. Now it gave way to a different, sweeter animal: doting, trusting, sublime.

Adam's phone buzzed on the night table. He picked it up and glanced at the screen. "Shit," he whispered, barely audible, putting the phone down.

Roi turned on his side toward Adam, propped one elbow. He could see Adam was worried. "Anything wrong?"

Adam hesitated a little too long. "Um . . . no. Merit just called." Adam's phone pinged a little tune. "Left a message, too."

"Who's Merit?"

Adam seemed embarrassed. "My fiancée." With a wry chuckle, he said, "Seems I've got some explaining to do."

Roi hugged him and smooched him on the back of the neck. He intuited that this was Adam's deal, but he could still offer support. "I'm here," he said, "if you need me." He slipped off the bed and headed to the bathroom.

Adam gazed after him. "I know that. I don't want any secrets between us."

Roi stood at the mirror, pausing briefly as he lifted his lip and examined his elongated canines. *Not bad*, he thought, *just a little sharp*. In their haze of lust, he doubted that Adam noticed.

Roi wondered how much control he did have over his blood lust. Now he wished he'd stayed and listened to his aunt. Maybe he's been taking her for granted. But then he thought, *Just another reason to go out on my own*. Self-reliance was what he needed to learn.

"Did you hear me?" Adam called out.

Roi emerged from the bathroom. "Yes." He pulled on his underwear. "I agree. No secrets."

"Good. So what's this about an argument with your aunt?"

"I told her to get out or I would."

"What brought that on?"

"It's been coming for a while. Time I was independent." Roi's expression was reassuring. "We both knew that it was inevitable."

"What are you going to do?"

"I'm not sure yet. A lot depends on you." He paused, testing the water. "On us."

Adam nodded. He knew it would be a hard life without Roi. If it was living at all. And duplicity was definitely not his style. Only one thing to do. "I have to tell Merit. She deserves to know."

Roi sensed Adam's consternation, then embraced him from behind, wrapping his arms around Adam's chest and kissing his neck, hoping Adam wouldn't suddenly turn and see his sharpened canines. "Wait until the time is right. No rush." he said.

Adam was thankful for Roi's patience. But he couldn't shake the feeling that Roi was holding something back. Then again, they couldn't learn everything about each other in a week. And he had plenty on his mind already.

CHAPTER 31

Eno sat at his desk, concentrating on the computer screen.

Chavi held her phone, sliding her finger across the display. "I know I've seen that somewhere."

"Seen what?"

"That three-leaf thing."

"The *Triquetra*?"

"Yeah." She sounded annoyed. "A website? A blog somewhere?" She looked over at Eno. "What else was it called?"

"A trefoil."

"T-r-e . . . "

". . . f-o-i-l."

She went back to pecking when suddenly Gaige burst into the office. He was breathless. He looked from Eno to Chavi and back again.

"Donuts on the desk," said Eno. "Probably a little stale by now."

Gaige's eyes were bright with zeal. He bolted around the desk and shook Eno's shoulder.

"Hey!" Eno objected, shrugging off Gaige's hand. "What gives?"

"I have to talk to that woman." He was breathless with excitement.

"What woman?"

"The one who got shot with this." Gaige held up the evidence bag with the arrow inside.

Eno eyes popped wide. "You didn't take that out of here, did you? That's police property!"

"Had to," he replied. "I needed another opinion. And their equipment. Your machine can't analyze cellulose. It was the only way I could confirm what I suspected."

Eno held out his hand, clearly pissed off. "May I have it, please?"

"Sure, sure." He handed it over. "But don't get brassed off."

"Thank you," Eno said stiffly. "What did you find?"

Gaige went over to his briefcase lying nearby and brought out an arrow—old, but still pristine. "Have a look," he said.

Eno sighed as he donned the latex and took Gaige's arrow in his free hand. He inspected the arrow under the magnifier, first one, then the other, comparing them. He sat up, brow wrinkled. A perfect match. Shaft, tip, everything. Right down to the trefoil. He had to admit it, this seemed more than coincidence.

Chavi appeared at Eno's shoulder. "May I have a look?"

Eno made room, and she bent to the magnifier.

Gaige's voice piped up. "My friend at the university carbon dated the wood cellulose on both and compared them." He paused. "Ten thousand years old," Gaige continued in a hushed voice, filled with wonder. "At least."

Eno mulled over the ramifications. "Are you going to resubmit your study?"

"Not right away."

"Then what was the point in carbon dating?"

"To prove my real theory." He whispered in Eno's ear. "You remember my digs in Germany?"

"No need to whisper. She's cool."

Chavi waved off Gaige's apology, and he forged ahead. "I took this arrow among the remains of an animal at the Neander Valley," he continued. "The extended dentition indicated some sort of predator. The remains were obviously those of a hominid. Look."

He went back to the briefcase, pulled out a book of photographs and handed them to Eno, who flipped through them.

He held out the book to Chavi. "Take a look at these."

She examined them in sequence. "The photos look genuine. As for the skeleton . . . " She shrugged.

Even to Eno's expert eye, it was impossible to determine if the skeleton itself was a fake, but the photos definitely were not. They had Gaige's stamp: meticulous, thoroughly professional. If there was tampering, it was a first-rate job.

"Well?" pressed Gaige.

Eno nodded. "Unusually wide jaw extension. And aside from the tiger-like fangs . . ." Eno hesitated, embarrassed, "Okay. Yes. I admit it. The remainder of the skeletal structure appears to have . . . a human configuration."

"But still skeptical, eh?"

Eno offered a noncommittal shrug. "What would you do in my place? Naturally, I'd have to examine the find."

"Give an old friend the benefit of the doubt."

"Fine. Let's say I do that. So what's the connection to Jane Doe?"

Gaige's smile was that of a delighted child. "That's a very good question. Let's find her and ask."

***

Chavi went home in a pensive mood, slumped onto the sofa without removing her jacket, and let her handbag fall at her feet. Devan sat nestled in his recliner, beer in one hand and playing couch commando with the remote, clearly in a bad mood.

"They postponed the game due to illness," he said telegraphically. "Only three players."

Chavi was astonished. She thought he'd be furious. Devan was even-tempered about most everything—even politics—but that did not include sports. "Couldn't they substitute?"

"No," he said absently with a shrug. "A sick-out. For real, I guess."

She didn't reply, overwhelmed by an uneasy feeling in her gut.

Devan smiled at her, a glassy one. He snapped off the television, went over to the couch and sat next to her, hugging her, but there was no warmth in it. "Still feeling down about the job? It's okay, sweets."

Sweets? Devan hated pet names.

"You'll survive," Devan continued, then forced a lighter tone. "Hey. Made something special for dinner. That should cheer you up."

She sniffed the air. "Pot roast?"

"Mom's own recipe. Better check on it." He smooched in her direction and made off toward the kitchen.

Her phone buzzed in her bag. She took it out. "Hello? . . . Hey, Eno."

Devan appeared behind her, large spoon in one hand, the other underneath to catch the drips. His expression was alert and watchful.

"You're kidding!" Chavi was incredulous. "When? . . . I don't believe it! . . . Thanks for telling me . . . Sure. Bye." She stared into space as she dropped the phone back into her bag.

Devan walked in even steps over to the couch, careful not to spill the contents of the spoon. He held it out for her to taste. "Who was that?" he asked, trying to sound casual.

Chavi looked uncomfortable. "Oh . . . Eno. Just called to chat."

"About the moving van case?"

She was a terrible liar. "Well . . . yeah."

"Chavi, you're suspended." His voice held a tinge of warning.

She mustered some courage. "I want to help out, that's all. Especially since I screwed up. It's on my own time. What could be wrong with that?"

"It could be seen as insubordination. That's what's wrong with it!" He was frankly angry. "And I'll be fucked if I stand by and watch that happen." He took a deep breath. "Dinner's ready. Go wash your hands."

"Don't boss me around!"

He stared at his feet, probably counting to ten. His voice was quiet, tense, and his fists were clenched. "We're done with this conversation. Wash up."

With a glare and a raised chin, she headed to the bathroom. Devan went back into the kitchen, and ladled out two generous helpings of pot roast and carried them to the dining area.

"Soup's on!" he called out, setting down the plates. After a few seconds he poked his head into the living room.

And noticed that her bag was gone. He stood for a few seconds, his face stone-cold with rage, took out his phone and punched in a number, glaring at the front door.

CHAPTER 32

In his lab, Eno paced back and forth, went back to his microscope, peered in, and then went back to pacing, rubbing his chin.

Sitting at a desk, Gaige peered into a microscope. "Eno, come over here." Eno didn't answer, but continued pacing, absorbed in thought.

"What's up?" Gaige asked, both concerned and curious.

Eno looked worried. After a pause, he said, "I'm not sure."

"That's nothing new."

"Don't be a wise-ass. I'm confused. Seriously."

"Sorry," replied Gaige. "What the problem?"

"Well . . . about this bug going around," replied Eno. He paused.

"Go on."

"I don't think it's a bug."

"What do you mean?"

"I mean it *acts* like a bug. There's a definite symptom complex. And there are plenty of antibodies. But it's more like a . . . ." He fell silent, then shook his head.

Neither Eno nor Gaige was aware of young man, spiky hair, black and frosted blond at the ends, crouched just outside the door, listening, clearly alarmed.

Eno opened his desk drawer and took out a pack of cigarettes.

Gaige frowned. "I thought you gave those up."

"I did. Except when I'm stressed. Or stumped," Eno replied defensively. "What about you? Anything more on that arrow?"

"Take a break. I'll tell you when you come back."

The young man listening in the hallway sprang to his feet. With a look of alarm, he sprinted toward the dark end of the adjacent hall without a sound, and disappeared into the darkness just as Eno emerged, putting a cigarette between his lips.

***

Chavi tried to control her alarm as she drove toward the ME's office. She'd always felt safe with Devan until now. She drove into the parking lot and parked a fair distance from the door. With some relief, she saw Eno's car among the vehicles. She reached for the door handle, and her phone rang. *Devan.* She debated whether or not to answer it, when she heard the slam of a door echoing through the lot.

Eno stood about fifty feet away from the door, cupping his hand to protect the flame as he lit a cigarette. He puffed a time or two before blowing out the match. Chavi opened the car door and called out to him. "Eno?"

He craned to see her through the darkness, but recognized her voice. "Chavi?"

"Hello," she called out, then noticed what she first thought was a shadow behind Eno, but soon shaped itself into a tall, obviously masculine form, moving so silently she still believed it was a trick of light . . .

Until there was no doubt the shadow crept up and reached out with both hands toward Eno's neck as he walked over to meet her.

She was so taken by surprise that she hesitated for only a second, in case she was wrong, before she yelled out.

"Eno! Behind you!"

He started to turn, thrusting up his elbow by instinct and thwarting the outstretched hands, but was knocked to the ground nonetheless. The cigarette flew with a shower of sparks on the tarmac.

Meanwhile, Chavi raced over to assist Eno. Though he was doing an admirable job of protecting himself against his attacker, it was clear he could use some help. She maneuvered behind the assailant and crooked her arm around his neck. With astonishing speed and strength, he bucked against her, throwing her to the ground on her back. He spun around and crouched over her supine body, his face close to hers, fierce and predatory.

She gasped as she saw a face that she recognized at once.

No mistaking it.

Then, close by, Chavi saw a backlit figure rush over from the building behind. His arm was raised, in his hand what she thought might be a stick or skewer. He cried out, "Hey, you!"

The young man straddling her turned—no, *twisted*—around to see the figure. He then leaped off, frank alarm on his pale face, backing away toward the shadows. Then he spun around and vanished, without a sound. Chavi could have sworn she saw the young man take wing.

The backlit figure—it turned out to be Gaige—hunkered down beside her. "Are you quite all right?" he asked, scratching his nose underneath his glasses. He placed one hand on her shoulder. In the other he held an arrow.

She nodded and tried to smile. Gaige turned to Eno. "How about you, sport?"

Eno was already getting to his feet. With his finger, he gingerly felt around the scrape on his cheek, but waved: *I'm fine.*

Gaige took out his phone. "The police may still be able to catch him."

"No!" shouted Chavi.

Gaige's hand froze in mid-air. "Why not?"

"Please," she pleaded, "just don't. My boss wouldn't like it. I could lose my job for good."

Gaige turned to Eno. "Your call."

"Besides, I think I know who it was," Chavi said. "And where you can find him."

Gaige and Eno exchanged looks of astonishment.

"Really?" asked Gaige.

Eno said, "Let's go inside and talk."

***

Eno sat at the lab table, sour expression, tapping a beaker. He held a cold compress to his cheek. He turned to Gaige. "What's going on over there? What's the big secret?" he asked Gaige.

"Trust me," answered Gaige, busying himself at the DNA processor.

"I do trust you. What I didn't do was thank you, though. That arrow sure scared off the guy. Think you'd had an Uzi or something."

"Indeed. Odd, wasn't it?"

Meanwhile, Chavi wandered around the lab. She tried to remember as much detail about Roi as she could, but her confusion kept distracting her. "I just can't believe this is the same guy I met before. This guy, Roi. He was really sweet."

"Are you quite certain he was the attacker?" Gaige asked. "After all, it was dark—"

She hesitated. "Yes, I'm sure." She paused. "I just can't *believe* it, that's all." She sidled next to Gaige, who was absorbed in his task, then snuck a look at Eno. "Why did you take a sample of his wound?" Chavi asked.

"He's cloning me," Eno called out.

Gaige ignored him and answered without looking up, writing in his notebook. "I don't want to say just yet."

Chavi shrugged and noticed what looked like a medallion loosely wrapped in plastic. She reached for it.

Gaige blocked her reaching hand. "Don't! Please!" His voice was sharp.

Chavi withdrew her hand, startled. "Sorry." She sounded hurt.

Gaige's expression softened. "No, I'm the one who should apologize." He gave her a little smile. "Let me explain."

"Here we go," muttered Eno. He was well acquainted with Gaige's "professor look."

Gaige shot him a withering glance before continuing. And sure enough, he did put his hand on the DNA reader as if it were a podium. "About ten thousand years ago, two new types of humans emerged."

"We've been down this road before," Eno commented.

"May I continue, please?"

Eno demurred with a wave of his hand.

"Thank you," Gaige chuffed out, then turned to Chavi. "As I was saying. Two new humans. The first were much like Neanderthals, very tall and strong, but clearly more powerful than both their Neanderthal contemporaries and our own sapient ancestors. And they had tools far earlier. Even metallurgy."

"That has never been proven," Eno said as he joined them.

"It has, now," replied Gaige. "But we can argue about that later."

Chavi was fascinated. "The other type of human. Who was that?"

"Ah, that's the onion," Gaige said, clearly pleased at her interest. "A type of predator. One we've never seen. They must have been elusive, possibly nocturnal. They were also very tall—six feet or more on the average—and with prominent canines nearly double the length of the surrounding dentition, which flattens on hinge-like structures when the mouth closes. Much like a snake."

Eno interrupted. "*That*," he said in a flat tone, "is pure conjecture. You found a single incidence. Those extended canines could have been caused by anything. An injury, maybe. Even an isolated mutation."

"Ssshh!" chided Chavi, scowling. "No harm in listening."

Eno rolled his eyes and grimaced. Chavi offered Gaige a bright smile. "Please go on."

"There was evidence of a battle, evidently. Carbon dating of this," he held up the ancient arrow, "placed it about eight thousand years ago. It was found among the remains of our long-toothed, long-dead friend deep in the Neander Valley."

"Still doesn't prove anything," Eno said in a sullen voice.

Gaige ignored him. "But my good friend Eno is right about one thing. There were no other sites or further evidence of these creatures around that time period. A few old bones. A single ancient arrow. And the token about which you were so curious." Gaige held up the medallion in its plastic case. "Nothing much to go on. Until now, of course." He offered the medallion to Chavi, who hesitated. "Go ahead," Gaige insisted.

Chavi took the medallion and looked closely. A three-leafed symbol was etched into the shiny black metal. "The Triquetra."

"Quite so," Gaige said. "Same as the symbol on these." He indicated the arrows. "This one was made recently, no more than a hundred years old."

Eno peered at the arrow and shook his head. "Coincidence," he sneered in a low voice.

Gaige retrieved the canister with its crystal bubble in the center, magnifying the slate-gray triquetra underneath. Gaige snapped open the cylinder and stretched out parchment from the roll. A large, ornate trefoil took up half the page, drawn in black ink that sparkled in the light. The lower half covered with a single huge word, in the same black ink. There was something hypnotic about the rich yellow of the page, the symbol, the graceful, joined cursive.

"'Vanator,'" whispered Chavi.

"Quite right." His blank look betrayed his disbelief. "You can read this?"

Chavi was nonplussed. "Sure. Can't you?"

Still surprised, Gaige said, "Some of it. The script is an ancient form of Sanskrit. The word, 'Vanator,' means *hunter* in Romanian. These people evidently did some serious migration over time." Gaige said. "And I believe they've survived to the present day."

"And so, this Jane Doe is supposed to be one of them?" Eno tried to soften his skepticism.

Gaige challenged Eno with a wide, appreciative smile. "Yes. That's my theory."

Eno shook his head. "Gaige." His voice was kind. "This is still just speculation. Anyway, where does this take us . . . I mean, you?"

"Speculation? Maybe. Maybe not. But this," Gaige held up the vial containing the sample from Eno's wound. "may give us another piece to the puzzle."

CHAPTER 33

Cezar sat in his armchair, scrutinizing Lorik. "You're confident the doctor called her, 'Chavi'?" he asked the sullen youth.

"I said so, didn't I?"

Cezar glared at Lorik. "Don't get cheeky with me," he warned, then produced a cellphone and poked at it. "Hello? This is Cezar. I've been assured it was she in the parking lot." He listened for a moment before he spoke again. "Agreed. Let's see what she does next." He hung up, stood up and aimed his gaze at Lorik. His voice was low and sharp with anger. "Why must you persist in disobeying my instructions? The plan was to retrieve the arrow covertly."

Lorik avoided Cezar's accusing stare. Even though he had long since learned his father's questions were rhetorical, he felt the need to defend himself. "I wanted to fix my own mistake. And you're always telling me to be more responsible."

Cezar's temper flared again. "By putting yourself in harm's way? That's reckless, my lad, not responsible." He sighed. "I cannot fathom which is worse, your impulsiveness or your failure. Either way, it was costly. The time for battle is closer at hand than we anticipated." His face was clouded with doubt. "And now, triumph is no longer a certainty."

***

Chavi let herself into the apartment quietly. She prepared herself for the scene that she was sure would follow. But though Devan's anger might flare, it never lasted long. She peeked into the living room. The only light was from the television. Devan was stretched out on his recliner, arms behind his head, watching the ten o'clock news. To her surprise, he gave her a slight smile as he rose from the chair. "You must be starved. Saved a plate for you."

"I went for a drive," she ventured. "To clear my head."

"Did it help?" Not a shred of anger—or any other emotion—that she could detect.

"I think so."

"Good." He sounded gratified, but cool and distant.

"Sorry for just bolting like that, without a word."

"That's okay."

He came over to her, gave her a light peck on the cheek and went into the kitchen. She slumped down slowly onto the couch, deep in thought. She considered telling him of the strange events of the evening, but something held her back. Her intuition, which told her that Roi wasn't Roi, now told her to keep silent. She sat back and watched the story on the news warning people to be aware of a new virus going around and what precautions to take.

CHAPTER 34

Merit was silent as she mulled over Adam's confession, then came out with a sad chuckle. They were sitting at the kitchen table with mugs of morning coffee before them. She was staring at a photo of Roi on Adam's phone, nodding appreciatively as she handed back his phone. "One thing I'll say, you've got good taste in men."

"Women, too, not too long ago. I went for you, didn't I?"

She gave him a wry smile, then shook her head. "I still can't believe it. Why didn't you ever mention you had these feelings?"

He shrugged. "Didn't even admit to myself. But when I met Roi . . ." He wanted to say he'd found his soul-mate, but he wasn't sure how Merit would take it.

"Adam, tell me something. I have to know. Is it something I did? Didn't do? Was I too busy with work?"

He shook his head emphatically. "We're both busy. That's our job. But no. This part of me was bound to come out sooner or later. Maybe it's better that I found out now, before things got too serious between us."

"Too late for that," she said. "I don't suppose . . ." She hesitated. ". . . that couple's therapy or something like that . . .?"

He said nothing, but concentrated on his coffee cup.

"Hey," she said, "I had to ask."

He took her hand. "I do care for you, Merit. Always have, always will. Truly."

"I believe you. I think I'd know if you were faking." She turned to him. She took his hand. "Which makes me wonder, Adam." Her expression turned anxious. "Is this what you want? Are you really sure? He's not in the best of health, you said."

He nodded. "It doesn't matter," he muttered.

She hugged him tightly, and then gave him a warm smile. "Then what the hell are you doing here?"

He kissed her hand and left the room. Only when she heard the front door close did she allow herself to cry.

***

Adam called Roi right away to share the news about Merit, but got voicemail instead. He was due for his shift in a couple of hours; no time to share the news in person, but he couldn't quite quell his excitement. He was already wearing his sweat suit, so he decided to jog. The effort would help him rectify the curious combination of joy and anticipation of a future with Roi, the grief with letting go of Merit, and a twinge of guilt about both.

The jog did help. He felt lightheaded and weightless now that the burden of secrecy was lifted. He was a little surprised that he found himself jogging into the hospital, just in time to shower and dress for work. With Roi foremost in his thoughts he sang in the locker room as he donned his scrubs, gratified to watch himself get half hard as he imagined himself nuzzling Roi's chest.

"Better get in there," said a man behind him. Adam turned to see Donny, one of the relief doctors in the ER, whose shift just ended. He looked exhausted. "Pretty crowded."

"Hey, Donny. What's up?"

"This new bug going around. People scared, mostly. The usual. Low-grade fever. Light sensitivity. No big deal." Donny got out of his scrubs and tossed them in the hamper nearby. "Strange food cravings, though."

"Like what?"

"Raw meat. Spinach." Donny yawned as he slipped into a jogging outfit. "One guy was even stuffing kale down his throat right as I was examining him."

"No shit."

"Yeah." Donny finished dressing and started warming up for his jog. "How's the weather?"

"Nice."

Donny called over his shoulder as he jogged out. "Good luck, man."

***

Donny hadn't been kidding. The ER was crowded, to be sure, a steady stream with no letup. But there was none of the usual murmurs or the occasional loud complaints. It was quiet and eerie, like a morgue. It seemed most people were unsettled without knowing why, eyes shining with apprehension, just wanting reassurance. He was kept so busy he didn't have a chance to look at his phone until early afternoon, when he was finally able to grab a few minutes for himself, take a bite of two of a sandwich and swill a cup of reheated coffee. He tapped at his phone and noticed that Roi had called three times. He tapped again to return the last one.

But it went straight to voicemail without ringing. "Hey, it's me. Just now got a chance to get in touch. Call me when you get this." He hung up, determined to answer Roi's return call whether he was with a patient or not—well, as long as it wasn't too serious. Besides, he was done in a couple of hours anyway.

Those couple of hours went quickly enough, but Roi's face kept forming in his mind's eye. He called Roi again as he walked down the hall to the doctor's lounge.

The same instant voicemail again.

He began to feel uneasy, which soon deepend into real concern. He jogged down the hall, pulling off the top of his scrubs as he went. He skipped his customary shower, instead going right to the locker and changing as Frank, his relief, came in. Adam had already dressed and headed toward the door.

"How's the man?" Frank asked in his typically cheery manner, as Adam rushed past without a word. "That good, huh?"

***

Adam parked behind Roi's SUV.

The house was dark but the front door was unlocked. Adam entered the foyer. He ventured into hallway and called out. "Roi?"

No answer.

He searched the house systematically, calling Roi's name now and again, his panic rising when the only answer was silence. He was about to ascend the stairs to Roi's room when he heard a soft stirring from the open door at the end of the hall.

He creeped over to it and poked his head in. He looked around the room. Roi sat in the corner, hugging a framed photo against his chest.

Adam started toward him. "Roi? Are you okay?"

Roi looked up at him. His cheeks were streaked with tears. His cell phone lay beside him, its display black. "I miss her," he whispered. "I don't miss the scolding and her goddam hovering. But I do miss her humor. The sound of her voice." He stood up and wiped at his cheeks. Now he was smiling. A welcoming one, it seemed to Adam—or could it be relief? He found himself not caring one bit. Roi's smile was enough for him. Adam stretched out his arms to receive Roi's own welcoming embrace. They stayed locked, close and warm, for what seemed like hours in the quiet dusk.

Roi whispered in his ear. "The place has been so empty. I'd be just as empty, too, if not for you."

He pulled back and looked Adam in the eyes. His voice turned savage. "And I'm pissed at myself for feeling so guilty that I'm free to live my own life." His eyes welled with tears, and his shoulders slumped. "Shit. I swore I wouldn't do this. I'm such a fucking wuss."

Adam stroked Roi's face, which looked drawn and gray. "When did you sleep last?"

Roi stopped to think. After a moment, Adam piped up.

"If you have to think about it, it's been too long. Let's get you to bed."

With arms around each other, they ascended the stairs. Adam held him close, tenderly stroking Roi's shoulder and torso.

Man, is he tense! Adam thought, tender strokes giving way to firm, massaging circles, evoking an appreciative groan from Roi.

They reached Roi's domain on the top floor. Adam guided Roi into his bedroom and began to undress him, slowly.

Roi didn't seem to mind that he was taking his time; his eyes were closed, the full, rose-colored lips parted in a slight smile, blissful. He took full advantage and savored the delicious disclosure of Roi's lean body as he unzipped Roi's cargo trousers and pulled them off, Roi lifting each leg without being told.

"Arms up," Adam whispered.

Roi obeyed at once, and Adam pulled the wife-beater over his head, tossing it onto the pile with the rest of the clothing. Adam nudged Roi over to the air mattress and gently sat him down. Roi opened his eyes—so trustful and open that it broke Adam's heart. He leaned down and pressed his lips against Roi's in a full, tender kiss.

"Lie down, sport."

Once again Roi obeyed with a contented sigh, lying on his side and watching Adam disrobe in his turn. Then Adam slipped in behind him, and after pulling the sheet over them both, wrapped his arms around him and pulled him close, snuggling his chest against Roi's back, spooning their bodies, nestling Roi's head under his chin.

"Just rest, kiddo," Adam whispered in his ear, then realized that Roi was already asleep. He drifted off himself as the last of the afternoon light, diffused by the window blinds, bathed the room in a deepening, quiet, tranquil blue.

CHAPTER 35

The light in his room was deep cyan when Roi awakened. He was ravenous. With the sight of Adam lying beside him, Roi clenched his jaw as he got aroused and, with some surprise, felt his canines poking against his cheek. He felt more powerful than he ever had. His hard-on roared up, and he pulled Adam over so they were face to face, gazing at each other.

They explored each other as if for the first time. In a sense, this was true. The galvanic urgency that had ebbed now returned, but with an undercurrent of surreal certainty, a *deja vu* that they recognized and embraced, together and at once.

With unhurried movements they paused, now and again, to taste each other's skin, now prodding or kneading with delightful surprise. Still locked in a kiss, they lay side by side, facing each other, renewing their shared fervor with eyes, lips, tongues exploring. They fondled each other's bodies in graceful play. Adam pinched Roi's nipples as Roi dandled with Adam's balls, which went tight and firm against the base of his cock.

With only the slightest hesitation, Roi reached around and stroked the silken skin of Adam's buttocks in gentle, lazy circles, then gingerly pressed his hand into the warm crevice. He stroked further and encountered the soft down surrounding the tight pucker of Adam's anus. Roi felt Adam stiffen slightly and backed off just a little. But with a soft groan and Adam's insistent tongue as they kissed, Roi decided it was his imagination and pressed in again. Adam bucked against his hand and gripped Roi's iron-rod cock urgently.

With this encouragement, Roi felt his loins smolder as he inserted a finger into Adam's sphincter. Adam bucked again and jerked against Roi's cock with frantic precision, bringing him almost to orgasm. Roi pulled away and willed back the jizz mounting up through his shaft.

Then with almost vengeful ferocity, Roi flipped Adam on his back and wedged himself between Adam's legs, hovering over Adam's face. Roi paused, buying a little time with a deep kiss to let his cream settle back into his loins.

Adam understood all too well. He gripped firmly, but didn't stroke Roi's cock, and focused on his lover's face, whose expression was tense with arousal, though his eyes were wide and steady. Then Roi looked deep into his eyes. With sudden resolve, he guided his cock between Adam's haunches, pumping slowly.

Roi pressed his cock against Adam's butt and bore down inside the silken valley, moving his massive head against Adam's hole, massaging it to relax the opening. Adam lifted his bum in eager acceptance.

Roi reached down and smeared the glans with pre-cum. He looked down and checked his erection, the veins glistening in the moonlight, more than slicked enough to slide into his lover's ass. Roi lodged his steel-hard cock against Adam's asshole, pressing with infinite patience. It could have been minutes or hours before Roi realized his pubes were rubbing against the smooth skin of Adam's behind. He paused briefly to cherish the delicious pressure inside Adam's ass before easing out, slowly, slowly—ever so slowly—now and again savoring the incredible friction. He looked down at Adam, whose face was filled with wonder.

Adam was lifted onto the crest of Roi's passion, his soul blazing and catching fire from Roi's loins. He wrapped his strong, graceful legs around Roi's torso and began to moan.

Roi took Adam's body, possessing it even as he himself was possessed, losing himself in Adam's half-open eyes. Adam's surrender was complete, his abandonment filled with the exquisite ache of savage submission. Spurred on, Roi now pounded Adam's ass in steady waves, first pulling out his cock, with slow and teasing gyration, and then following, after a second's pause, with firm thrusts deep inside. Hearts racing, cocks swelling as their loads rose, each laid

his claim on the other beyond question. Roi looked down at Adam, whose face was filled with

serene amazement, almost ethereal. He felt Adam stiffen in his arms and the repeated pulsations

of Adam's rock-hard cock as he spewed column after column of cum, coating Roi's belly.

Seconds later Roi slipped his cock from Adam's ass and pressed him close, writhing against him,

chest to chest, pressing them together hard and close, so as to make them one. A loud groan deep

from his chest escaped in triumph as half a dozen spurts of cum shot from his cock, mingling his

seed with Adam's. He felt Adam's skin tighten as he dragged his fangs over Adam's throat and

down his neck. He tongue-flicked his nipples, lips tracing down his torso into his groin, ending

with a firm bite on Adam's inner thigh. Adam took in a deep, shuddering breath as Roi sucked

on the raised flesh and took several draughts of the warm, red, salty flood, which Adam

rewarded with a deep, soft sigh. Roi licked Adam's skin clean.

Then Roi slid up atop Adam, grinding against him. He ran his fingers through Adam's

hair and tugged gently with his fist before letting go. Adam's head rolled back, and Roi buried

his face in Adam's armpit, breathing in his scent.

Adam traced a line of soft kisses over Roi's body as he drew back. They exchanged one

glance; they recognized in each other a perfect knowledge—that they were a special part of the

infinite, a conjoined being that went far beyond the sum of its parts, a vital organism with a

persona all its own. The deep, dark sky was close enough to touch, as if starlight were their life's

blood, their bodies subject to their souls. They were more than one flesh; they were one spirit to

which their bodies were vassals.

So as one flesh, in each other's arms, they slept into the night that had forged them into

one spirit.

***

The ringing of Adam's cellphone woke Roi. Adam lay motionless; his tan skin had paled to ashen. Roi gently poked Adam, who stirred and groaned softly. He opened his eyes, and Roi held up the phone, the display of which read "HOSPITAL." Underneath the time read, "8:53." Adam's eyes popped, and he shook himself awake, snatching the phone from Roi's hand. "Hello?" His voice was hoarse with sleep. He cleared his throat. "Yeah. Sorry. I'll be right there."

He got out of bed and collected his clothes. Roi slipped out of bed and stretched. "Good morning."

Adam turned to him and gave him a smile, brief but genuine. "Morning." He looked down at the dark red stain on his thigh and poked at it. "Wow, babe! You went berserk!"

Roi looked at it, distressed, but a bit proud, nonetheless. "What can I say? You drive me wild." He peered closer. "Does it hurt?"

"Nah. I'll get a rabies shot when I get to work." He looked at Roi, who looked even more distressed. "Kidding!"

Roi did a poor job of smiling. "Coffee?"

Adam finished dressing, went over and hugged him tight. "I can't. Regular doc called in sick, and I'm next on rotation."

"Adam, I have to talk to you."

He looked at his watch. "Shoot."

"Have a seat."

Adam hugged him again. "Sorry, babe. No can do. My shift starts in twenty minutes. I'll probably be late."

"Can't they wait a little longer? It won't take long to tell you." He paused. "But you may need a little time to absorb it all."

Adam stopped. He'd never seen Roi like this before. Sure, a little spacey, introspective and quiet. He was an artist after all. "In that case, I'd rather wait until I can give you my full attention."

After a pause, Roi said, "Sure. Get going. You'll be late."

"Why don't we have lunch later? Come to the hospital."

"Too sunny."

"It's supposed to rain later." Adam hunkered down and held his hand. "Look, Roi. I *have* to go in. The guy I'm replacing has been on his feet for eighteen hours. Not to mention if I want a shot at getting admitting privileges."

"We all have our priorities."

"I know you're disappointed. But we'll make it right." He gave Roi a peck. "You okay?"

"Yeah." Roi produced a grin.

"Are *we* okay?"

"Of course." Then, adding sheepishly, "I really am sorry about the bite."

"Forget it. I've been known to draw a little blood in the throes of passion, too." They shared a full kiss on the mouth, and Roi watched Adam rush out the door.

Roi craned his neck toward the window. Adam was right about the weather; it was already clouding up. *Fine then*, he thought. *Lunch it will be.*

***

Adam drove toward the hospital, stopping first for coffee and a quick bite at the convenience store; no time for a sit-down breakfast at the cafeteria. Time not withstanding he found he hadn't much of an appetite. Their spat that morning, if one could call it that, had left him unsettled. Despite his frustration, he felt more confident than ever that he and Roi belonged together. But he was still concerned about Roi. Concerned in some specific way that felt familiar but which he couldn't put his finger on.

He thought that it was more than anxiety and fear over his missing aunt that put Roi in such a mood. He never got the impression that Roi was clingy. Maybe Roi had found some sort of empty comfort in solitude? *Until I came along*, he thought.

Anyway, their life together wasn't Adam's decision alone. As much as he knew they belonged together, he also knew that Roi must come to him with a full heart, or not at all. No one person can have trust enough for two. Even the richest soil spread too thin can't allow a seed to even take root—much less grow into a full yield—of a life worth sharing. Adam only hoped that there was harvest enough left for him in Roi's heart when it came time to reap.

And vice versa.

CHAPTER 36

A sky full of clouds with the promise of rain prompted Roi to visit his studio. He'd been working there for several weeks, and the investment in his own space paid off. He hadn't been so productive since his teens, and the spaciousness allowed him to work on larger projects. His neighbors were perfect: informed and friendly, yet respectful of his privacy, as he was of theirs.

Today, however, after his tiff with Adam, he didn't feel exactly inspired. He worked on the armature anyway, set it, and started slapping on the clay, but his heart wasn't in it. Several hours passed. He wiped his hands and sat on the sofa, savoring the silence for a minute, when there was a soft knock on the door.

"Come in!"

The door opened, and Imogen entered in her wonderfully timid way.

"And how's my favorite sculptor today?" she chirped. Since fully half of Imogen's questions were rhetorical, Roi didn't bother to answer. How many sculptors did she know, after all? But he did manage a smile. "Well enough, thanks," answered Roi. "Sorry I don't have anything to offer you."

"I don't want to hear it," Imogen said. "I come bearing gifts," and pointed to a case of bottled water in the hall. He thought that in a way she was a proxy for Aunt Roz. Still, she didn't visit often: *This is your domain,* she had promised, *And I won't pester you unless invited.* And although she didn't stick to her word, Roi didn't mind; her impromptu visits were always pleasant diversions. But this occasion, it turned out, was especially pleasing.

"Not making much progress," Roi said ruefully. "Guess I'm a little blocked."

"No matter. I have some news that will inspire you!"

***

Roi sat across from Adam in the hospital cafe. "My own show!" he chanted. "Can you believe it?"

Adam tried to muster as much enthusiasm as he could, but his smile was wan. "Sure I can. You're terrific." He took Roi's hand. "In more ways than one."

Roi answered with a worried frown. Adam looked even more ashen than he had that morning. "You look pale."

"Pale? With this tan?"

Underneath it," Roi said, "if that makes any sense."

Donny, the other ER physician, had noticed it too, as well as his lackluster demeanor. Adam could always be depended upon for an upbeat attitude with patients, but today he seemed slack, his decisions robotic. Adam forced a broader smile. "Must be the hours I'm keeping." He winked. "Especially at night." Then his expression got serious. "So. About this morning. You need to talk about something important, you said."

Roi hesitated. The moment of truth had come . . . and gone. "About the exhibition. That was all." He said apologetically and cursed himself for his cowardice. Maybe the time wasn't right. At least, that's what he told himself.

Adam knotted his brow. "Didn't you just find that out a little while ago?"

Roi stammered, "Yes. But they hadn't decided yet, and I guess I just wanted some moral support."

"Oh." Adam sounded relieved. "Because when you said it might take you some time, I thought . . ." He trailed off, sounding contrite.

Roi offered a broad smile. "No, forget it. It was just me, being insecure." He got to his feet. "Finish your lunch. We'll talk later, okay?"

"Absolutely."

Adam watched Roi, loving his retreating form, tall and graceful. He seemed to glide without effort among the plodding crowd. He looked down at his food. No appetite at all. He picked up his tray and maneuvered through the crowd, not paying particular attention to the incredulous stares he was getting.

Then Baxter approached him, squinting with concern. "Adam, are you all right?"

"Hey, Bax. Sure. A little tired. Why?"

Baxter said nothing, but pointed right at Adam's groin. A large spot of dark red stained his scrubs.

Right at his inner thigh.

***

Adam lay on the the gurney, staring at the ceiling. Donny was giving him a close once-over. He gently prodded the twin wounds. Pinpoint, dry, and not a drop. "Right over the femoral artery," Donny said, taking off his gloves. "Should have bled even more. You lucked out. You poke yourself or something?"

"Not that I remember," Adam said.

"Anything different in your routine?"

Roi's naked form popped into his head, but before he could answer, Baxter came in with a sheet of paper and handed it to Donny, who perused it. "Red cells a little low. Whites, a little high, but within normal parameters."

"Platelet count?" Adam queried.

Donny shrugged. "Perfect."

"So?"

Donny considered. You're skipping meals, probably, right?"

"Just lunch today. Had some breakfast on the run."

"Start getting more iron. That should take care of the red cells. The leukocytosis is probably stress related. Or fatigue. Hell, we're all working doubles this week. Right, Bax?"

Baxter nodded. "You said it."

"Take it easy for the next couple of days," Donny continued. "I know that's not easy, but see if you can't squeeze in a few hours' shut-eye in the doctor's lounge."

Adam got up and stretched. "I'll see what I can do."

"Doctors make the worst patients," Baxter retorted.

CHAPTER 37

Chavi was in the living room, listening on the phone when Devan walked in, pulling on his toque. To Devan, she looked happier than he had seen her in days. She turned a bright face to him and pointed at the phone.

"Of course I'm available!" Her voice quivered with excitement. "Who's the artist?" Her face went slack in an instant. "*Who?*" She went very still and listened closely. "Spelled like it sounds?" Her eyes opened wide and wary. The elation drained from her voice. She paused, then said, "I'll check my schedule and let you know. Thanks again."

She hung up the phone, deep in thought.

"Who was that?" asked Devan.

"My old photography instructor. He got me a photo assignment. At an exhibition."

"That's a good thing, right?"

"Uh-huh." Her voice sounded far away.

"Where's the job?"

"Beaumont Gallery."

"Nice. You gonna do it?"

"I don't know," She said in a flat tone, staring into space.

He looked at her curiously. "How come?"

"Not sure if I should."

"Why not?" He sounded a little irritated.

"I know the artist. Well, sort of. I met him once."

Devan went very still. "I think you should take it. Get your mind off things. Doing what you love." His voice was hypnotic. "What's wrong with making a few bucks?"

She seemed to come out of her trance. "Nothing." She shook her head with a slight smile. "You've got a point."

"Now you're talking. He hesitated for a quick second before giving her a perfunctory kiss. "Call them back, okay? Ham and provolone on rye. Want one?" he asked as he disappeared into the kitchen.

"No, thanks," she said as she sank onto the couch and asked of the thin air, "What's going on with you, Roi Kirkland?"

***

"So, I was wondering, what he's up to," Chavi said to Eno, who sat behind his desk, which was littered with papers. He looked pale and tired.

"You mean aside from hawking his wares? You'll get a chance to find out. Go to the exhibit. Take photos." He read the anxiety on her face. "You still have that feeling, don't you? That it wasn't him in the parking lot."

"Yes. More than ever."

He got up and sat on the desk close to her. "Look. I thought about reporting it anyway. But you said not to, and there's something about you I trust. And like you," he said, looking her right in the eye, "I don't always follow the rules. Sometimes I have to rely on what's right here." He pointed to his chest.

He went over to a device that looked like a printer. "On the other hand," he continued, "science has some useful tools. This is a DNA analyzer. Anything the subject touches can be used. A glass, a spoon . . . anything."

"What will it prove?"

"Who knows? Like Gaige said, another piece of the puzzle. Just promise me one thing."

"What's that?"

"Take me with you."

Chavi gave a hearty laugh and then realized how much she liked Eno, how deeply she trusted him as well. "Where's Gaige?" she asked.

"At the university, doing his part. He should have spectrograph results any time now. And he's talking to a philologist."

"A what?"

"An ancient language guru." He paused and looked at her critically. "You know, you really threw Gaige for a loop. Being able to read those inscriptions."

"Just one word. Lucky guess, that's all." She zipped up her jacket. "Well, I'm off. Thought I'd go to the Beaumont and check the lighting." She held up a light meter.

"The Beaumont? That's where it's gonna be? Sweet!" He sat down at his desk again and picked up his pen. She headed for the door when Eno called out. "Chavi?" She looked back. "Don't forget. We're behind you."

She smiled her thanks and walked out.

***

Chavi arrived at the Beaumont in a fine soaking rain. She made a dash for Building 2 and followed a cheerful voice that rang out in what sounded like a spacious exhibition hall. "Careful now!"

Chavi turned the corner into the room—and spacious it was. A striking woman—the owner of the cheery voice—turned to face her. In bright colors with a turban to match, she seemed like a modern abstract, animated into a hologram. Two moving men in green coveralls stood by, holding an object covered with a tarp at each end, evidently awaiting instructions.

The woman strode toward her, arms extended. "And you must be Ms. Kapur."

"I am. Please call me Chavi. Ms. Fuchs?" she queried, taking the offered hands in her own.

"Yes. 'Imogen,' please. So happy to meet you. Thank you for accommodating us on such short notice."

"No problem."

"Now then, you're here to check the lighting, I believe?"

"That's right. Especially crucial when it comes to sculptures."

"Of course, of course!"

One of the moving men called out. "Lady, where do you want this?"

"Oh, my dear! Sorry!" Imogen called back, pointing to a far corner. "Right over there, sweetie, at the taped X-mark. Number four," she said, rushing over to him.

Chavi took out her light meter. "Gorgeous place," she commented.

A man's agreeable voice piped up behind her. "It is, isn't it?"

Chavi spun around to face a tall, well-groomed, well-formed middle-aged man—taller even than Devan—attired in understated elegance: navy blue, slate gray and khaki dominated the expensive fabrics, and his black shoes were spit-shined. He held pearl-gray gloves in one large hand. The other he held out to Chavi. "Cezar Balanescu. Charmed." She held out her own hand, and he kissed it lightly, continental style.

A peculiar emptiness washed over Chavi. "Chavi Kapur," she stuttered. "Nice to meet you, Mr. Bala . . ." she stuttered.

"Cezar, if you please. If I may call you Chavi?"

She didn't speak, merely nodded, open-mouthed. She couldn't identify his slight accent, but with his salt-and-pepper hair and deep-set eyes, he seemed to have leaped right out from the pages of the latest romance novel.

Imogen marched over. "Cezar! So good to see you! Mr. Balanescu is on the board here," she murmured to Chavi, "besides which, he's our landlord." She turned back to Cezar. "To what do we owe the pleasure?"

"Board meeting," Cezar answered, then leveled a steady gaze at Chavi. "I was just leaving when I caught sight of the young lady and felt compelled to introduce myself."

"Would you care for something, Cezar? " asked Imogen. "I believe we have some chilled mineral water. Or perhaps coffee? Herbal tea?"

"Nothing, thank you."

"Chavi?"

"No, thanks."

"I understand we have an exhibition in several days," said Cezar. "A local sculptor, I believe?"

"Yes, a most talented young man," offered Imogen. "New to the area, but already fitting in splendidly. Chavi was good enough to find time to photograph his installation for us."

"Very fortunate," Cezar agreed. "And the name of this talented young man?"

At that moment Cezar's phone rang. "Excuse me," he said, answering it. "Yes," he said in a low voice, then listening intently. "I'll be there at once." He put away the phone and faced the company. "Please excuse me, but I must go. The best of luck with the exhibit." With that, he swept out in a blur.

Chavi was impressed. "Wow!" She took her light meter and started scanning the room. "Quite a guy."

Imogen beamed. "A thorough-going gentleman."

"Yes. Where's he from? He sounds foreign."

"I'm not quite sure. Perhaps Austria. At least, that's what I once heard. He's been a board member for . . ." She paused, pondering. "Well, now that you mention it, I don't know. Before we arrived, and that was twelve years ago. He's deeply involved in the community, but he travels quite a bit. Business interests abroad, I believe. Anyway, we don't get much opportunity to mix."

"So where is the artist himself? I'd think he'd be here to supervise."

"Oh, no, my dear. He's quite shy. We all agreed that the set-up—catering, positioning the pieces and so forth—should fall on our shoulders."

"But he'll be here at the exhibition, right?"

"Oh, yes, of course! It took some convincing, but he finally agreed. Though he did insist on an evening event. Usually the gallery prefers noon to six."

One of the movers called out. "Hey, lady! Can we wrap this up?"

"I'll be right there." Imogen turned back to Chavi. "Pardon me, dear. And thanks once again. See you at the show!" She breezed out, leaving Chavi to her task.

Cezar's face and his continental kiss lingered in Chavi's mind like a painting on glass— flat and slick. Suddenly she felt rustic and untutored, and more than a little out of her element. She decided she needed some moral support for tonight. She pulled out her phone and tapped, then said, "Eno? Hey, do you still want to come to the exhibit?"

CHAPTER 38

Lorik put his jacket on and slipped the invitation into the jacket's interior breast pocket. He tiptoed through the foyer and entered the kitchen. He thought he heard something—a sound like shuffling, maybe, or a wet sheet on a clothesline flapping in the breeze. He froze in mid-step, listening. *Must be my imagination*, he thought as he went to the cupboard next to the door leading to the garage and opened it.

Not a single key hung on the hooks labeled for the three cars in the garage. Before he had time to wonder about it, the door opened wide.

And there stood Cezar, eyes glinting. There were the keys, all three of them, dangling from his long fingers. He jingled them.

***

Showered and made up, her hair twisted into an elaborate braid, Chavi was ready to dress for the exhibition. She rummaged through her closet, looking for just the right outfit. She glanced at the clock—an hour at most, if she were to get there before everyone else. Since she never paid much attention to trends, indifference laid an easy path to understatement: a pair of dress jeans she wore out on the town, a white silk blouse and her so-called "good" jacket, an unadorned burgundy leather, the real thing. Then a misting of Chanel Chance, a gift from Devan.

She decided against jewelry.

The shoes were a problem. Dress up with heels or down with flats? She was working after all, and agility was a must. She settled on low sling-back pumps that she thought would pass muster, fashion-wise. She slipped them on and grabbed her shoulder bag and camera on the way out the door.

She looked at her watch. 5:05 PM.

She had one more stop to make, but had plenty of time to beat the VIP crowd.

***

Eno perked up when he saw Chavi. "You look nice." He had gone with the preppy look, probably in deference to the high-toned venue. He had on a blue blazer over a white shirt and striped bow tie, khakis, and deck shoes with no socks. He produced a long-stemmed yellow rose and presented it to her with a flourish.

She took it and held it up to her nose. It was the real thing, not a hothouse job. "Thanks, Eno," she said with some caution. "You know I'm seeing someone right now, right?"

"Sure I do. That's why I picked yellow. The color of friendship. My intentions are honorable; I want to see you work. Maybe I'll put in a good word with your boss. Hear anything yet, by the way?"

"No. He's doing what he can, so he says. But thanks for the offer. Shall we? I want to get there first. Speaking of arriving, where's Gaige?"

"Still at the university. Shoulder to the wheel and all that. Says he's close to a breakthrough."

"Is he coming to the exhibition? I invited him, too."

"He may show up later. Maybe in his lab coat." Eno bowed and with a sweep of his arms, indicated the door. "Shall I drive?"

CHAPTER 39

Adam drove to the women and children's homeless shelter in Surrey, where he volunteered twice a month. It was an urban variety of pro bono house call, and he found it very gratifying on a personal level as well. The families he tended, he supposed, were proxy for the one that disowned him. In deference to tradition he carried a Gladstone bag which held his equipment, medicines and, of course, treats for his favorite patients—the kids.

And there were plenty of kids today, so he was kept busy from the time he walked in. But there was none of the scuffle and shouts of children at play that he was used to, none of the fidgeting or ticklishness when he examined them. They seemed as preoccupied and somber as their parents.

When he was finished he spoke with Sheena, the director, because of one major concern—bite marks on some of the residents. It didn't appear to be a widespread problem, he said, but she should inspect the bedding and linens just in case. She replied with a perfunctory nod and a wan "thank you." Adam thought she looked tired, which didn't surprise him, and said so.

"You look pretty tired yourself, Doc," she observed.

"Just too many shifts," he replied, which she acknowledged with a tiny smile.

Later he sat in his car, making notes, and reflected on how much he loved children—and how much he would love one, or more, of his own. He reflected on Merit's query—*Are you sure this is what you really want?* As sure as he was of Roi, he was just as sure he wanted children of his own.

He felt the energy flow back into him.

He couldn't wait to share his idea with Roi.

CHAPTER 40

The last golden casts of the afternoon were quickly fading as Eno and Chavi drove into the Beaumont parking lot. The lot was nearly empty. They parked close to the door and got out. The autumn evening couldn't have been more beautiful: the air, cool and crisp; the sky, moonless, clear, and starry after the rain.

Inside, they approached the exhibition gallery. Chavi stopped just outside its entrance, stopping Eno with a tug on his sleeve.

"What's the matter?" he asked.

She pointed to Imogen who was setting out pamphlets.

"Classy looking," commented Eno. And she was, a far cry from the bohemian attire of only days before.

Chavi looked down at her jeans with mild disgust.

"Should I duck home and change?"

"What for?"

She decided it would take more explanation that it was worth. "Oh, fuck it," she muttered, straightened her back and marched into the room, Eno in tow, his question unanswered. Imogen spotted them and breezed right over.

"Chavi! Good to see you!" She gave Chavi the once-over. "How lovely you look, dear."

"Thanks. You look terrific," she said, and meant it. "Oh, and this is my friend. Eno, this is Imogen. She organized the exhibition."

"Pleased to meet you. Delighted you could join us this evening," Imogen said.

"Thank you," Eno replied, blushing with pleasure and giving Imogen's offered hand a gentle shake.

Caterers continued setting up canapé trays. Floral designers were strategically placing the abundant arrangements. Chavi felt a bit more confident when she caught a young man who was setting up the champagne bar staring at her. He gave her a sly smile and a wink. She smiled back.

"Are you here to help out Chavi?" Imogen asked Eno. "Not that she needs any, of course."

"No, ma'am. I begged an invitation, since I've never been here."

"In that case," said Imogen, "we hope you'll return often." She reached over and picked up a brochure from the spread nearby. "Here is some information about us. You may consider joining our arts league." She took in the displays with a wave of her arm. "And if a particular piece happens to catch your eye, the hyperlinks in the brochure will display the pricing for each work. Just click on your choices on our website."

"Well, if you'll excuse me," interrupted Chavi. "It's time I got started."

"Of course, dear. I must finish with the caterers. The other guests will be arriving soon. Please help yourself to the canapes and champagne. Don't stand on ceremony." She smiled and headed off to instruct the wait staff.

Chavi took her camera from her bag. "I have to get ready," she said to Eno. "Why don't you look around?"

While Chavi worked with her camera, Eno strolled around and viewed the exhibits. Eno was impressed. Whoever the artist was, he showed extraordinary talent. The sculptures themselves certainly showed variety. Whimsical but charming curios gave way to larger and more substantial works of solitary males and females—and a few group pieces—flanked with framed sketches, obviously the studies on which the sculptures were based. The dominant figure in the exhibit was that of a muscular male form in dramatic pose. More than six feet tall, its facial features were strong and proud, arms reaching out as if either to embrace or proselytize.

"Good ambient light," Chavi said. Eno wasn't sure if she was talking to him or making a general comment. She first kneeled in one place and checked her light meter, then another, and then another.

"I love this one." He indicated an abstract piece, small but vivid, of a splay of intersecting arches—which in fact was the title of the piece—carved out of wood and buffed to a high gloss. "He sure knows his stuff." But Chavi was too absorbed in her work. She had moved onto another *objet d'art*, trying different angles. "So glad I could keep you company," Eno wisecracked with a wry smile.

He turned his attention back to "Intersecting Arches," and wondered if it was worth the asking price, whatever it may be. He didn't know his ass from an easel when it came to art, but the more he looked at it, the more intrigued he became. He heard a mellow voice at his elbow. "Excuse me."

He looked up and found himself face-to-face with a lovely woman dressed in what looked like homespun cloth in an intricate pattern, which she filled out very well. Eno wasn't short, but she towered over him, as did the man by her side, dressed in similar garb, as though from a unisex store. She pointed to the far corner of the room. "That's our spot over there," she said, adding, "we're the music. Violin and keyboard."

"Oh! Sure," answered Eno, giving way. They passed by and went to a far corner and started setting up. Despite their robust frames, their moves were quick and graceful in the confined space, almost delicate. In short order, snippets of Mozart and Marsalis wafted through the room as the musicians warmed up.

As the first guests began to arrive Imogen pulled Chavi aside. "These are the *bon ton*, dear. *The* cream of local society. Some complimentary photos of this well-dressed cadre may just find their way into the paper's arts and leisure section. Then, who knows? Maybe a few assignments for the glossies? And the internet exposure?" Imogen gave Chavi a subtle wink. "Make the rounds, dear. The paper's staff photographer is not exactly absent by oversight."

At that moment one of the impeccably dressed company, the male variety, sidled over.

"Imogen!" he crowed. "Congratulations! You have outdone yourself this time. These pieces are marvelous! You say the artist is new to our bailiwick?"

"Yes. And very shy."

"I hope that won't prevent him from making an appearance."

"Not at all. He promised to be fashionably late. And speaking of marvelous . . ." Imogen gently pulled Chavi to her side, "Please meet Chavi Kapur, our gallery's new photographer. Chavi, this is Bryce McFadden, the Third."

"Call me Tripp. Glad to make your acquaintance, Ms. Kapur. Have you had a show of your own?"

Chavi felt abashed. "I did win some prizes as a student. But nothing really professional. Yet."

Tripp offered a charming smile. "We'll have to do something about that. Right, Imogen?"

"Splendid idea!"

"I've already begun a new portfolio," Chavi said, omitting the fact that she had only just begun it that evening. "In fact, may I add a photo of you two together?" Imogen gave Chavi another approving nod and sly wink.

Tripp looked delighted. "Of course, Ms. Kapur!"

Chavi smiled as she brought the camera to her eye. "Please. Call me 'Chavi'."

CHAPTER 41

Cezar pushed Lorik back into the kitchen, still dangling the keys. "Going somewhere?"

Lorik's shoulders slumped a little. He gave Cezar an evil-eyed, sidelong glance. "Yeah. Out," he muttered.

"Out where, may I ask?"

"Nowhere special."

"Are you certain?" Cezar's hand was a blur as he snatched the engraved invitation from Lorik's inside jacket pocket. Lorik looked away and rolled his eyes.

Cezar held out the invitation and began to read with dramatic flair. "The Beaumont Gallery cordially invites you . . . " Cezar turned around the envelope. "Which means *me*, evidently." He broke off again to grab Lorik's shoulder as he tried to retreat. "'Cordially invites you to attend the opening of the exhibition of Roi Kirkland, and to meet the artist." Lorik struggled to retreat again, but winced as Cezar used a crushing grip. "And not just to meet the artist, it would appear. What's this? Musical entertainment by . . . " He treated Lorik to a look of mock surprise. "Ms. Sabine Burgess!"

Cezar released his hand, and Lorik took a deep breath and exhaled with relief, then looked dead-keen at Cezar. There was no mistaking Lorik's anger: fierce and hard-bitten.

Cezar rewarded the look with a full-on slap across the face, knocking Lorik to the floor.

"You stupid *boy*!" Cezar spat the words like venom from a cobra. "Reckless . . . mulish . . . *little* boy!"

Lying there, Lorik mustered some courage. "I am *not* a little boy!" he yelled back. "What I am is a prisoner! Going crazy with boredom!"

"Crazy with infatuation, you mean."

"What's that supposed to mean?"

"It means, my dear son, that your father is not a dolt. Sabine is clearly more than a friend. Much more. Isn't that so?"

"Yes! She is! Why should I deny it?"

Cezar nodded with satisfaction. "At least you spared yourself the embarrassment of lying to me. I know very well what your intention was."

Lorik, knowing he was caught, remained silent.

Cezar grabbed the lapels of Lorik's jacket and pulled him close, nose-to-nose. His voice was tight with fury. "Don't you know what even touching a Vanator's arrow will do to you?"

Lorik's voice was a weary sing-song. "Yes. Kill me. Even a single scratch. You told me. And told me and told me and told me."

"Even brushing your skin against that cursed fletching. Yet you shot that woman . . ." He broke off once more.

"I made a mistake," Lorik yelled back. "I'm was aiming for—" He bit off the last words.

"Yes. Her partner, Coleg, who took issue with that stunt, by the way. Fortunately, in defending herself, Sabine defended you as well. Otherwise, we would be in a far worse predicament." He hunkered down. His voice was soft and gentle. "Son . . . why?"

"To have a companion."

Cezar was incredulous. "A companion? But you have Yago." He stopped short. "Incidentally, where is your consort?"

Lorik crossed his arms and stared straight ahead.

Cezar nodded. "I see." He grasped Lorik by the front of his shirt, twisted the collar noose-like around his neck and dragged him through the house, ass skidding along the floor, pausing in the central hallway. Lorik gasped for breath.

Cezar glared down at him, no nonsense. "Where?"

"Den," Lorik choked out.

When they reached the den, Cezar released Lorik, who collapsed on the floor, chest heaving.

Yago lay sprawled on an armchair, unconscious. His silk bathrobe lay open. Cezar gave Lorik a mean quick glance before striding over. A thick black metal choker encircled the man's neck. Cezar turned to Lorik. "You've been in my quarters." His voice was quiet, steady with suppressed anger.

Lorik said nothing.

Cezar grabbed Yago's hair and gently pulled his head forward. With his free hand Cezar pulled off his ascot and, careful not to touch the metal, used it to unclip the stud-and-hook clasp, removed the choker.

Yago's eyes opened at once. He sat up, looked down at his groin, then looked around, astonished. "What happened?"

"What do you remember?"

"Well . . . " He looked from Cezar to Lorik and back again. "We were going to, you know, have some fun. Then Lorik said he had something for me. A bonding gift, he said."

"This one?" Cezar held up the choker.

"Yeah. It was wrapped in silk. He said he would put it on. And then I woke up here." He knit his brow, and his voice got sharp. "What's going on?"

Lorik started to get to his feet.

"Stay right there!" Cezar shouted. Lorik slumped down with a sullen expression.

"Platinum black," Cezar said, holding the choker higher. "A form of platinum that can be forged, with the proper skill. Even so much as *dusted* on any object, it could kill." He looked sidelong at Lorik. "Isn't that so, son?"

Lorik mumbled.

"Speak up!" Cezar commanded.

Lorik growled through gritted teeth. "Yes. It can."

"Now," Cezar's tone was reasonable. "You may get up and apologize to Yago."

CHAPTER 42

Eno milled through the crowd, sidling up to Chavi holding a glass of champagne. "I think I'm going to buy that wooden arch thing. See over there?"

She peered around the milling guests. "Oh, yeah." She nodded. "Nice." She reached for his glass. "May I?"

He pulled the glass away. "Uh-uh."

Chavi was indignant. "Why not? I'm doing all the work."

"You're driving."

"Is that why you're getting plastered?"

"Why not? This is the good stuff. Quality." Eno didn't know wines any better than he knew art. Outside of the laboratory, his natural habitat was the man cave in his basement with a cold Corona or Molson's and a football game. "Want something?"

"A soft drink? With ice?"

"You got it," He nudged his way through the patrons over to the beverage table. Imogen was there. She noticed him and smiled. "Eno! Are you enjoying yourself?"

"Absolutely."

"May I get you a refill?" She pointed to his glass.

"Sure. Something for Chavi, too, please. Nonalcoholic."

Imogen poured ginger ale into a wineglass and handed it to him. "At least it looks like the real thing." She took his and filled it with a very good year of Veuve Cliquot Ponsardin.

Eno pointed to the violinist. "Who is that?"

She followed his pointing hand. "Sabine Burgess? Comes from a prominent local family. An expert in survival training. Even works with the RCMP."

"Impressive." He pointed to the violin and keyboard. "Interesting side-job for such an outdoors type."

"Oh, yes. Knowledgeable about all sorts of media. Music, television, electronics. We were lucky to get her. She's very busy. Divides her time between events like ours and running survival camps for her father." Eno shrugged, but then stopped short when he caught sight of Sabine. There she stood, stock-still, dead-keen focused on something across the room.

He followed her gaze to the front of the gallery. No doubt about it, that "something" was a handsome young man hovering near the entrance to the gallery, looking around and blinking as though he might have stumbled into the wrong place. He took something out of his pocket and gave it a nervous glance. *Cellphone*, Eno thought, but then it shined as it caught the light—a silver locket of some type, but—wrong again—he flipped open the cover, revealing a watch face.

Suddenly Imogen's expression brightened. "You must excuse me, Eno. I see that our man of the hour has arrived."

Eno watched her greet Roi Kirkland. Then he looked back at Sabine. Her earlier thunderstruck expression had vanished. Now her eyes squinted with cold calculation as she whispered in her associate's ear. He crouched slightly, as if ready to pounce, but then nodded and slipped away.

***

Once the three men were seated, Cezar's tone became reasonable. "Now. What's this about a companion? Why Sabine?" he asked Lorik.

"I need someone I can talk to, confide in, with no strings attached. No agenda. So I thought maybe a girl. Like a sister."

"A Vanator to join our ranks then. Is that it?"

"Why not?"

"Because we would then have two enemies instead of one, you dolt!" Cezar said hotly. "Have you any notion of the difficulties we would face in the event of a two-front war?" Cezar was practically screaming.

Lorik yelled back, on the verge of tears. "But I feel so empty…" He trailed off into a pout. "What's the use. You don't understand."

Cezar went quiet and pensive. "You're wrong. I do understand. Better than you realize. But more importantly, we Primes follow the natural order. Hierarchy. To reach the height of existence we must tower above all else. And we must subdue those over whom we build that tower."

Lorik hung his head, sobbing quietly.

Cezar rose and went over to him. "You will fully realize your destiny, son. This I promise." He pulled Lorik to his feet. In a flash, he spun Lorik around and held him fast, whispering in his ear, "But only at the proper time." He pulled back, releasing the young man.

Lorik glowered and said nothing.

"What's this petulance?" chided Cezar. "That will soon be mended. We may kill two birds with one stone." He held up the choker in his gloved hand. "Let's return it to its rightful owner, shall we?" He tossed a set of car keys to Yago.

***

Roi's timidity actually served to ingratiate him to the crowd. His shoulders were slightly hunched as if in pain, arms folded, hands tucked away, his eyes wide and tentative as he chatted in a low voice. This peculiar stance was taken by those present as modest, almost self-effacing.

Now Eno understood what Chavi meant. It was difficult to believe that this handsome, quiet young man could have perpetrated the fierce violence Eno had suffered in the parking lot.

Chavi caught Eno's eye. Her expression said: *See what I mean?* Eno nodded with a raised brow, when he noticed Imogen approaching him with Roi, his arm tucked through hers.

"It's time you two met. Roi Kirkland, please meet . . . " She broke off with an apologetic smile. "I'm sorry, Eno, but I never got your last name."

"Velazquez. Inocente Velazquez. Eno for short." Eno held out his hand to shake as he watched Roi's expression, to gauge some sort of recognition in the artist's eyes. But they were guileless. Eno's doubt that this was the perpetrator deepened even more.

When Roi took his hand, Eno was surprised by the feel of fabric. He looked down and saw that Roi wore gloves, the kind one would wear at a very formal affair, pearl gray and soft as fur. Roi's grip was firm. "Velazquez, like the painter?"

"Yes," answered Eno with more than a little surprise. "No relation."

"Eno is interested in one of your pieces," Imogen said. "With that, I'll leave you two to haggle while I make the rounds." She patted Roi on the arm and disappeared into the milling crowd.

Roi locked eyes with Eno, who began to feel lightheaded. "Which one do you like?"

It took a few seconds for Eno to answer. When he did, his tongue felt thick. "'Intersecting Arches.' Beautiful."

Roi countered with a modest smile. "Well, thank you. I think I can be persuaded to part with it."

"What a relief," joked Eno. Then he added, trying to sound casual. "How about that one?" He pointed to the large centerpiece statue in the corner, around which there were several admirers. "There's no hyperlink for it in the brochure, so I was wondering."

Roi was about to answer when he stopped short and stared straight ahead, as if he were being called from faraway. His head jerked around toward the entrance to the gallery just as a tall, robust man appeared, who for some reason looked familiar to Eno. Roi murmured, "Pardon me," as he lit out toward the door. The tall man at the door scanned the room back and forth like a beacon until his eyes rested on Roi gently elbowing his way through the crowd and gave his friend a slight, warm smile. They met with hands outstretched, drawing close, looking in each other's eyes and shared a few whispers.

Chavi snapped a few photos of the two men at a distance before honing in for close-ups. Out of nowhere, it seemed, Imogen appeared at her elbow. "Handsome couple."

Putting it mildly, thought Chavi. "And close, it seems," she said aloud.

"Not surprising. He's been so lonely since his aunt left."

"She left?" Chavi asked, startled.

"Why, yes," answered Imogen. "They had a falling out. I gather she was moving out anyway. You don't know Rosamund?"

"Oh, no," Chavi stammered. "I overheard someone make a remark, so I thought . . ." She trailed off. "Well, I'd better hop-to, if I want to get some close-ups."

"Too late, dear," remarked Imogen, nodding discreetly. "It seems the boys have slipped away."

***

Merit sat in front of her computer at home paying bills. The engraved invitation to Roi Kirkland's exhibition tucked into its envelope was propped against the lamp. Since the medical center was a benefactor of Beaumont, Merit as a staff physician received invitations to its exhibitions as a matter of course, and Roi Kirkland's was no exception. She recognized the young man from his photo and was again struck by his good looks, and his work certainly looked intriguing. Aside from the fact that she was covering for a sick colleague in the ER that night, she felt it was better to give Adam some space—*and me, too*—she had decided after some thought. Not to mention avoiding any awkwardness if she were to meet Roi face to face with Adam so close by. And even though it had only been a few weeks, she had to admit she missed Adam terribly. Maybe she would catch the exhibit later, when the hoopla had died down.

She returned to her task when the doorbell rang. She went to the front door and looked through the peephole.

There stood a tall, slender but well-built woman, really not much more than a girl, by Merit's estimation. A backpack was slung over her shoulder. She looked familiar somehow.

Merit opened the door and got a better look. Her eyes were deep blue, but it was her hair that was so striking—a rich chestnut brown with a few blond streaks—either natural or nothing less than a session at a high-end salon. The expression on her face was anxious under a smooth tan.

"May I help you?" Merit asked, trying to place where she'd seen the girl before.

"Yes. Hello. My name is Zelie Giroux. Are you Merit?" Stunned, Merit could only nod. Zelie looked anxiously over Merit's shoulder. "Is my brother here?"

CHAPTER 43

Roi and Adam slipped into Roi's studio down the hall, closing the door behind them, hushing the hubbub of the crowd. Rough sketches and sculptured works in progress, like mutants, stood silent among the litter of clay-stained sheets.

"I'm so glad you're here," Roi said with obvious relief. "I felt so scared out there by myself. So alone." He offered Adam a plate of food. "Just for you," he said with a smile.

Adam smacked it out of his hand, looking right through him. Brie and canapés went flying. Caviar splattered against the wall, pitting it like buckshot.

The gentility he had come to expect from Adam had vanished, with ravening hunger left in its place. Adam's brows lowered and deepened the shadows against his eyes—unblinking eyes that seemed singularly empty of all but lust, and his skin was hot. The soft ambient light reflected the perspiration misted on forehead and cheeks. His breath came fast and hard as he approached Roi.

Roi took a few steps backward, eyes wide with fear. "Adam? What's going on?"

Adam lunged forward and wrapped one hand around Roi's neck, making him cry out, pawing with his other and sniffed Roi from neck to groin like an animal, yet gentle and loving. "Man, you turn me on. Let's fuck," he demanded, his voice a soft rumble, like the purring of a lion.

Though Adam's newfound aggression excited Roi even more, he shoved him back, and the force of it surprised Adam.

"I can't do this right now," Roi said with regret, but obviously meaning business.

"The hell you can't!" Adam's eyes were steady, calm, and ferociously bright. He jumped on top of Roi and straddled him, pinning his torso and legs. Adam looked around, and then grabbed at a spool of armature wire nearby. "Wanna see what happened to prisoners we captured who gave us a hard time?" He held Roi's wrists together and pulled wire from the spool. And in what seemed like split seconds he wound loops of wire around them with expert precision, tightening so that he couldn't move. Roi was so taken aback it didn't occur to him to resist—and he found himself not wanting to—but he struggled nonetheless.

Adam gave him a wicked grin. "Yeah, go ahead. Fight me," Adam whispered, his face inches from Roi's. "Let's have some fireworks."

But there was already fire in Roi's eyes; they seemed to spark and flash, and his gaze seemed to bear down on Adam like a weight. "You think I have no idea what's it's like to be a prisoner?" Roi snarled, with ferocity so primal that Adam didn't notice him pry the tight loops of wire apart and throw them to the ground. He pushed Adam away and crouched like a cornered wolf. Tears brimmed in Roi's eyes as he approached Adam, looking through him, licking his lips, saying softly, almost lovingly, "To have a thirst an ocean couldn't quench?"

Holy shit? Adam thought with sudden fear, feeling terribly, alarmingly vulnerable. Then, as if yanked back, Roi stopped short, shoulders slumped. "You have no idea, my man."

But suddenly, Adam did have an idea, an especially knowing one as he recalled Roi's sculpture in London, the figure trying to leave a pedestal, as if removed from life by a prison of blown glass. Tears of his own came as he went over to Roi and enveloped him in his arms.

He yanked Roi's trousers to the floor, then peeled his underwear from his crotch. Without ever breaking his gaze from Roi, he undid his own zipper, spit in his hand, and then pulled out his cock and slicked it up. Pressing it against Roi's anus, he pushed it in just far enough so that the head was nestled inside the tender flesh of the opening. Then he halted and whispered in

Roi's ear. "We're one. We belong to each other. Never forget that. Be loved and free to be yourself forever."

Roi felt himself relax, wrapped in the rich sincerity of Adam's voice. In response, Adam slipped his cock shaft into Roi, at first grinding slowly, sensually, then battering at Roi's inner sphincter with conquering force, driving Roi to the edge of climax.

"I'm waiting for you," Adam said, but he didn't have to wait long. Roi gasped as he came. Adam shot his load deep inside Roi seconds later.

Afterward they lay together for a minute or so in silence, then Adam got up. He was sheepish as he put his cock away and zipped up. He went to remove the restraining wire from Roi's wrists. "I wish I knew what came over me . . ." But then he finally noticed that the wire had been stretched out, lying on the floor. Roi was free, straightening his clothes. Adam was flabbergasted. "How the hell did you get loose?" He pointed at the wire. Roi had good strength, and the wire was flexible to a point, but it was tough. There was no way Roi could have freed himself.

"There's something you don't know. Something important." Roi's tone was foreboding.

"Okay. What?" Adam didn't move a muscle, caught in the crossfire of desire and apprehension. "I'm a creature . . . of a different kind."

A hitch in Roi's voice jolted Adam out of his reverie. "*Creature?*"

"Yes. It's hard to explain."

"You started. So try."

"It's hereditary. That much is true. But . . . well . . . "

Adam lost patience. "Out with it!"

"You said before, free to be myself. You said that."

"Sure I did. So?"

Roi licked his lips and took a deep breath. He opened his jaws wide. His canines shone as he pressed himself against Adam in an instant. His breath was hot and moist at Adam's neck. "I'm a vampire."

***

Merit showed Zelie into the kitchen and made coffee. "So, are you out here for a visit?" Merit asked. "Adam didn't mention we were having a guest."

"Oh, he wasn't expecting me. I just needed to talk to him. And lately, on the phone, he's been . . . well, sort of distant.

Merit nodded. She'd felt the same way, of course, but now she knew why.

"At first I thought it was my decision about school."

"What decision was that?"

"He didn't say anything?"

"No. He never mentioned his family much."

"Oh." She looked surprised. "I applied to medical school. I thought maybe he disapproved. We talked about it before, and he was always telling me that it wasn't easy giving up family."

"Yes, I remember now. Because of religion, right?"

Zelie nodded. "I told him he was the only family I really wanted to keep. He didn't say anything, and I haven't talked to him since." She fell silent. "There's something else going on. I know there is. He's not answering his phone or returning my calls. I got worried, so here I am."

She wondered if she should tell Zelie about her brother's recent confession, and if so—how? And how much? When Zelie asked when Adam would be home, Merit decided to play it safe and mention nothing for the present.

"That's strange, all right."

Zelie looked disappointed, so Merit offered the only encouragement she could muster off the cuff. "There's a bug going around the city that's been keeping us pretty busy at the hospital. As a matter of fact, I should be getting ready for work myself. But why don't you try calling him again?" she suggested. "You can hang out here if you like, and he can meet you here when he's finished doing whatever."

Zelie smiled her gratitude. "Good idea. Thanks."

***

Adam stood as if turned to stone. The seconds ticked by in deafening silence. "A vampire," he said, barely moving his mouth.

Roi nodded. He approached Adam, who halted him with an upheld palm.

"You mean like . . ." He crooked two fingers at his grimacing mouth in makeshift fangs.

"I don't know much about it myself. Aunt Roz told me—"

Adam interrupted, his words calm, even, measured, not bothering to mask his sarcasm. "Oh. Is she a vampire, too?"

"Well, no. But . . ."

Adam stared at his shoes. "This is really an insult." He glared at Roi. "If you're having second thoughts, just say so, instead of all this gothic bullshit." Then an idea struck him.

"But I can prove it! Here, see for yourself." Roi put a finger to pull back his lip, but a knock on the door interrupted him. Imogen's head popped in. "Sorry to interrupt, Roi. But Sabine has a question about one of the pieces. She says it can't wait."

"Thanks, Imogen. I'll be right there."

Imogen left the door ajar. Roi turned back to Adam, who was still wide-eyed, wary and still as a statue. "I'm serious, Adam. I know this is weird."

"Oh, you think?"

"Just promise me you'll wait 'till I get back?"

"I don't know . . ." Adam began, then his phone buzzed. He took it out and shrugged. "My sister."

"We'll talk later?" Roi pleaded in a loud whisper.

Adam shrugged. "Sure. Why not?" His tone was noncommittal.

Roi left as Adam spoke into the phone. "Honey, this isn't a good time to talk. Can I call you back?" Then his jaw dropped. "You're *where*? . . . Stay put. I'll be right over." He pocketed his phone as he hurried out of the room into the hallway.

He paused for a moment to rest against the wall and wipe his brow. He spotted the back exit a few feet away and went through the door into the parking lot.

He heard the door open and close behind him. He only got a glimpse of the man, as tall as himself, who spun him around and cracked him against the jaw. The snapping of his head is the last thing Adam felt before he slumped to the ground.

CHAPTER 44

Roi joined Sabine at the sculpture of Adam. In a loud voice, she said to Roi, "I hear you don't want to sell this piece."

"That's right. It has sentimental value. But if you're interested, you can commission a copy."

Sabine edged closer, her face deadpan. In a soft voice, she said, "You don't seem very happy to see me."

Roi looked surprised. "Should I be?"

Sabine considered. "No, I guess not, after that stunt you pulled. But after the risks I took for you?"

"Excuse me? Stunt? What risks?"

A few seconds passed, heavy with antagonism. Her smile was cold. "All right. I understand this isn't the time or place. But it did give me an opportunity for payback. So we're even."

Roi's response was cut short as Sabine leaned over and whispered in his ear. "And don't think for a minute the Burgess won't back me. Boyfriends are a dime a dozen. The Truce is what matters."

Roi knitted his brow in confusion. "Truce?"

She answered with a look of utter contempt. "Just remember what I said. We're square. Got it?" Then, above the murmur of the crowd, she indicated the sculpture and announced, "Thanks just the same. But I don't want a copy." She offered a tiger's grin. "I insist on having the original."

Roi's jaw was still slack as she grabbed her violin and gave him a lingering, ugly glare as she stalked past him—which did not go unnoticed by Chavi or Eno, who exchanged curious glances.

***

Sabine rushed across the parking lot over to the figure hoisting an unconscious man, who had been bound at the wrists and feet, into the back seat of an SUV. She joined her assistant and looked closely at the motionless figure.

"Any trouble?" asked Sabine.

The man shrugged. "Not much. Big guy, though."

"He looked bad."

The man nodded his head and pointed to the blood stain at Adam's crotch. "Sure. He got nipped."

Sabine flashed a broad, gratified smile. "Perfect." She handed her instrument to her partner. "Stow this and let's get going." She opened the driver's door and got in as the man opened the trunk and carefully stashed her violin case alongside his electronic keyboard. A well-dressed couple emerged from the exit, saw them and waved. "Nice night!" one said.

"Gorgeous!" Sabine called back cheerfully, slammed the door, and revved up the engine.

From the far end of the parking lot Devan sat in his prowler, reporting the pair's every move as he spoke into his cell phone. "They took the boyfriend." He paused, then said, "Yes, Maestru. No mistake." He nodded as he listened. "Yes, I know her. The one with the arrow. She left the hospital against medical advice." He listened again. "Sure. Crown Mountain. About fifteen kilometers, stone marker. Got it," he said and tossed the phone aside. He started the engine and paced Sabine's SUV at a good tailing distance.

CHAPTER 45

Roi was perplexed by the exchange with Sabine, but he didn't have time to ponder it long. Chavi came up to him, grinning.

"Hello, Roi. Do you remember me? Chavi Kapur?" She watched his expression closely.

It took only a second or two for Roi to recall. He extended his gloved hand with a warm smile. "Of course. How are you, Ms. Kapur?"

"Call me Chavi, please. I'm doing well, thanks. I'd like to get a few solo shots with you and your pieces."

"I saw you taking photos of the crowd." He gave her a curious look. "But I thought you were a police officer."

Her smile slipped a bit. "This is just a side job. A hobby, really." She looked closely at him. "May I?" she asked, holding up her camera.

"Certainly. Where would you like me to stand?"

"Right next to this big piece right here," indicating the centerpiece figure. She peered at the piece's title plaque and read it aloud. "'Adam.'"

Roi moved next to it. "That's right. Want me to stand anywhere special?"

"No. Just be natural." He assumed a relaxed pose. She aimed the camera and took a photo, speaking as she did so. "Your 'Adam' here looks familiar."

"He should. The model is here."

Her expression lit with recognition. "Of course! The man you met at the entrance." She took another photo. "I'd love to take a photo of all three of you. Artist, model and creation."

"This really isn't a good time."

"Oh." Chavi sounded disappointed. "Not even one teeny little photo? It'll be quick, I promise."

Roi looked uncomfortable. She tried another tack. "Look," she started in a low, pleading voice, "I'm trying to make a name for myself as a photographer. And it would really help my portfolio if I could get all three of you." Roi considered. She charged back in. "And I'll give you all the prints you want. Enlargements, the whole works. I'll even throw in framing." Then, remembering the cost, added in a low voice, "For one of them."

Roi started to give in. She seemed so sincere. And really very sweet. *She must really hate being a cop*, he thought. He was sure Adam wouldn't mind his effigy for all the public to see, if it came to that. "All right. I'll see if he's up to it." He was gratified, noting that she was quite pretty, when she smiled.

"Do you mind if I tag along?"

Roi was used to visitors milling around the gallery, and often enough they stopped in. He didn't mind. It was part of the public relations of the place. "Not at all," he said, to her delight. They made their way through the crowd, which had thinned out. Chavi spotted Eno at the buffet table. Imogen was handing him two glasses of champagne.

Eno addressed Roi. "Awesome party, dude. Wonderful stuff." He lifted his glass and took a sip. "Too bad you won't sell 'Adam' over there. Everyone's talking about it. Who knows what you could have gotten."

Roi offered a friendly shrug. "Glad you're enjoying yourself."

Chavi said, "Eno, I'll be taking some photos in Roi's studio. Down the hall."

"Oh, yeah?" He already focused his attention on an elegant young woman in the far side of the room, who parodied a pout and waved him over. "Excuse me. Damsel in distress. Have fun, you two." He made his way toward the Damsel.

"Why didn't you sell it?" asked Chavi.

Roi countered with a smile. "Maybe I should have. After all, I have the original." He stopped, his smile fading as recalled Sabine's parting words. Chavi frowned with concern.

"Something wrong?" she asked.

"No. Follow me."

He moved off toward his studio, Chavi following behind. He opened the door and flipped on the light.

No Adam. Roi's worried frown returned, deeper this time. He turned to Chavi. "He could have gotten a call. He's a doctor," he said, as if to himself.

"Maybe he's in the bathroom," Chavi suggested.

Roi resisted the urge to go look. "Could be. Let's wait a few minutes," he added, leaving the door open.

"Fine. I'm in no rush." Chavi strolled around, examining his half-finished work. "How long does it take you to finish a piece?"

"Depends. Sometimes I have to tweak a little. Other times it just sits there for a while."

"Mellowing?"

"Something like that."

She gave the studio a broad once-over and scanned around with light meter. "The lighting here is superb."

"Doesn't the camera do that for you?"

"Yeah, but I'm old fashioned. I like more hands-on. I'm an artist too, you know. Like you." She paused. "How about standing over there?" She pointed to a table with a sculpture in its early stages. "Stand right next to it." He followed her direction. She backed up, adjusting the angle. "Could you back up just a bit? I can't go back any farther." She pointed to her backside. Her buttocks were against a table littered with instruments.

Roi shuffled back and bumped into another table. The armature tottered and started to fall, but Roi caught it in time. While he carefully replaced the object, Chavi snuck a look behind her and spotted a clay-caked spatula lying within reach. She recalled Eno's words: *Anything that's been touched. This baby can handle it*, patting the DNA reader with affection. In one quick motion, Chavi slipped the spatula into her pocket.

"This okay?" asked Roi. He had positioned himself behind the armature, moving it to one side, not looking at her.

"That's great." She aimed the camera. "Now, look right at the camera, as if you're looking at someone who's *inside* the camera at the back. Good. Now, please don't move."

There was a soft knock. A man's face appeared, timid, in the open doorway, backlit from the hallway. "Hello?"

"Gaige!" Chavi cried. "What are you doing here?"

"Eno is responsible," Gaige replied, stepping into the room, briefcase in one hand. "He was in the company of a rather tipsy lady of generous proportions and obvious means." He noticed Roi and went over to him, hand out in introduction. "Gaige Sutton."

"Sorry. Where are my manners?" Chavi said. "Gaige, this is my friend . . . " She looked to Roi for confirmation, who nodded in agreement. "Roi Kirkland."

Gaige observed Roi with great interest. "Oh-*ho*! The suspect!"

"Excuse me?" Roi queried.

Gaige approached Roi slowly, eyeing him critically as though he were an exotic totem.

"Gaige!" Chavi scolded.

Gaige withdrew but continued to scrutinize Roi.

Roi was indignant. "What's going on? Who are you?"

"An associate, sort of," Chavi said. "Let me explain."

Roi crossed his arms and gave Chavi his full attention.

"A few nights ago," Chavi began, "we were attacked in the parking lot."

"We?"

"Me, Gaige and Eno."

Roi seemed at a loss. "Eno? The guy who came with you tonight?"

"Yes. "Anyway, this attacker . . . well . . ."

"Looked very much like you," Gaige put in, turning to Chavi. "You're right. Remarkable likeness!" He returned to scrutinizing Roi. "We all witnessed it."

Roi was confused, then alarmed. "But—"

"We don't think it was you," Chavi was quick to say, then with a quick glance at Gaige, "At least, *I* don't."

"I'm inclined to agree," Gaige replied. "But we're not interested in laying blame. Not yet. Not until we've solved a mystery. You said yourself," he said to Chavi, "you found it difficult to believe Mr. Kirkland here—"

Roi interrupted, his sarcasm tinged with amusement. "Hell, with cheerful accusations on such short notice, you might as well call me Roi."

"Of course, Roi," Gaige said with a winning smile. "We think it highly unlikely that you could be the culprit."

Somewhat mollified, Roi found it hard to resist Gaige's guileless charm and found himself more curious than irate. "So what's next then?" he asked with genuine interest.

"Document that you were not the attacker. And here's how," Gaige said, opening his briefcase and donning his gloves. He took out a cotton swab and small plastic bag. He approached Roi with the swab, ready to poke. "Would you be so good as to open your mouth?"

Roi's stepped back. "What's that for?"

"Test for DNA. If yours matches what we have at Eno's lab . . ."

"Then what?" Wariness crept back into his voice. "You turn me in?"

Chavi didn't give Gaige a chance to reply. "Like Gaige said, we think you're innocent," she said with finality.

"Exactly," Gaige said. "Until proven guilty."

"That's reassuring," Roi told her, then addressed Gaige. "Should I get a lawyer anyway?"

Gaige thought about it for a second. "No, I shouldn't think so."

"Swell." Roi didn't seem entirely convinced. "But you'll keep me posted?"

"Naturally." Gaige beamed a smile. "Now, open wide!"

***

When Roi returned to the exhibition hall he wished more than ever that Adam was at his side. Standing close to the sculpture afforded him some comfort, as he greeted those offering compliments and congratulations. He noted with relief that the crowd was very sparse. The exhibition was technically over at nine o'clock, and it was getting close to that now. He began to relax when he spotted a young woman, late teens or early twenties, he guessed, standing next to

Imogen, who pointed in his direction. As the woman approached, Roi thought she looked familiar.

She rushed over to him and demanded, "I was told you would know where my brother is." The lovely timbre of her voice tempered her Southern accent.

It suddenly dawned on Roi. "You're Zelie!"

"That's right. Adam was supposed to meet me. I called about an hour ago. He said he was leaving then. And he's not answering his phone."

Roi shook his head. "I have no idea where he is. We talked earlier, but when I returned later, he'd already gone." He paused, wondering whether he should mention Adam's peculiar behavior, then decided against it.

Zelie looked as if she might cry, and Roi's heart went out to her.

"I'm sure he's all right. He might have been on call. Maybe he's at the hospital. Vancouver General."

Zelie nodded. "I know. I'll try there."

Roi pulled out a card and gave it to her. "Call me anytime."

Zelie smiled through brimming eyes, her face a study in disappointment. "Thanks." She dabbed at her eyes. "Adam says he really likes you. I can see why," Zelie added as she made her way toward the entrance.

CHAPTER 46

The first thing Adam noticed when he came to was that his jaw hurt and his vision was doubled. *Shit, probably have a concussion,* he thought as his head began to clear. The second thing he noticed was that his hands were bound with what felt like rope and tethered from behind to his bound feet. He lay facing the rear of the back seat of an expensive vehicle, judging from the unmistakable aroma of leather. He craned his neck around to see behind him, and he felt a jolt of pain in his jaw, making him groan. He had just enough peripheral vision to see the two people in the front seat. There was a ringing in his left ear as a result of the assault, so that the passenger's voice—a woman's—seemed to come from another room.

"Our guest has awakened," she said in a low but pleasant voice.

"But has he come to his senses?" asked the man in the driver's seat.

She gave Adam a sidelong squint. "Time will tell," she said.

"Who are you?" asked Adam in a thick voice; his voice sounded far away as well. Instead of an answer, he saw the man lean over to kiss the woman, who pushed him away.

"Eyes on the road," she said with irritation.

"I don't get it," he said. "He's not one of us. *Or* one of them. He doesn't stand a chance in the Revel."

"You might be surprised, Coleg. I heard this dude was like a *mega*-soldier. Smart, too. And we can even the odds. He might just make it."

Adam piped up from the back. "Nice to be discussed as if I'm not here. Where are you taking me? You could tell me that at least." Still no reply.

Adam felt himself shift slightly as the vehicle turned and soon rolled to a stop. The front seat passengers got out, slamming the doors. Some muffled conversation; it sounded to Adam as though they continued their earlier argument, the man protesting, the woman defending first more loudly, then with a final word, yanking open the door. Now wide awake, Adam stared up into the face—a lovely one—of a tall figure of a woman. An equally tall man joined her, and with a quick glance between them, the woman leaned down close. "Save your strength, bucko," she said. "You'll need every ounce."

***

Baxter eye-smiled at Zelie over his sandwich. "Adam left right after his shift. Went to some art thing," he said through a mouthful, then swallowed. "Sorry," he added, dabbing his mouth with a napkin. "About seven o'clock. Won't be back for . . . " He leaned over and looked at a schedule. "Another two days." He looked at Zelie. "Is this a follow-up? Someone else could see you."

"No, I—" Zelie began.

"Wait! I know you! You're Adam's sister. Uh . . . um . . ." He wracked his brain for the name.

"Zelie."

"Right! Zelie! Good to meet you." His face showed sudden concern. "He has been acting a little weird the past week or so. Like real distracted." Actually, Baxter had thought Adam more than distracted earlier that evening—almost seductive, in a cruel way, as if he were stalking quarry and would pounce any minute, especially with men. Baxter had been frightened, and very worried about Adam on recollection, but he said nothing of it to Zelie. Instead, he leaned forward and asked softly, "Is everything okay at home?"

"Like always," answered Zelie.

Baxter smiled with relief. "That's good." He shifted his attention to the elderly couple

shuffling toward the desk. "Sorry I can't help. I'll tell him you were here the minute I see him."

CHAPTER 47

Cezar drove the SUV while Lorik sat shotgun. Yago stretched his legs across the back seat. They rode the first fifteen minutes in silence, leaving behind the busy highway and driving on a two-lane forest road. Yago pondered his recent bout of unconsciousness. For the first time in his hyperlife Yago felt a twinge of fear. "When I was out, was I . . . *really* dead?"

Cezar chuckled. "More like slumber. Comatose, really."

"Just from touching a piece of metal," Yago whispered.

"That's correct," Cezar answered with a hint of warning. From what I've heard, there are other substances are used in its making. Silver, I've heard. Different alloys have different properties, evidently. *And* different purposes."

"Don't you know?"

"Neither vampire nation is privy to that, and never has been since time out of mind. One of the most ancient and closely guarded secrets of the Vanator. The discovery of which, I suspect, fueled my son's foolish venture to participate in the Revel."

"Revel? Some sort of religious thing?"

Cezar lolled his head toward Lorik and gave him a sly look. "Would you care to clarify, my son?"

"And take away your chance to show off? Hell, no." Lorik's tone dripped with more than a little sarcasm. Lorik turned to Yago. "Nothing personal, man. But you see how he is," nodding his head toward Cezar.

Yago's answer was a noncommittal shrug. As attracted as he was to Lorik, he wasn't particularly inclined to trust him.

"The Revel is a ritual, but there ends the similarity to religion. A trial by ordeal in which the Vanator demonstrate their prowess over Primes and Sympaths alike. A hunt on the grounds of their compound. Which is where we're headed now."

Then, to everyone's surprise, Cezar pulled over, slammed on the brakes, and stared straight ahead. In a flat voice, he said, "They have arrived."

By now Yago had become accustomed being on the outside looking in, but Lorik looked just as baffled. "Who has?" he asked.

Cezar opened the door and leaped out. He crouched and looked around, as if trying to locate a distant sound. His head dipped slightly, his eyes wide and wary.

Cezar looked at Lorik, rather *through* him, which chilled Lorik to the bone. "I haven't had this feeling since . . . " His voice trailed off. He looked up into the sky and stood very still, then yelled. "Is that you?" he asked of the night air, his voice loud and shrill. "Already?"

Lorik leaned over toward the open door, his face scrunched with concern. "Father?"

Cezar's expression was pensive, but he said nothing. He got back into the vehicle and drove on, the headlights beaming a small morning on the tarmac.

CHAPTER 48

Chavi hovered at Gaige's elbow as he looked at the display on the DNA testing device, which looked much like an ordinary desktop printer. Eno flanked his other side, also peering at the screen.

"Uh-huh!" Gaige sounded fascinated. He turned his head to Eno. "You see that?"

"Sure do."

Chavi was irritated. "See what?" she hissed at Eno. "Is Roi the same guy who attacked you?"

"Well, yes," Eno said uncertainly.

"And no," Gaige added, sounding no more certain than his colleague.

"What's that supposed to mean?" Chavi snapped.

"Don't get cross," Gaige said. "It's good news."

"It seems our friend Roi has an identical twin," Eno said with confidence.

"And it means we're a little ahead of the game. The person in the parking lot certainly was not the agreeable young man we met at the gallery," Gaige said.

"And now," Eno proposed, "we need only track down that guy in the parking lot."

After a moment, Chavi stood and said with finality, "And that agreeable young man could help. He may not be a thug, but he may not be telling the whole truth either."

CHAPTER 49

The customs officer at Vancouver International Airport was cheerful, despite the early hour. "Purpose of trip?" he asked.

"Visiting relatives," Gedrec Kirkland answered. He glanced at his wife, Elspet, at the next cubicle. He caught her eye, and she smiled at him. Despite the eight-hour flight from London offset by the time zones, neither looked any worse for the wear.

"Thank you," the officer said with a smile, handing back his passport. "Enjoy your visit."

He joined Elspet in the seating area. "Hungry?" he asked, sitting down and reaching into his carry-on for a thermos.

Elspet remained standing. "I'd rather get going." She sounded rather peevish.

Gedrec had already taken a long swallow. "I know you're anxious. But you haven't had anything since we left. Come now," he chided. "One mouthful. No argument."

With a sigh she took the thermos, gulping down the liquid while Gedrec looked on with approval. He was used to this. If he didn't keep after his wife, she'd keep going until she desiccated in mid-stride. This time, though, he understood and even sympathized. Her constant contact with her niece, Rosamund, had ended too abruptly for comfort.

She handed back the empty thermos. He took out his handkerchief and dabbed at the red stain at the corner of her mouth.

"Guess I was hungrier than I thought," she conceded.

"Mm-hmm," he agreed.

They followed the signs for the rental cars and spotted the strip-mall of car rental agencies across the street.

"Which one?" Elspet asked.

Gedrec pointed across the street at the familiar logo.

"And I even ordered a GPS," Gedrec said with his crooked grin. Elspet squeezed his hand. They trotted across the busy street and entered the air-conditioned storefront.

The girl at the counter—whose nameplate announced "Sharon"—was as chipper as she was helpful. "Where are you folks from?" she chirped as she photocopied their international driver's licenses, waiting for the credit card to go through.

"London," Gedrec offered, with his crooked smile again.

"Oh, I have relatives over there! What a terrific place!"

She went down the bullet-point list of questions on a form, ending with: "Will you be driving out of the province or plan on crossing the border?"

"We don't plan on leaving the area," Gedrec answered.

"Did you want basic or extended coverage with your insurance?"

Gedrec looked at Elspet with a wrinkled brow.

"Extended, please," said Elspet, then to Gedrec. "It's been a while since either of us drove."

Gedrec nodded.

"Okay!" Sharon extended a clipboard holding a form. "Then sign here, please, and then initial . . ." She pointed to several spots, continuing, "there . . . there . . . and there."

Elspet asked, "Do you have any idea where Crown Mountain is?"

Gedrec scratched with the pen as directed. Sharon grabbed keys and form and motioned them to follow her.

"It's one of our most popular hiking trails! As a matter of fact, we have a brochure that tells you all you need to know." She snatched a pamphlet from a display and handed it to Elspet.

They followed Sharon out to the car, and after the routine inspection for dings and scratches, handed the keys to Gedrec, who insisted on escorting Sharon at least as far as the door.

"How charming!" she said, smiling. "Good manners are one of the things I love most abut the English."

Elspet stood behind their car and looked on, amused. Sometimes Gedrec liked to put on a little show—why he insisted on doing this, she knew was an old habit. *Very* old.

Sharon said, nodding to Elspet, "You folks enjoy the day."

"Same to you," Elspet said with a friendly smile.

"And remember, if I can be of any assistance, give me a call. My number is right on the contract. I'm here until eight o'clock. But anyone will be happy to assist you."

Gedrec gave a slight bow as Sharon headed toward the office. "Thank you," he called out.

As he walked past Elspet over to the passenger's side, she leaned on the trunk. "Oh, am I driving?"

He looked and saw her look of mock-surprise. He looked in at the passenger's side and laughed. "That's right. I'm the navigator," he said, and tossed her the keys, which she caught neat. They opened the door and got in.

"It's been years. *Decades.* Are you sure you know where to go?"

"Of course I do, my dear."

As they buckled up, Elspet said quietly, "It sounds good to hear you laugh."

"Yes, we haven't done much of that lately, have we?"

He leaned toward her with a tender expression on his face. "Or this," the tenderness reaching his eyes. She took the cue, and they exchanged an affectionate kiss.

Then Elspet started the car, and the GPS display lit up. Elspet poked at the screen, pecking in Rosamund's address in Richmond.

The mechanical female voice announced, "Please drive to highlighted route." Sudden worry flooded Elspet's face.

Gedrec looked over. "You all right, love?"

Elspet gave him a worried frown. "Now that we're actually here, it just hit me. How do you think Roi will take it?"

Gedrec put his hand over hers. "In stride."

"He's never laid eyes on us, really. That he'd remember, I mean."

"Another reason to find Rosamund. But even if we don't, I'm certain he'll understand."

She paused again. "Do you think he found out? About Lorik, I mean?"

"My dear, I have no idea. How could I?" His voice was weary.

Changing her tone, she added, "Sorry. I'm worried about Rosamund on top of everything else. Guess it's made me nag."

Gedrec was solicitous. "She may have good reason for her silence. We've only one place to start, and that's with the Burgess." He was going to say, *don't you worry,* but he knew how little comfort that would offer in the face of the inevitable. Rosamund's sudden silence was at first unsettling, then as much as they tried to quiet their fears—ominous.

The first battle, very possibly.

The harbinger of a much-anticipated war. Elspet knew that too.

But always the optimist, a smile tried to poke through Elspet's worried frown as she put the car in reverse.

"I know it's been a while since I've been to the compound," Gedrec commented, "but I think I can find the way. Besides," he added, pointing to the screen, "that's not going to help any more than the brochure. That way," Gedrec said, pointing at the exit to Route 99 North.

Elspet turned off the GPS and headed for the exit.

***

Sharon stood at the door and watched them drive off into the early morning dark. She had worked the counter for six years. People rented cars for all sorts of reasons, some even criminal. As a result, Sharon became good in judging people's moods. She looked at her watch. Two-thirty. She poured herself a cup of over-brewed coffee, hoping it might carry her through quitting time. There was something special about the Kirklands, she decided, and hoped that whatever was making them sad would work out in the end.

CHAPTER 50

Cezar was silent for the few minutes that remained of the drive. He turned onto a gravel road past a stone marker, man-high, to which a metal plaque was bolted. The plaque had a bas-relief trefoil. Immediately Cezar slowed down to a virtual crawl.

There was no sound but the crunch of tires on gravel as they rolled into a large clearing a moment later. There was a Vancouver P.D. cruiser parked next to a large SUV, but no other vehicles. Without a word Cezar killed the engine and snapped off the lights. Lorik got out first, then Cezar, who indicated with a look for Yago to do the same. No need for flashlights, of course; they could see very well even on a moonless night like this, a novelty that Yago still found both astonishing and delightful.

They found the wide path easily. The tramp of their footsteps was the only sound above the occasional hoots and twitters of the night creatures in the forest.

Then through the thinning trees appeared a large clearing, in the middle of which was a long wall of closely set flat stones, about fifteen feet high. There were no lights or windows, but there was a hinged door of heavy steel, displaying a trefoil like the one on the marker, studded in silver rivets like a mosaic. Next to the door stood a tall, uniformed officer.

Cezar raised his hand in greeting. "Good evening, Devan. Glad you could accommodate us."

"Looks like nobody's home," Devan commented.

"The compound is rarely used except for the Revel," Cezar replied. "But tonight we have a special guest. We're expected." With that, he crouched slightly and leaped over the wall, followed close behind by Lorik. Yago stood there, wondering what to do next in the presence of the stoic police officer.

Lorik's face appeared at the top of the wall. He looked down at Yago and said, "We still need to bond. That means I start showing you the ropes." He leaned forward. "Squat."

"Excuse me?"

"Squat. Hunker down. Sit your ass on your heels."

Yago did as Lorik asked, and waited.

"Okay. Now push off."

"Push off?"

"Yeah. You know. Jump up and push off with your legs. Raise your arms straight up when you do." Lorik looked on expectantly.

Yago leaped, his heart leaping, too, as he glided through the air, up and over the wall, landing in the courtyard with no effort at all. "Damn!" he said. He was getting to like this vampire thing more and more. He looked up. Lorik was there, hovering at the top of the wall, arm resting on the top, legs dangling, looking at him with a gratified grin. He floated down next to Yago and clapped him on the arm. "Cool, huh? Good job."

Inside, the courtyard was bare sand except for a few shrubs and flagstone walkways. Lorik strode toward a low building at the far end of the yard, where he joined Cezar, who was smoking a long cigarillo.

Cezar called over to Yago. "Open the gate, if you please."

Yago did so—with little effort, even though the door was quite heavy. Devan strode in, not looking at Yago, straight over to Cezar.

Yago began to close the door. "Leave it," ordered Cezar, "and join us."

Low buildings were set against the perimeter wall at the back of the compound. The four of them stood at the center building which had a single, dimly window next to a door. Cezar and

Lorik stood well away while Devan pounded on the door. At once a tall, well-built, young woman answered.

"Greetings, Sabine," Cezar said.

Sabine nodded and stood aside. They all filed in, and Yago noticed that the black metal door handle had a peculiar sheen. Sabine led them to an anteroom with little furniture—a table and two chairs.

"You're late," she said.

"I had a family dispute to settle." Cezar looked at Lorik. "Speaking of dispute, my son has something to say."

Lorik was sheepish as he mumbled an apology.

"Makes no difference," she said to Lorik. "As I told you at the exhibition, the score was settled."

Lorik looked confused. "But I never made it to the exhibition."

Cezar intervened. "I'm afraid my son isn't privy to our arrangement, Sabine. And Dr. Giroux has never laid eyes on him."

Sabine was nonplussed. "But I saw them together! And trust me, they were more than acquaintances!"

"There are some facts which you know nothing about, my dear. I have it on very good authority," here Cezar snuck a look at Devan, "that the doctor has interests elsewhere. Which, at the moment, is not your concern," he answered. "Suffice it to say that I have my part of our bargain right here." He patted his breast pocket. "But first, it's time you produce yours, as agreed."

CHAPTER 51

Chavi was glad Eno and Gaige had decided to come along to visit Roi. Chavi was doubtful about her powers of persuasion. She felt that Roi was as reticent about his private life as he was very reserved in mixed company, as he had shown at the exhibition. They all decided it was worth a try.

They pulled into Roi's driveway and turned off the ignition. They sat for a minute, discussing who was going to say what.

**

Inside, Roi stood at the kitchen sink. He was starving. He sucked desperately from the bag marked "O-POS." He felt strength slowly flow back into his body. He straightened up and felt momentary dizziness. He gripped the sink until he steadied himself. "What the fuck?" he whispered in disbelief.

Outside he heard a car door slam. He made his way as quickly as possible to the front door, clicked on the porch light, and popped his head out the open door, peering in the direction of the vehicles. "Hello?" he called out.

There were three people standing there. A woman's voice piped up out of the gloom. "Roi?"

"Yes?" He emerged and stood on the porch. "Chavi?" he asked with a hint of amazement.

"Yes, it's me," she answered.

"Who's with you?" He sounded frightened.

Eno spoke up. "It's me, Eno. And Gaige."

"Salutations," Gaige said.

"We have to ask you something. May we come in?"

Roi said nothing, but held open the door as they approached the house. Chavi came up the stairs first, and noticed his painful expression.

***

Roi didn't think to offer his guests refreshments, and they didn't ask. They sat, looking at each other, speaking between long pauses. Roi glanced over at Chavi from time to time as though looking for clues about how to react.

Gaige began by explaining his research, in a nutshell, about the arrow, the cylinder, the possible connection to Roi, the mystery man in the parking lot, and the elusive Jane Doe. Gaige was quite persuasive, but it wasn't as if Roi didn't have a story of his own, just as bizarre.

They had more information about Roi's attack on Eno in the parking lot—and the most puzzling evidence of all. They had determined he wasn't the perpetrator, but—

Roi looked stunned, then managed a chuckle. "*Twins?*" He shook his head. "Sorry. No siblings. I'm certain." His words were slightly slurred, and Chavi noted that he was careful to move his mouth as little as possible. She also noted how pale he was—or rather, how much *more* pale. His complexion seemed more like wax than flesh.

Eno produced a printout. "Here, look for yourself. The highlighted part."

Roi gave it a quick look, but none of it made any sense. A scientist he was not, and never would be. "I don't get it." He squinted at the printed number. "I thought identical twins were . . . well, *identical*."

"They are, but they still develop as individuals," Eno said.

Gaige helped out. "Identical twins *do* have identical genes, but the *number* of copies are usually different. One twin may have ten copies of a gene, the other may have none."

"But you could still be wrong?"

"Virtually impossible."

Roi still looked doubtful. "Aunt Roz would have told me." *And maybe would have, if she hadn't gone,* he thought, as he closed his eyes and sank into a chair.

"What's wrong?" Chavi asked.

Roi nodded. "Nothing. Just tired. Busy night."

"Hey, I was just as doubtful as you," Eno said to Roi. "And I found a lot of Gaige's notions . . . fanciful," Eno added, avoiding Gaige's fisheye. "But I had to admit the facts are intriguing. Just too many coincidences."

Roi listened in silence as he tongued his canines, which hadn't blunted in hours. His normally pale skin had taken on an ashen hue, which alarmed Chavi. "Maybe we should let you get some rest," she suggested.

"Want me to take a look at you?" asked Eno. "I may be an M.E., but I can still tell the living from the dead."

"I may still pose a challenge," Roi managed a weak chuckle. "But no, thanks. I'm under a doctor's care. And Chavi's right. It's been a long night."

"Morning, is more like it," Chavi said. "It's going on three o'clock."

They got up to leave. Gaige said, "Think about it, Roi. There's something odd happening, and you could be the key player."

Roi gave him a nod, and said, "Chavi? Would you mind staying?"

"We all came together," she said.

"I'll give you a ride back." Roi sounded a little desperate. "You could stay in Aunt Roz's room." He had a pleading look. She wanted to get home herself, but she felt a closeness to him, and maybe responsible, in some strange way, for his predicament. *Maybe this is what having a brother must be like,* she thought, and said aloud, "Yeah. Sure."

CHAPTER 52

At first Sabine objected that Lorik accompany Cezar to the cell. While she no longer had an issue with Lorik, she was no less incensed that he had duped her. But Cezar still had leverage—the purloined choker—so they left Yago behind while Sabine led the pair to where Adam was being held. Even though Cezar could hear Adam's breathing through the walls, the bar latch across the door at the end of the hall was a dead giveaway. They approached the door and Cezar halted immediately.

The bar latch was black and glistening.

Cezar waited as Sabine walked forward and gripped the bar latch, which wasn't locked at all. The bar slid easily.

"Please stand aside," Cezar said to Sabine.

But she stood her ground, blocking the open door. She held out her hand. "All right, hand it over."

Then Cezar squared his shoulders. "You know our arrangement. When my son has finished here."

She tensed—then stood aside. "Make it fast."

Cezar turned to Lorik with a stern look. "You. Wait here until I call for you." He stepped into a dimly lit, small room. A thick mattress lay on the floor, and on the mattress sat Adam, less feverish and frantic than he had been at the gallery, but looking a little worse, scruffy, and not in the best of moods.

Cezar slipped in and looked around. A bowl and its contents were scattered in one corner. "The victuals not to your liking?" Cezar asked Adam, amiably enough. "Not much point in a hunger strike."

Adam answered with a glare, and spoke with as much antagonism as he could muster. "Who the fuck are you, and what the fuck am I doing here?"

"Neither of those questions matter right now. What does matter is that you have made a foolish decision, in a very particular way. Are you aware of that?" Cezar indicated the mess in the corner, then kneeled next to Adam, who managed a weak shove. Cezar caught Adam by the wrist and squeezed. He whispered in Adam's ear. "But it's not too late, young man." His tone was urgent. "Under my guidance, you could still have a cadre of your very own. Just think, *dozens* of Roi's at your beck and call! And I hear you like the fairer sex as well. Why not dozens of *them*? Or both, in whatever combination you choose," he said with a wink, then appraised the doctor's body with an appreciative eye. "You seem up to the challenge under the usual circumstances. Why deny yourself?"

In spite of his desire not to play Cezar's game, he answered. "Don't you worry. I won't deny myself—to the person of *my* choice. Not to someone who chooses for me."

Cezar rose to his feet. "That's quite true. You must choose your path freely. But what of the person you *have* chosen?" He chuffed out a cynical snort. "Hardly someone of your equal. But I shouldn't be surprised. You couldn't be expected to know better at this stage." His cold stare never left Adam as he tapped twice on the door.

The door opened to reveal a back-lit figure, tall and well-built, who seemed very familiar to Adam.

As Adam's eyes adjusted, he recognized the youth standing in the doorway. His jaw dropped. He couldn't believe what he was seeing. "*Roi?*" He gave the figure the once-over and noticed the blond-on-black spiky hair. "What have they done to you?"

"Something that can't be undone," the young man answered. But it *couldn't* have been Roi—not with that callous undertone. Roi's toughness was rooted deeply—a quiet inner strength, not the brash insolence Adam was experiencing now.

Adam's confusion was beyond words. He thought: *What's happening?* But aloud he said, "Roi, take me out of here."

"Just what I had in mind," the youth replied. The young man bit at his left wrist; dark blood flowed thickly. Then in one sweeping blur was upon Adam, straddling him, forcing his other hand under Adam's jaw to hold him steady.

The young man jumped back, hissing, hands held out, palms up—which were red and steaming. The youth, his eyes pained and full of tears, looked at Cezar, whose own expression was frozen with surprise. Adam crouched against the wall, not certain what to do, then slid to the floor, semiconscious.

"What's going on?" demanded Lorik.

"He's been cleaved to another," Cezar declared, his voice quiet, barely controlling his rage and disbelief.

"Cleaved? What the hell is that?" Lorik saw something in Cezar he never thought he would: uncertainty. "What are you hiding from me?"

"Now is not the time for this discussion," Cezar answered.

"It's never the time!"

"Hold your tongue!"

A cellphone rang. It lay next to Adam, but before he could grab it, Cezar stepped on Adam's wrist and arched over to look at the display.

"'*Sis*,'" he pronounced, sounding like a snake. "This may be quite interesting. And fortuitous." He reached down and picked up the phone. He tapped the screen and spoke into the mouthpiece. "Hello. May I ask who's calling?"

CHAPTER 53

Elspet sat parked at a convenience store in Squamish, B.C., fortunately only less than an hour, according to the GPS, north of the Capilano exit they should have taken. They sucked on bottles of water.

"I didn't remember that the compound was so close to the city," Gedrec stated in wonder.

"The brochure said it was about 30 minutes," offered Elspet. She too was surprised she missed the exit, but they were distracted—by worry and apprehension. Or maybe they were avoiding the whole issue.

"Just an estimate," Gedrec answered.

"Well, at least we're not that far away. Let's get back on the road."

***

Chavi and Roi had started on smoothies when his phone buzzed. He looked at the display—area code 843. "Hello?"

A youthful female with a Southern accent piped out. Chavi had no trouble hearing it.

"Roi? This is Zelie Giroux."

"Hello! Are you all right? I mean—"

"Fine. Just wanted to let you know I finally found Adam."

"Thank God! Where?"

"Someplace out in the boonies. A retreat at Crown Mountain. Off Capilano . . .? Wait. Yeah, Capilano Road. Partied a little too hard, went off with a friend. Now he's zonked out."

"What friend?"

"Some guy named Caesar, or something like that. Sounded kind of foreign. Classy."

The name sounded familiar to Roi, but now his main concern was Adam. "But Adam's okay?"

"Oh, yeah. This guy Caesar says this retreat is too hard to find at night. Just to let him sleep it off, and I can go and pick him up tomorrow. Which suits me fine," she said through a yawn, "I'm dead on my feet. Jet lag, you know?"

"Yes, I surely do. How about brunch tomorrow, all of us?"

"Sounds good."

Thanks, Zelie."

"You bet. Have a good night."

"You, too."

He put his phone away, pursing his lips. His eyes were narrowed and thoughtful.

"Chavi, something's wrong. Adam's in trouble."

"But his sister said that he's okay."

"I know. I'm going to get him myself."

"Dude, you can hardly stand."

Not exactly true. The smoothie helped, though not as much as usual. Still, he felt compelled to find Adam. "You don't have to come."

Chavi wanted to argue, but there was something in Roi's voice that meant business. She sighed. "Fine. Then let me drive. We're halfway there already, and I know the area. Where was it?"

"Crown Mountain, she said."

She sat up straight as a poker. "Crown Mountain?"

"Yes."

"On Capilano Road? That's what she said?"

"That's right."

Chavi's eyes widened as she recalled. "Now I remember!" She pulled out her phone and zipped her finger across the screen, stopping abruptly and giving the screen a triumphant tap. "That's where I know that symbol from!" She held it out for Roi to see.

A photo of a stone monolith with a weather-worn plaque, a trefoil engraved into it.

"Part of my senior portfolio in school. Supposed to be some sort of survival camp. I knew I'd seen it before! And the one place I didn't look," she said mournfully, holding up the phone.

***

Having carefully replaced Adam's phone, Cezar turned back to Sabine. "I think we're finished here."

Sabine's tone was sullen. "Took you long enough." She held out her hand again. "Now?"

"The doctor is of no use to me. But that bodes well for you."

"What do you mean? How so?" She looked wary.

With one last look of disgust at Adam, Cezar turned to Sabine. "He's ripe for the taking. He'll give good sport." He stalked off down the hall.

Sabine turned to Adam with a wicked smile. "Hear that? You're in for some fun, my friend. We all are," she promised as she slammed the door and replaced the black bar.

Sabine joined the others in the courtyard, where Yago stood waiting, chatting with Coleg, who welcomed her with a smile. "You look happy," he commented.

"You don't know how much," she replied. "Go back and guard the cell. I'll join you in just a moment."

"You have good quarry," Cezar said to Sabine. "May I consider our arrangement concluded to our mutual satisfaction?"

"Not what I expected," she replied, "but he'll do. And Coleg and I were looking for a little spice in our life, isn't that right?" She regarded Coleg with a smile.

"He looks to be a fine man, in bed and out," Coleg answered.

"That's entirely up to you, of course. Do with him what you please. But mind you, he's strong of purpose. Not easy to subdue. *Mult noroc*, Sabine."

"Thanks. Good luck to you, too," she replied, nodding toward Lorik, standing nearby, grim and silent. "I'll leave the gate open. Coleg will stay, in case he comes in handy. Meanwhile, why don't I shed a little light on the subject?" She walked through the open gate and a second later the exterior lights, recessed into the wall, flooded the clearing.

Cezar next addressed Lorik, avoiding his eyes. "Hands out, please. Palms up."

"Fuck that. You tell me what happened to me in there," Lorik said, "Or I'll tell the Burgess. About the choker. What you've done with that woman Rosamund. Everything." His grin widened to a sly, wicked grimace.

Cezar said nothing, looking like he'd been stabbed. Lorik got Cezar's full attention by a rough shove to the shoulder. Cezar struck Lorik across the jaw, knocking him to the ground.

"So be it, young master!" Cezar's voice was rife with cold fury. "Perhaps it is time for you to know the *whole* truth." He leaned over Lorik, hands on his knees, his voice hoarse with resentment. "Your mother abandoned you. *Both* of us."

Lorik's jaw slackened as though he'd been struck a second time—and harder. His eyes narrowed. "You said she died."

Cezar pressed on, his eyes narrowing as he twisted the knife. "Only to spare you. She left you in favor of your older brother. You were certainly dead to her, so why not the reverse? Had it not been for me, you would be nothing but an insolent brat with blistering skin, crouching in the shadows, an urchin feeding on vermin, with a dim past and no future."

Lorik rose from the ground, his shock giving way to hurt and resentment, as the tears spilled from his eyes.

"As you see, my son, we must comfort and protect each other. The trials of tomorrow will be sterner." He straightened and offered Lorik a hand up.

Lorik struck away his hand and stood on his own, shoulders squared in a gesture of defiance, his face filled with rage and disbelief. Then without a word and fighting back sobs, he darted off into the forest, disappearing into the gloom.

Cezar called over to Yago. "Go." He jerked a thumb at Lorik's retreating form. "Keep an eye on him."

Then he turned to face Devan, who was all attention.

"Seems we are too late for direct recruitment to undermine the Sympaths. If so, a pity. But not entirely unexpected, I fear. A most stalwart man, this Adam Giroux. Staunch, principled and compassionate. He will indeed make a formidable adversary." He paced back and forth. "Formidable, but hardly invulnerable." He put a hand on Devan's shoulder. "We should proceed at once with a contingency plan. There is a young woman on whom you must pay a call. Her name is Zelie Giroux."

"What about you, Maestru?"

"I'll remain here. My son will need me, once his temper cools. Now, off you go."

CHAPTER 54

Gedrec took the wheel as soon as they hit Capilano Road. He turned off the GPS and since then had been driving in silence, staring straight ahead, as if in a trance. Elspet had never seen him in this state before. He had his bouts of pensive silence, to be sure, but nothing to suggest the depth of fixation she saw now. Perhaps he was preparing, as she was in her own way, for the imminent challenges—first, their progeny and, second, the unknown.

Even though Gedrec muttered to himself, it shattered the silence. "I hope I recognize the turnoff." Elspet had nothing to add, never having been there herself.

"Here it is," Gedrec announced, with something like relief.

And so it was. Elspet saw the flat-stoned monolith. On it was a plaque with a weather-worn symbol, what looked like three intersecting spokes turned outward. But no other words, letters or identifying marks. There was no gate. With a quick look and firm hand-hold, they advanced slowly past the marker, following the well-worn, well-tended road.

"There should be guards here," Gedrec said.

But they saw no one as they drove through the woods into the spacious parking area. Three vehicles were there: a sensible, fuel-saving sedan; a gas-guzzling, sporty SUV; and a large luxury sedan.

They stopped abruptly at the foot path leading away from the parking area into the woods. Gedrec glanced sharply at Elspet. "Do you—"

"Yes," she said, cutting him off. "I feel it, too. Stronger than ever. He's here." Her feeling of vague antagonism somehow bolstered her confidence. Gedrec evidently felt more confident as well. He held her hand. "Are you prepared, my love?"

Elspet nodded with grim resolve. "Let's go."

Then without another word he climbed along the rough path. Determined. Witt Elspet right behind him. They both felt there wasn't a moment to lose.

As they proceeded they felt they were slogging through an ever-deepening bog, until they saw the clearing not far ahead, and as the trees thinned out, the squat walls of the compound.

They pressed on and stepped into the clearing.

There stood the tall, proud figure neither had seen in decades, yet knew so well: Cezar himself. "Welcome, welcome!" he said, spreading his arms in greeting, then put an arm around Coleg's shoulder. "Coleg, you have the pleasure of meeting the Kirklands, Gedrec and Elspet."

Coleg stood with bow in hand. The Kirklands took special note of the full quiver slung on Coleg's back. Cezar and Coleg stood still as Gedrec and Elspet approached them, steady and purposeful, halting a little more than an arm's distance.

Coleg stepped forward, pulled an arrow, in an obvious move to protect Cezar, who stopped him with an outstretched hand. "No need for that, Coleg. Our friends here are well aware of the risk they take in challenging us." Without a word, Coleg stood down, and Cezar returned his gaze to the couple.

There they stood, unmoving, appraising. Gedrec and Cezar gazed at each other in silence, with more curiosity than animosity. Then, after a few seconds, they managed to share a ghost of a smile, one based in memories long past.

Cezar was first to yield. "You've changed a tad—just a tad—since . . ." He frowned. "Refresh my memory, good friend?"

"Baltimore. Twenty-one years ago."

Cezar nodded as he smiled, as though approving. "Yes, quite an auspicious day." He scrutinized Gedrec. "Yes, you have changed. But only a tad." He offered Elspet a sidelong glance. "Must be the company you keep."

Gedrec ignored the comment. "You look the same, Cezar. No different than when we first met."

"Baltimore again," Cezar replied. "Those were exciting times."

"Not exactly the word I'd use for a nation split in two, brother against brother."

Elspet piped in. "And you may find the battles less profitable this time around, old friend."

Cezar's arched a disparaging eyebrow. "Elspet!" He made a courtly bow. "And still so fetching. But such a sharp tongue! What a pity the years have not yet blunted the barbs." He turned to Gedrec. "You should take a leaf from your more dignified husband."

Gedrec's voice was tight with controlled anger. "Your manners have decayed as much as your ethics."

Cezar's reply was calm and chilling. "Ethics! Neither of you have grounds for that argument. But I meant no disrespect, none at all." Cezar's retort was sincere. "Your wife is exemplary. Strong, intelligent—and brave, if somewhat reckless. And of course," he grinned widely at Gedrec, "both of us know how admirably she dispatched her maternal duties."

Elspet couldn't keep still. "Where are they?" Her gaze was fierce; her voice, low, measured, threatening. "Where are my boys?"

In the heavy silence that followed, the company heard the snap of a dry twig, not far away amongst the trees and turned in the direction of the sound.

Coleg strode past Gedrec and Elspet, took out his bow and fitted an arrow onto the bowstring, then systematically skirted the trees close to the edge of the clearing. Coleg's eyes rested on a deer, who ceased her foraging as she stopped dead and fixed her eyes on Coleg, who listened intensely for a moment, then relaxed and strolled back and joined the others.

"Anything?" Cezar asked.

"A doe," Coleg said. "Lucky for her, it's buck season. Please, Maestru, be careful with that." He was referring to Cezar's cigarillo.

***

Meanwhile, Roi and Chavi barely had time to get under cover when Coleg approached the forest.

They had arrived only minutes before Cezar and Sabine appeared from inside the compound. Fortunately, they heard them chatter and had had just enough time to plunge into the forest, just within earshot of the throng. "I met that guy!" Chavi murmured when she saw Cezar. Some minutes later Roi and Chavi tried to sneak past again, when they heard tramping up the path. Roi was barely able to stifle a gasp when a couple emerged into the clearing and approached Cezar.

Chavi didn't dare even whisper, but it was obvious from Roi's fixed, wide-eyed stare that he recognized these people, and that they were more than casual acquaintances.

They were stealthy enough when they had snuck away from the path among the trees and circled the clearing, but Chavi had stepped on a branch. The dry snap echoed clearly in the early morning quiet.

The company in front of the compound fell silent. A young man snuck toward the forest in a methodical fashion, shouldering a bow and strung arrow. He peered among the trees. But for a doe which strayed about five feet in front of them, blocking the young man's view, they might have been seen. Then the man halted and tramped back into the clearing, leaving them in the shadows of the forest. They both breathed a soft sigh of relief as the man rejoined the group and the conversation continued.

"All right," Elspet's clear voice piped out, no-nonsense. "Enough chatter. First, where is Rosamund?"

Listening in the nearby woods, but still at a considerable distance from the others, Roi gripped Chavi's hand by reflex, so hard that she nearly cried out in surprise. *He knows who they are,* she thought.

***

"The so-called aunt? I have no idea," Cezar replied, and it had the ring of truth. No one questioned it.

"Then what about Roi?" Gedrec asked.

"As far as I know, he is at home. Resting up after what was no doubt a very lucrative exhibition. Or should have been, with the irrepressible Imogen Fuchs at his side. He's quite a talented artisan, though not much of a salesman. "And as for *my* son," Cezar continued, "he made off not long ago, probably on some cavalier adventure, as is his wont."

"*Your* son!" Elspet spat.

Gedrec tried to calm her. "Now, my love—"

"No!" She shouted back at Gedrec. "I will not be silent. I don't care about The Burgess or The Truce! I care about our sons. *Both* of them!"

"Kindly restrain your shrew, Mr. Kirkland," Cezar's silky tone did not disguise its coldness.

"I will not," answered Gedrec. "Rather, I will add my voice to hers. Perhaps we should take the matter to the Burgess himself. Is he inside?"

Cezar held up his palms in mock surrender to quell Gedrec's affront. Then he regarded Elspet and began to declaim, not unkindly.

"Madam." He softened a little more. "Far be it from me to find fault with your maternal instincts. I understand fully, I assure you. Nothing prepared me for the arduous task of child-rearing. A task which, if you will recall, I was not at all pleased to have thrust upon me. Yet I shouldered it all the same, just as you rightly shouldered yours.

"*But*," His voice now took on a steel edge. "Remember that this situation was decided decades ago. And it is far, *far* too late to undo the compromise brokered by the Burgess. I suggest you continue to respect that arrangement, as I have.

"Now, I implore you, for the time being at least, let us enjoy a respite from conflict, however brief it may be."

Elspet nodded, her better judgement appealed to.

"You've heard the rumor?" Gedrec asked.

"What rumor is that?" Cezar shot back.

"That the Amaranth has been discovered?"

"Yes, I have heard," Cezar replied quietly.

Gedrec didn't respond right away, but managed a slight smile. "If true, and we both survive, maybe we can rehash old times. Better times."

"Are you saying we will all look back on this one day and reminisce in front of a cozy fire? Charming, but unlikely." Cezar offered a sad smile, and quoted: "Two roads diverged in a yellow wood, and I—"

" . . . and I took the one less traveled by,' is the end, I believe," finished Gedrec. "Until then?"

With a sweeping gesture Cezar indicated the path back to the parking area.

Gedrec put his arm around Elspet and guided her toward the path leading back to the parking area. "We're both tired, my dear. A couple of days without a break, all the stress—"

Cezar called out, interrupting him. "Elspet!" They stopped and looked back at him. "You asked me about the boys. I imagine they might find each other . . . intimidating. They share the same blood, after all. *Exactly* the same, do they not?"

CHAPTER 55

Still hiding amongst the trees, listening to the conversation in the clearing, Roi resisted every fiber of his being that compelled him to burst into the clearing and declare himself—if not for a deeper instinct, one which rose to sheer panic when Coleg drew near. He had felt himself in the deadliest danger, and to make a sound would be disastrous—and not only to himself. So he dared not speak. All he could do was listen and muffle his cries.

Slack-jawed, he sidled up to Chavi and mouthed, *Twins.* She sported a crooked, knowing smile that said silently, *told you so.*

They moved off toward the compound. As soon as they were out of earshot, Chavi spoke up in a low voice. "Your parents, right?"

"We're here to get Adam," was his clipped response, and Chavi took the hint.

Roi skirted the perimeter wall, careful to avoid stepping on any more twigs. Chavi followed close behind. When they spoke, they whispered in each other's ears.

"I thought you said they'd have a back entrance," Roi mumbled in a sulky tone. When they saw the compound wall, Roi was discouraged, but Chavi had told him not to worry, that she had it covered, remembering the meticulous map her father drew. But there was no time for particulars.

"I said they *usually* have one. Compounds have underground tunnels, too."

"How do you know all that?"

"My dad told me. He was an insurgent in Punjab back in the eighties. Almost got hanged." She paused and scanned the wall. "He stayed in a place like this until he escaped and joined my mom in England. I couldn't get enough of his stories."

Roi looked at her with new respect.

The leaves crackled as the coterie trudged on. "Do you think they'll hear us?" he asked. But Chavi had stopped and was standing still.

"What's wrong?" asked Roi.

"I feel strange. Like a tingling. Pins and needles, like."

"Where?"

"All over." She inspected her arm, poking at it. "Does my skin look strange to you?"

"Strange how?"

"Well . . . " She didn't exactly know how to put it. "Rainbow colored, marbled and swirling. Like oil standing on the surface of water."

Roi peered at her arm. "Looks fine to me."

Chavi shrugged in confusion.

"It's nothing," Roi said. "Probably the excitement."

They resumed searching around the wall. Suddenly she slipped on a patch of wet leaves and nearly fell on her butt, steadying herself against the wall in time, her foot landing on what seemed to be metal. "I think I found something," she said, sweeping away the leaves.

It was a flat metal hatch with no handle or lock, snugly recessed into its concrete frame, making impossible any jimmying along its edges.

Roi appeared at her elbow. "For all the good it'll do. Looks like they wanted a way out but no one getting in."

Roi stood at the wall, measuring it, concentrating. As though an afterthought, he abruptly squatted and sprang up.

He hung onto the wall near the top, as if magnetized. He was just as surprised as Chavi as he hung there, but he soon understood. Chavi, on the other hand, remained astounded.

"How . . . how are you doing that?" she asked, aghast.

"I'll explain later. Just trust me, okay?"

She wanted to protest, but she was overwhelmed by that odd prickly feeling, now stronger than ever. "All right," she said.

Roi hoisted his legs over the wall and disappeared.

***

Once over the wall, Roi found himself on a narrow strip of lawn between the back of the building and the wall. A grate, large as a manhole cover, was practically at his feet, which he guessed led to some sort of passageway, and eventually to the the hatch on the other side. It was dead quiet and he saw no one outside. He lifted the cover on its hinge and climbed down the rungs to a good-sized culvert about eight feet deep, at a junction, with the tunnel going in opposite directions.

He headed toward the rear of the compound and soon saw another set of rungs. He climbed up and pressed up on the metal hatch.

***

Though it couldn't have been more than a few minutes, it seemed a lifetime to Chavi when the hatch opened and she saw Roi's face peering up at her.

"How do you feel now? Less tingly?" he asked.

Actually, she felt more tingly than ever, but said, "I'm okay. What now?"

He told her the tunnel led under the building.

"I think we should stay up top. Never know what we're going to find down there, and there's not much we can do if we're caught in close quarters."

That made sense to Roi. "I don't know what kind of shape we'll find Adam in," he whispered, "*if* we find him."

"When."

"Fine. *When.* Or how to get him out."

"Well, we've come this far. My dad described some of his guerrilla tactics. Maybe it'll spark an idea. We should try, at least."

They saw no one as they snuck around the back of the buildings, pausing at corners and peering around, until they reached what looked like the courtyard.

Chavi looked around. "Deserted."

Roi pointed to the door. "Let's go." He crept over, but he jerked his hand back from the sparkling black handle. Intense fear washed over him like a tsunami.

"What's wrong?" Chavi asked.

"I don't know. But . . . " He backed away slowly, never taking his eyes off the handle, as though it might strike like a snake. "You'd better open it," he said.

Chavi pressed on the handle. The door was unlocked. There was no sound or anyone in sight. The building was dimly lit throughout. They crept along the corridor. Neither spoke to the other, and Roi was consumed with worry and confusion. Meanwhile, Chavi's tingles had graduated to rivers of pins-and-needles roving over her skin, though the sensation was not an unpleasant one. In fact, her senses were heightened; she fancied she could even hear the rustle of leaves outside.

Roi, for his part, felt stronger.

They heard mumbling and followed the sound, stopping at the junction of a hallway, where he recognized the low throaty voice that could only belong to Sabine.

Roi peeked around the corner, down the perpendicular passage and saw Sabine hunkered down in the open door of a small room. He could see Adam lying supine a few feet away from his captor. He held his breath as he watched and listened to what looked like a one-sided conversation.

"Nice tan," Sabine commented. *That's so true*, Roi thought. Since he discovered Adam could touch him—and vice-versa—without a problem, he loved kneading and caressing Adam's smooth, sun-drenched skin.

"I love the sun, too," Sabine continued. She paused for a few seconds before she spoke again. She leaned over and gave his shoulder a gentle shove. "Hey, look, I'm sorry," she said. "Like I said, this isn't personal. But your boyfriend shouldn't have fucked me over."

Roi pricked up his ears, and his brow furrowed in confusion. *What had he ever done to her?*

Sabine's voice became more ominous. "One thing's for sure. You won't be keeping that gorgeous tan of yours."

Then all at once, Roi understood fully, for the first time, the gravity of Adam's sacrifice. Adam would never see the sun again, if they stayed together. For him, the ashen half-light of dwindling days would be all he could stand.

Chavi poked his shoulder from behind, jolting him out of his trance. She gestured: *What's going on?*

Suddenly Adam groaned and his body jolted in a spasm, knocking into a tray nearby. Sabine sprang to her feet and rushed to his side in a few quick steps. "Hello there! Glad to see you're coming around." Her back was turned as she busied herself tidying up around Adam.

As they approached a passage on the right, Roi held up his hand, halting Chavi. He put his back to the wall, his expression full of fear and doubt. By what seemed like instinct, Chavi moved toward the passage. Roi caught her arm and mouthed, *what are you doing?* She looked at him—actually, *through* him—deadpan, and shook off his hand.

Chavi turned the corner.

She saw Sabine at the open door, leaning against the doorsill, arms crossed, her outstretched foot tracing a pattern on the floor.

Sabine looked up with surprise. She nudged Adam with her foot. "Well, look who it is!"

Oh, shit, was the only response that came to Chavi's mind.

Sabine sounded delighted. "What are you doing here? I thought you were out front with Cezar."

Chavi opened her mouth, hoping an appropriate response would come forth. But she was spared.

"Never mind," said Sabine, her voice tinged with relief. "I've been so fucking bored, Coleg."

This only added to Chavi's surprise. *Coleg?*

Sabine offered a mischievous smile and groped Adam, who groaned at her touch. "Get over here. Somebody I want you to meet." She whistled. "A *big* somebody."

And since retreat was inadvisable, if not impossible, Chavi did as asked, passing by a framed print of an abstract painting of deep blues and black, affording Chavi a good reflection of herself—

Which was *not* herself, but a man, large and strong, with wide eyes, irises so black that the whites practically glowed. She—or rather, *he*—stood there stunned, in equal parts of surprise and admiration, taking in the reflection for a few long seconds.

"Yeah, don't worry, you're still gorgeous," Sabine called out. "Now, do you mind getting over here and sharing some of that beauty with someone besides yourself?"

Chavi looked over at Sabine, who beckoned her . . . or him.

"Sure," said Chavi, startled at the deep basso that emerged with that syllable. It was a good thing that years of teenage rebellion against her parents honed her skill at concocting plausible stories on short notice. "It's just that somebody wants you out front."

"Who?"

Chavi feigned indignation. "Who do you think?"

Sabine was surprised. "What for? The deal's done."

Chavi nodded and shrugged. Resigned and a little concerned, Sabine marched down the passage. "Watch him, will you?" she called over her shoulder. "And no sampling the merchandise until I get back, hear?" She looked over her shoulder and tossed a little wink as she turned right at the junction.

Shortly afterward Roi turned the corner, astonished. "What was that all about?"

Her face was dark with disbelief. "Something my mother told me about. That I never believed. So it wasn't bullshit after all," she said, standing still and and staring ahead in amazement.

"Roi?" Adam's groggy voice sounded from inside the closed room. "Is that you?"

Chavi was coming out of her reverie when Roi rushed to Adam, who was on his side, leaning on one arm, the other arm stretched out toward the open door. His face was anxious and tearful. Roi kneeled next to him and put his arm under Adam's shoulder, lifting him up.

"You came back." Adam's voice was pathetic with relief. Then, accusingly, "Why did you leave me here?"

"What do you mean?"

"You looked so pissed when you left," he answered, thick-tongued, "I thought you'd never come back for me."

"Well, I'm here now. And we have to go right now. Can you get on your feet?"

"Think so. Feel stronger." He did in fact sound more alert as he struggled to his feet. "Much stronger now." He gave Roi a wide smile. Roi smiled back, and they embraced each other. Adam's head lolled back. Roi's eyes glowed with hunger as he stroked Adam's throat with his fingers, then licking it.

"Roi!" Chavi hissed at him. "What are you doing? There's no time for that now!"

Roi looked up, incredulous, ravenous. He wavered.

"Let's go, or we'll never make it," she insisted.

With what looked like tremendous effort in waking from a trance, Roi released Adam, pulling his arm over one shoulder and hoisting him. Chavi did the same on the other side and lifted Adam, supporting him as his knees buckled a bit. Adam looked at her curiously. "Who are you?"

"A friend," she answered.

They made good time down the passage after securing the door behind them. Adam indeed got stronger with each step, and by the time they turned the corner toward the direction of the hatch, he was on his own two feet with only a little unsteadiness.

They backtracked until they saw a shadow on the far wall advancing toward them. They stole into a dark room to one side, and not a moment too soon. They held their breath as a red-faced Coleg stomped by, muttering angrily under his breath, an arrow in his fist. After a few seconds Chavi checked the corridor. She motioned for them to follow her, and rushed in the opposite direction toward the front of the building.

The front door was open. They had just reached it when the doorway was blocked—by Sabine, looking both angry and amused.

They heard footsteps behind them.

Coleg stood at the end of the hallway, trapping them. He still clutched the arrow and held it, point up.

"Pretty good trick, whoever managed that disguise," Sabine said. "Maybe you'll clue me in later. For right now, your presence is requested."

They marched to the front of the compound.

CHAPTER 56

Sabine and Coleg pushed the captured trio through the gate into the clearing in front of the compound, where Cezar stood waiting. He strolled over to Roi, hands behind his back, and inspected Roi as though he were a soldier in formation. "Extraordinary," he whispered. "Yes, very nearly identical. Aside from the ingenuous expression on this one, who could tell the difference?"

He straightened up, crossed his arms, and then addressed Roi directly. "I am Cezar Balanescu. Your stepfather, of sorts." He backed away and gestured to Coleg, who grabbed Roi from behind in an instant, arm around his throat, and held the point of his arrow inches from Roi's cheek.

"Do you understand, stepson," said Cezar softly, "the peril you face right now, at this minute?" His gaze moved to Adam. "Does your . . . *intended*?" He put a snide spin on the last word. "But for you, the doctor might have been a captain—or a king—in our world."

Neither Roi nor Adam said anything, but both looked wary and terrified. They understood that whatever the threat was, it was real and imminent.

Adam knew what he had to do.

"All right. Take me!" he cried out. "I'll do what you want. Willingly."

"That's a good lad," Cezar crooned. "Better a living dog than a dead lion, as the saying goes."

Roi started to struggle against Coleg. "No!" But Coleg held fast.

"Don't struggle so, stepson," Cezar warned him. "The smallest scratch will end your life. And I would have you live, if only to watch my own son triumph! Now, doctor," he said, turning toward Adam, "prepare yourself."

Cezar crouched, ready to spring toward his quarry.

A huge light, not daybreak, but a shimmering bluish-white nova engulfed the entire company and bleached the surrounding trees, obliterating the shadows. A deep voice thundered from the orb. *"Kee-leh neer-kah!"*

At once Cezar flung himself to the ground, cowering. The others shielded their eyes, turning away from the small purple nova burning at the edge of the clearing—except for Chavi, who stared at the orb, transfixed and unblinking.

Coleg dropped the arrow as he shielded his eyes from the blazing light. Adam scrambled over to Roi. They kneeled and embraced, not knowing what to expect.

The violet orb, from which emanated the aura of dazzling light, moved toward them. But not so blinding that all couldn't see Burgess standing at the open gate, holding out the blazing spike. "All are bound by the thread of time!" His deep chant resounded through the woods. "We Vanator alone guide that thread to its proper purpose! Stand down, Maestru of the Primes!"

The blinding blue light ebbed with the close approach of dawn, and the aura vanished by degrees, leaving behind a substantial dagger, blade and handle both black as pitch with a glittery cast in Burgess' fist.

With a measured stride Burgess approached Roi and Adam, as they clung to each other. They looked up at him. "Go now," he instructed. "These walls are no protection and hold no answers for either of you. Go and face whatever awaits you." With a nod of his head, Burgess indicated the forest beyond. They got to their feet. Sidelong they saw the others, evidently frozen in their places. Only Cezar dared to turn his head cautiously, his mouth a rictus of fear and fury.

It was a full half hour until sunrise, and the day promised to be as clear as the night had been. The growing light slowly banished the blazing blue aura from the dagger, which was now pristine black only, save for a few glimmers and flares of violet.

Cezar got to his feet. His fury had waned, but his resentment still burned embers in his belly. "Testing the stepson's skill, Burgess?"

Burgess's face was grim. "In part. His wisdom also. Not to mention his character, as well as his partner's. One last test remains. Incidentally, speaking of stepsons, I believe you have something of ours."

Cezar reached inside his topcoat and pulled out the silk-wrapped package and held it out. Burgess reached out and with one quick, strong pull, snapped away the silk.

Cezar had a single moment to see the choker dangling on his palm before falling to the ground, unconscious.

Then Burgess addressed Sabine and Coleg. "As for you, your selfish folly served our purpose."

"What about him?" Sabine asked, pointing at Cezar's unconscious form.

"He will learn he cannot always command. He serves, just as we all do." There was an edge of disgust to his voice as he regarded the pair. "You included. Wait inside, both of you." Sabine looked defiant, Coleg contrite, as they went without a word into the compound's middle building.

Chavi, stunned with shock—which was quickly wearing off, leaving exhaustion in its wake—gingerly skirted Burgess, sneaking toward the open gate. She had almost reached it when Burgess called out. "Rakshasa!"

She halted mid-step, not daring to turn around. A memory—until now, buried by years of denial and skepticism—invaded her inner vision, in which her mother, towering over her as a toddler, pointed with a shaking hand, and uttered a terrible word—*Rakshasa!*—and how her mother's expression of surprise and fear had shocked her, and made her afraid then, too.

"Don't go exploring," Burgess warned. "Stay on the path."

At first, she didn't know which he meant, a spiritual path or the one through the forest. She didn't dare ask or look back, merely moved on.

Burgess knelt beside the still-unconscious Cezar. "Have a nice rest, old friend," he said. "Can't have any more meddling. Not until it's time." He hoisted Cezar over his shoulder with no apparent effort and walked toward the building.

Chavi marched down the path, partly angry, mostly relieved, but thoroughly confused. Roi had some explaining to do. And so, probably, did she.

CHAPTER 57

Adam and Roi had gone only so far when they realized that while the compound was no shelter, the forest offered little more, nothing but a small rise that would give them no more than a few minutes of shade from the sun which was already peeping over the horizon.

And neither was at his strongest. They stumbled, arm around each other's shoulder for mutual support until Adam fell. "I'm all used up," he gasped.

Roi cradled Adam's face in his arms and looked into his eyes. Songbirds began heralding the dawn, chirping in the treetops above.

Adam and Roi looked at each other, furtively at first, then steadily. With the sunshine eating up the shadows, there seemed too little time for apology or regret. Just the same, they tried.

"I should have told you about me sooner," said Roi.

"I should have listened to my gut when you did."

"Guess we were both under the gun." He smiled. "Thanks for doing what you did back there. Saved my life. Only wish it had been worth your while."

"It *was* worth it. Still is. We're here, together." Adam paused. "What'll happen to you?"

"Burn to ashes, I guess."

"How about me?"

"I don't know. Wish I did. Better keep your distance, though, just in case."

"You could turn me."

"You might have a chance to live if I don't."

"That wouldn't be life. Now that we're in the foxhole, I realize that now. If we can't live together, then at least we can . . . " He didn't want to say it.

"Die together? What would that prove?"

"Don't you know?"

Roi thought for a few precious seconds. "Yes. I do."

The sun crept over their feet.

Reluctantly at first, but seeing Adam's desperate sincerity, he bit down hard on the soft flesh in the crook of his left arm and offered the ruby-colored rivulet. Adam grabbed Roi's arm, and stemmed the flow with his tongue, following it to the wound, then slaked the oozing wound as though he'd been thirsting for a thousand years. He pulled away, breathing as heavily as Roi was himself, retreating from the dappled sunlight which stretched out, and then over them, like an amber tide, over their bare skin, which started to hiss and smoke.

Adam turned to Roi and said, "Whatever lies ahead . . . " He planted his blood-stained mouth on Roi's, kissing deep and long, Roi obliging in kind.

They embraced in a blaze of perfect joy.

CHAPTER 58

The first thing Adam saw was Roi's face, looking away from him, in profile, looking up. His skin alabaster smooth and clear, without charring or blister. His lips were smeared with blood, now burgundy colored and flaking. Adam's eyes roved down to Roi's left arm, bare and white, still hugging him across the chest. Something seemed odd about the arm, but he couldn't place it until he realized—there was no sign of the bite wound on Roi's bicep, or even a scar.

Adam lifted himself off the ground, feeling light as a cloud. The weakness he'd been experiencing for days had vanished, leaving vigor in its place. He surveyed the forest around him as he basked in the sunshine he thought he would never see again. He lifted his face to drink up the warmth.

He felt Roi stir beside him and mutter, "What . . . ?" Then with a fearsome cry he raised his hand to block the morning light from his face as he buried himself against Adam's body, frantically writhing in the bright sunshine.

It was then Adam saw the couple, arm-in-arm staring down at them, a woman with lovely, cider-colored hair and a tall, lean man with strong features and a head of thick hair like wet coal, silver-gray at the temples. Though Adam was fairly certain he had never seen them before, they looked familiar. Adam pressed a hand on his companion. "Roi?"

Suddenly Roi gave up his struggle, looked around, bleary, then lifted his bare hands into the sunlight, amazed. Then he saw the couple staring down at them. And judging from Roi's expression, they looked familiar to him as well. He sat up and regarded them for a long moment. He reached in his pocket, took out the pocket watch, and flipped it open. He gazed at the framed photos, then up at the couple.

"Hello, son," Gedrec said.

CHAPTER 59

Even though Roi had left the keys in the car, Chavi didn't leave. She had crawled into the back seat, and never before had she slept as soundly as she had those few hours that morning. The morning which changed her life. Actually, it didn't *change* her life—it awakened her to it.

Just then Roi tapped on the window, smiling, arm-in-arm with Adam, also smiling. She thought she might have been smiling, too. They got in, Roi on the driver's side. They looked like crap, as though they'd spent the night in the woods, which she later discovered they had.

"We have to talk," she said, by way of 'good morning.'

"Yes. And we have plenty to tell you," Roi said. Adam held his hand.

Roi was a vampire; now Adam was, too. They had shared blood, in a particular way that gave them certain abilities and protection, apparently at the cost of immortality. Just like Roi's parents, who stayed at a distance and waved at them as they got into their rental car. "You'll meet them sometime soon," Roi promised. Chavi remarked on their good looks.

Otherwise, she listened. Speechless, because . . . what could she say? Her mind, overwhelmed, spun down to low-level autopilot.

She asked to be dropped off at Eno's office.

"Are you sure that you're okay?" asked Adam. "We've all been through a lot."

"That's putting it mildly," she answered with a chuckle. But she *was* all right, she said, and declined Adam's offer of a tranquilizer.

And for the most part, she *did* feel fine—at peace, even. She knew they were fast friends now, and she felt the warmth of it. The problem wasn't the fellowship they shared. It was the netherworld they'd entered, and which she knew, down deep, they must now inhabit, at least in large part. It couldn't be ignored. She was overwhelmed and silent.

The sunny start of the day at the compound had given way to a fog so thick that driving down from the mountains was treacherous and slow. While Roi was warm and talkative with Chavi, he was quiet and pensive on the way home after they dropped her off. Adam didn't press him, keeping the conversation light.

Roi opened up again after they got home and installed the Kirklands in Rosamund's room. They didn't ask about Rosamund, which seemed odd to Adam, and Roi didn't volunteer anything. Roi was brightly cordial—he was clearly pleased to see his parents—but acted more like a well-trained butler than a son—keeping a respectful distance yet never letting them out of his sight. He was quiet and preoccupied, but not sullen.

Meanwhile Adam was distracted by the change in his appetite. He was ravenous, downing smoothies in single gulps, even before the others had their mugs filled.

That night after their transformation in the woods, they clung to each other. Roi said little but seemed to smile constantly. Adam, like the Kirklands, felt it unwise to push further, hugging him closer. When he woke the next morning, he saw Roi standing at the window in the sunlight, elegant as a statue. He felt himself get aroused and was again surprised—and not for the first time—at the pinprick sensations from his tined canines at the inside of his lip.

Roi's turned his head but kept his back to Adam. "I haven't been very good company," he said. "Maybe this will make up for it." He turned to face Adam, his arms outstretched. Cradled in his hands was a sculpture: strong, shapely, masculine hands clasped in a Roman handshake, loosely bound by a graceful loop of ribbon. Adam went over and admired the meticulous, delicate hues in the acrylic finish, then noticing the inscription across the ribbon—*amor omnia vincit.*

Roi said, "It means—"

Adam interrupted. "I know. 'Love conquers all.' Do you believe that?"

"I used to. Now I wonder," Roi replied. "Maybe love isn't a conquering spirit. Maybe it's the strength left behind that people can share after all the hurt and sorrow are gone." He looked into Adam's eyes. "Forgive me?"

***

A thick fog blotted out the sun in the woods where Lorik and Yago lay in each other's arms deep under a large outcropping, well away from the dawn's blistering rays they had barely escaped a few hours before. Lorik found Yago's instinctive panic at the approaching daylight endearing and took great comfort in protecting his new consort. He felt his cock stir as he watched Yago's face as he slumbered, groping him gently and impressed by Yago's endowment. *He'll do nicely*, thought Lorik, wondering if his father hadn't been right about everything all along.

Lorik drew the locket hanging around his neck and flipped it open. He studied the image of a lovely, sweet-faced woman with cider-colored hair, the woman whom Cezar said did not die after all, but abandoned him for his brother. Cezar hadn't said *mother*—he had said *'she'* with contempt that Lorik suddenly understood all too well. He sat up and crushed the locket in his fist, cracking the delicate porcelain and leaving the silver case slightly warped, and it wouldn't snap shut. A single tear rolled down Lorik's cheek. Yago stretched and sat up, smiling.

Lorik stood and held out his hand to Yago. "Time to get moving."

CHAPTER 60

One day soon after the ordeal at the compound Gedrec pulled Roi aside, and the two had had a long conversation to which Adam was not privy, but their discussion clearly had a profound effect on Roi; for some time afterward, he was silent and distracted. Adam knew that Roi felt ambivalent about the sudden appearance of his parents, especially after such a long absence. He wanted to support his lover however he could—but how? He decided to mention it, and Roi dismissed Adam's heartfelt concern in the sweetest possible way. But Adam was yet only reassured by half when they had settled down for a nap afterward in Roi's bedroom shortly after midday. He was curious as hell about that conversation, but thought, *No, let him rest awhile*, as he nuzzled against Roi's neck.

Adam woke up first. He leaned over and watched Roi as he slumbered, nestled against him, his face so handsome in repose, when he became aware his cock stiffening against the curve of Roi's buttocks. Adam found he couldn't resist the desire that was mounting in his groin. Roi rolled onto his other side, and Adam saw that Roi had oak in his penis as well. With his hand he rubbed and playfully swatted it against Adam's, as though dueling. He crooked his arm against Adam's neck and pulled him close. They kissed, tongues poking and batting as they did with their cocks. Their arms interlocked around each other's necks and wrestled into a mutual full nelson, when suddenly they stopped, face-to-face, as though seeing each other for the first time and appreciating more than the beauty of stalwart manhood. Now they were locked in perfect knowledge and commitment—to each other, to be sure, but also to something so profound, neither of them could quite grasp it. Not yet, anyway.

But it did propel them to a new height of understanding; they were so absorbed that neither realized they were riding on thin air, spinning slowly. Free of the fetters of gravity, it seemed to free up their lust as well. Adam thrust himself against Roi, slamming him against the wall, then kissed him with such tenderness that Roi's body relaxed in supplication—but only for a quick sweet moment. Still in Adam's tight embrace, Roi pushed off with his feet, and they bumped against the door, knocking it ajar, then drifting toward the center of the room.

There they continued to wrestle with each other, trying, it seemed, to explore their bodies in so savage a way as to sate a soul-hunger. Adam seized Roi and pulled him back into a leg lock. Roi's eyes flashed, and he grimaced—not with pain, but frustration; he struggled and writhed. After a few seconds, he slipped free and reversed the move; Adam was now on the defensive, but soon freed himself as well. Still grappling, after headlocks and takedowns as best they could in mid-air, they found themselves locked tight, an arm encircled around the other's thigh—face to groin. Floating gently, bound to each other, they exchange a glance, not unmindful of hard knots in their loins, begging for release.

But they didn't loosen their grip. Instead, in the same moment, their jaws gaped wide; fangs protruded, and with infinite care, using tongues at their guide, they swallowed each other's cocks, sucking ferociously. Adam let out a growl. Roi was working a miracle, tonguing the sweet spot; he countered by using his own skill, ramming Roi's cock deep into his throat, then slowly inching up, allowing the suction to mount, bringing Roi to even greater hardness—and was rewarded with a long groan from Roi. It seemed that both of them competed, as they had done moments before in their mid-air struggle, to triumph by making the other cum first.

But in the end, it was no use—as it happened while wrestling, the best they could manage was a virtual stalemate; they came at the same time, equally copious. Afterward they held fast, descending slowly as they relaxed, nursing on each other, refusing to let go of the wonderful moment. When they settled back onto the mattress, they lay together, face to face, hand in hand.

No words were necessary.

CHAPTER 61

It took some explaining, once all four were together again, to bring Adam up to speed on the impending conflict between vampire nations and the Vanator's brokered peace, now possibly nearing its end. His amazement at the world of which he was now a part wiped out any resentment he felt about his abduction. In a way, he thought, he had already been abducted by the nature of his own desire, the call of his innermost heart when he saw Roi lying on the gurney. It seemed years ago now.

The inevitable conflict was near, but no one knew exactly when. The mystical tome (and to some, mythic) known as 'The Amaranth' might disclose the hour, but no vampire could look upon it without sustaining harm, and the Vanator evidently no longer had the skill to read it. Gedrec, however, believed in its existence as part of the triad of icons known as "The Three."

"We know the other two exist," Gedrec insisted, "so why not the third?"

Why not, Adam didn't know, and he didn't care. He cared only for Roi and their life together.

And it seemed to Adam that Roi was different now—bolder and more self-assured, but not the fierce, ravenous creature he now realized was Lorik. He was his own, beloved Roi, with eyes that no longer peered inward, but looked at Adam himself with a new confidence, deep and searching, trusting, which Adam felt he'd had a part in bringing out.

***

Gedrec and Elspet stood in the living room and watched Roi and Adam strolling, arm in arm. Their expressions were pensive as they spoke, and no wonder: they had learned much in too little time—but time was precious now, especially if The Amaranth had resurfaced.

"Do you think they realize what's at stake?" Elspet's voice was edged with worry.

"Hard to say," answered Gedrec. "One thing for certain: Nothing is as formidable as a force whose time has come. No battle is as fierce as that between factions of shared blood, whether it be between brothers or lovers."

<<<◇>>>

www.ingramcontent.com/pod-product-compliance
Lightning Source LLC
Chambersburg PA
CBHW051409170626
46809CB00006B/2081